Restored

A Second Chance Romance

Nikki Kiley

She Wrote What LLC

RESTORED: A SECOND CHANCE ROMANCE

A CHANCE BROTHERS SERIES

NIKKI KILEY

WWW.NIKKIKILEY.COM

ISBN: (eBook) 978-1-955808-04-0

ISBN: (Paperback) 978-1-955808-12-5

To my husband,

My Forever Muse

Love you

Chapter One
Rebecca

Thank God for Fridays, four p.m., and no traffic on the causeway.

I approached the Intracoastal Waterway (IWC) the three-thousand-mile path along the coast that stretched from the Atlantic Ocean to the Gulf of Mexico. As impressive as that was, I had my eye on something bigger. Every mile forward took me closer to my parents' Star Island retreat and further away from the tedium of the last few hours.

I pressed the car's play button on my mother's Bentley and called the main office in Nashville. Producing a televised home renovation show for the Home Design Network had me run ragged, but I hadn't asked to be so good at this. I'd kill for a partner I could trust.

I'm not conceited. I'm not.

But the proof was in the real estate deals I'd negotiated for the studio—and the fact that our show Renovated was now a green light in Miami. Renovated was my TV baby. I gambled on the chemistry of my hosts and their ability to win over a national audience, and it had paid off. Marisa Sanchez and Levi Chance were the new darlings of the Home Design Network and the home renovation world.

Surely my family would have to recognize what I'd done for the family business.

Right?

My last task had been to close the real estate deals for the show. Fueled by desperately thin hope, I'd accepted my brother Charles's offer to sign the papers in his place.

Three quick pen strokes and it was done. Not even a snide remark to push me out the door.

I'd figured it was a trap—he and Mom not so secretly did not want me on the show—but there wasn't much he could do to sabotage me. The show was all but a guarantee to hit the top of the ratings.

The phone rang three times before Sarah answered. A smile hits me when I hear the low "a" and "o" of her delightful Cajun accent that makes so many people think she's from Boston.

With her attention to detail and her drive to grow in communications, she was the best associate to come out of the admin department. Although a graphic artist by profession, she took the personal assistant job to get a foot in the door at Home Design, hoping it would pay off in the long run. On the few occasions she talked about her past, she'd revealed she was raised in one of the toughest neighborhoods of Louisiana, and that her survival instinct had helped her ever since.

My smile grew wider. Few knew how much work went into this negotiation, and to get under contract so fast, Sarah had put in late nights to make today possible. It wasn't just that I saw a little of myself in her. I saw in her a person I wanted to be more like, too.

"Rebecca Walton's Office, how can I help you?"

Accomplishment wrapped around me like a cloak. "It's me. Rebecca, how are things panning out over at home base?"

"Wait, aren't you supposed to be in a meeting?"

"Just finished. Signed and delivered."

"Was it a trap?" she said, as aware of my brother's bad habits as I was. After all, he wasn't subtle.

"If it's a trap, he's the one caught. Charles owes me big time."

"What happened? Legal told me it was a sign and date type of meeting."

I almost laughed at the irony of what happened. "Imagine a conference room with three lawyers, two realtors, and myself. We dissected each clause ad nauseam in the contract. I almost heaved from the stench of overpriced men's cologne."

"Oh, no."

"Yes. Only self-control and a strong gag reflex kept my bagel from coming up. The realtor in front of me checked her watch no less than ten times. She wasn't even stealthy about it. I was this close to asking her if she had someplace, she'd rather be. I know I did, well not really—but any place would have been better than there. And the personal assistant to the lawyer who sat to my right was busy swiping on some dating app on her phone."

She barely contained what at first sounded like uncontrollable sneezing—only it wasn't sneezing. For a few seconds, it was uncontrollable laughter. And after a few more seconds,

I was laughing with her. A sense of humor was important, if I wanted to keep my sanity.

"Sorry," she finally said. "Please continue."

"I'm not kidding. I watched as the personal assistant confirmed a date for tonight. Hey, and I saw the guy's photos. How could I be mad? He looked like a mix between Chris Hemsworth and Chris Evans."

"Honestly, it sounds like you should go on the date too, at this rate. Do you have any plans for tonight?"

"I have a pool beckoning me to the house," I answered, which I planned to dive into as soon as I arrived home. And given I'd be the only one there, screw the bathing suit. This heatwave in Miami made me feel like it was only a matter of time before I melted into a puddle and evaporated.

I'd seen some big puddles, but none that impressed me. I had to cool off, and if the cost was solo skinny dipping... I was in dire need, since I had arrived in Miami not even a singular pinkie toe had breached the surface of the pool.

Everyone needs a bit of self-care.

The first dip would deflate me like a hot air balloon. A desperately needed deflation before the pressure made me explode.

"I'm just happy I can get back to focusing on Renovated," I said.

"What's your magic bullet?"

"Sarah. If you've got doubts—"

"That's not what I'm saying. It's just..." Sarah's voice lowered as if she was making sure that no one overheard our conversation on her side. "Don't you get tired of proving your-self all the time? I've become well acquainted with exhaustion from handling the back end of the paperwork and being the go-between here at Home Design. And I'm only doing a fraction of what you do every day."

I rolled my neck as I answered her, keeping my eyes on the road. "Tired? Who has time? I'm running on coffee and adrenaline most days. I think sometimes it's the only way I know how to function anymore. Full throttle ahead, that's the only speed I know how to work at."

I felt sorry for her. We had just started working on choosing and setting in motion the guests that would start their home renovation, and then I added this to her pile.

"Once you leave to come here, there will be no one to keep me in the loop."

"Don't you worry, I've got you covered? I've become excellent friends with the girls in the admin division. All those pastries from Blue's Bakery have paid off."

"Are you..."

She cut me off before I could ask another question.

"Go, relax, boss, all work and no play make Rebecca grouchy, so celebrate, drink something bubbly by the pool. Life's short. Take some time to smell the roses."

"Thank you. I was thinking like a dirty martini to start. Lots of olives."

My finger paused over the disconnect button on the car's console before I heard her say, "Before I forget, word around the water cooler was that the previous hosts that Levi and Marisa replaced accused the network of blackballing them on other networks."

I sighed. Deep down, I knew Home Design had distanced themselves from the previous hosts, and they had been a super popular couple. Their rating had been through the roof, so of course getting canceled tasted like sour grapes.

But in all honesty, did they think the audience would forgive his affair with the nanny? Or his mad as hell suddenly ex-wife waving her gun at the newly married couple? Scandals were a dime a dozen, but this one even made the cover of Home & Renovations magazine. No one was forgiving or forgetting this anytime soon.

One host's loss is a prodigal daughter's gain...

I was aware the public might turn a blind eye, but the network wasn't, and as a conservative station, they did not condone the behavior. The show was now, as they say, mine to lose.

"Tell me you'll be here," I begged, already accepting she wouldn't.

"I promise you'll be okay," she said. "I'm flying in on Monday if everything goes as planned. I should be ready to hit the road running by Tuesday."

"You're a godsend. Has anyone told you that lately?"

"I'm actually really excited to start in Miami. With all that my mother made us move around, we never made it to Florida," she answered.

"Well, welcome to the Sunshine State. I can't wait to get started working with you again in person rather than Zoom. Send me the files with the families requesting *Renovated* do their homes. I'll vet them myself. We need at least three more projects at the same time to make sure we've produced enough footage for a show."

"Done and sent," she said in her efficient manner.

"You're heaven sent. I won't take any more of your time. Enjoy your weekend!"

I planned to. Starting with no clothes, a martini with my name on it, and not a soul around me for miles.

* * *

Driving the ICW always filled me with elation, between the skyline of the buildings and the cerulean blue of the water there was nothing that beat it in my book.

The Atlantic Ocean on my right reminded me of all the summers I had spent here with my family. Although it was close to five p.m., the sun was still out and wouldn't set for another three hours. The blue of the sky, a reflection of the water, not a cloud in the sky. I couldn't believe that I had stepped away from all this for over eight years. Jet skis and boats on the azure waters passed me by as I drove toward my home.

All I wanted to do now was relax by the pool and work on my tan. I was still as pale as when I'd arrived in Miami over a month ago. These last few weeks had been a nightmare, but maybe Sarah was right. Perhaps it was time to take a break.

Once I passed the gatehouse to the only entrance in and out of my waterfront neighborhood, large homes lined both sides of the road. They ran the gamut in architecture from sleek minimalist glass mansions to traditional Spanish haciendas. I drove by the manicured lawns, lush tropical landscapes, and private security guards making the rounds on golf carts. As I neared my parents' home, I purposely avoided looking to my right at the natural stone bench that jutted out of my neighbor's retaining wall. But like a witness to a car accident on the road, I couldn't help but look at the disaster, no matter how cringe-worthy it was.

Yep, the dull ache in my chest was still there, and I scowled at my sentimentality. As I passed the monumental fixture, I repeated the affirmation I'd started saying as part of my journey to self-healing.

"Screw you, bench."

I gave the bench the proverbial middle finger, and though I kept it up in silent defiance, I closed my eyes as I passed the location where I'd suffered my biggest delusion and humiliation—all within a mile of my house.

* * *

After being surrounded by people all day, I craved the quiet. I needed to decompress and looked forward to having the house to myself.

I entered my parents' Miami home through the kitchen, with its pristine marble floors and stainless-steel appliances gleaming from lack of use and impeccable care. The house staff should have already left for the day since Yolanda, our caretaker, had notified me she had planned to drive her husband to his dialysis appointment.

Although I was the only one living in the six-bedroom mansion, I was never alone, and there was never any privacy. If it wasn't the pool man, then it was the landscapers or the household staff underfoot. Never a moment alone. As the central air enveloped me, I unbuttoned the small delicate buttons of my blouse and shrugged off the silk top. My body already felt lighter. Softer. Cooler.

I crossed the entertainment room with its colossal microfiber sectional that took up most of the room. Already down to my bra, the zipper of my pencil skirt undone, I slid every piece off me and savored the delicious sensation of literally nothing between, my body, and the open air, my lace bra and under—

A cough sounded behind me. My heart shot to the moon. Then slammed back into my chest.

Turning toward the sound, like a deer caught in headlights, panic tightening my chest. I was frozen in my tracks, as I clutched what I could grab of my clothing in my fists.

Good going, Becca.

Someone's in my house, and I'm practically naked. The news headline writes itself.

Woman Does Striptease for Burglar, Gets Robbed Anyway

The indignity of it all.

But when I spun in place to face the thief, my blouse held up in front of my breasts, I saw his face and realized nothing about today would be easy, light, and refreshing.

Was this a robber? Well, not technically. A robber couldn't hold a candle to the man who'd stolen my heart.

Chapter Two
Dale

I'd known seeing Rebecca again would be an event, but finding her like this?

When it rains, it pours. And I'm about to drown.

Her scent filled my lungs and my senses. She still favored delicate florals with a hint of vanilla. Once upon a time, that scent made me feel like I was home. *It still does—but home is also where the girl you crushed lets you know you might be done with the past, but the past isn't done with you. Eight years had passed. I had destroyed any chance of being the man she needed me to be.*

I'd breathed her in as I lowered my head to whisper in her ear. The moment felt like forever.

But I'd proven myself a coward when I wasn't brave enough to tell her the truth, and here I was just staring at her, as silent as ever. I shook my head and looked away. I wasn't a moron, and the feelings rising up in me would quickly turn me into one.

"Don't stop now," she said. "The show was just about to become interesting."

I was powerless to hold back my smile, even if there was something harder behind her joke. She was comfortable in new ways, less comfortable in the old, no longer the easygoing eighteen-year-old I knew back when.

I turned away as she picked up the blouse from the floor and shoved her arms back into it. When she indicated to turn back to her, she was standing stiffly and straightened her skirt.

I needed to wipe this stupid grin off my face, particularly before she did it for me. How was I *still* staring?

Does she see me as differently as I see her?

The man before her wasn't the nineteen-year-old boy who'd once promised her his heart, then just as cruelly taken it away.

She leveled me with a stare of her own. The show was over. "Ugh, can you not be that obvious?" Sarcasm dripped from her words, but I heard a hint of the girl I'd known. She wasn't gone. She'd just retreated far within her.

All thanks to me.

Self-loathing never struck me as a good hobby. I'd let a chance for forgiveness go all this time, but now that she was here?

"I promise I didn't see much."

"Your dog has more manners than you," she barked back.

I smiled sheepishly. "Becca, what did you expect? I walked out when I heard a noise only to find you doing a striptease."

"And you didn't see much."

"Nothing I haven't seen before."

"There's the Dale I remember, except this time I'm not buying all the sugar. What was this, anyway? An ambush?"

I furrowed my eyebrows. "Yolanda, let me in. Levi told me he texted you to let you know I was coming today." Now it was her turn to be embarrassed. I hadn't ambushed her at all. We'd been forced to be in the same space since her network had contracted with Chance Brother's Construction, but she avoided me like the plague. I'd ended our relationship by humiliating her. Embarrassing her today wasn't going to fix that. "But those texts get lost in the abyss all the time."

She let out a long breath and—I prayed it wasn't my imagination—the corner of her mouth almost looked like a smile. "As nice as it is to see you, I had planned to enjoy my first day off the set."

She looked too happy for me to break the bad news to her just yet.

"And you want me out of here," I said.

"Bingo. What were you even doing here, anyway?"

"Levi's on my case to finish this and get it over with. And once we received a P.O. on behalf of Charles to do the built-in library cabinets—"

If I'd thought she looked mad when she saw me, she looked downright furious at something I'd said.

* * *

Rebecca

Of course, Charles was behind this.

Anger swelled in and out of me. I'd come here to release all this, and instead I was wound up hotter than ever.

He'd manipulated the situation like a chess piece on a game board. A heavy feeling in my stomach came over me as

I realized that this was payback for Mother taking my side and backing the decision to start Renovated. He probably justified it to himself as if this was some sort of hard-love therapy to make me confront my past. But this was going too far, even for him.

I crossed my arms and mimicked Dale's stance. Not intimidated by the big man, and this was still my home. He needed to go. His eyes followed my movements and focused on my chest.

"Ahem ... eyes up here, mister." He lifted his face, and once again, those emerald greens pierced me with a hungry look. "Well, I don't care what they sent you to do. I want you out."

He pushed himself off the doorframe of the library. I couldn't help but take in his built arms, tanned from his work in construction, crossed in front of him as he shook his head. "No can do. A job's a job. Your mother requested we work on this project with some architect she hired for this. If I don't do it, someone else will. And we both know, no one can do a better job than me."

I'd forgotten how cocky he could be. Or how impossibly attractive it made him.

Of all the infuriating obstacles fate could have thrown in my path, it had to be the one person that trips me up with every step.

I walked toward him, determined to keep my footing. My fingers shook, glad that he couldn't see my erratic heartbeat, but my steps stayed steady. He didn't have the power anymore. From the way his eyes narrowed and his skin flushed at me getting closer to him, it was me who had the power. With so much at stake...why not use it?

"Then we will simply ignore each other if we happen to both be in the same room." As I passed to enter the library and verify the details of his assignment, I brushed against his arm and chest—

My heart somersaulted as if I'd touched a live wire, with just that tiny graze between us. My reaction to his physical presence had always left me wanting more—no wonder I'd avoided being around him while in production. Plastic cloths covered tufted chairs, sofas, and ottomans to protect them. Pushed against the wall was the large dining table that doubled as a desk. Bookcases were now empty. My favorite room in this house was now a construction zone. Dale was here to stay if the job had to get done.

He followed behind me, and in defiance of the laws of me walking upwind, his scent filled my nose. Wood, man, and an indescribable pheromone that may as well be called Love Potion #9.

I swiveled to confront him. I couldn't help but focus on his lips as he bent to whisper in my ear. His breath on my skin brought a shiver of electricity that traveled from my upper spine and down my back. "Whatever you want, Becca. I was finishing up anyway. I'll leave you to your swim. Enjoy yourself."

My skin pebbled as his breath blew across my neck, reminding me again of the effect he had on me. It was me who was supposed to have this effect on him.

Instead, it's me getting aroused.

Unacceptable.

Since I started production on Renovated for Home Design Network, this was the longest we had been together. A question burned in my mind after all these years. I didn't want to seem pathetic, but its existence alone made me doubt the intentions of any man that proclaimed to love me. I trusted no man, much less one with my heart.

My insides churned as I looked into his eyes and asked, "Why?"

His back stiffened, his whole body tensed as he turned to face me. His broad chest expanded and retracted with each breath. "Why what?"

It was now or never. Maybe I'd achieve the closure I hadn't gotten back then. I was not that girl anymore. His betrayal had made me grow up like nothing else could have done. I steeled my features as our eyes met.

"Don't act all innocent, you know what I mean. What happened? I waited for you that night." The heat grew in my cheeks as I spouted out what I had bottled up for so long. "You never answered my calls. Was it all a lie?"

His eyes reflected sadness, and if my eyes didn't deceive me, a little pain. He clenched his hands at his side. "No, it wasn't a lie. You were too young." He stepped away from me, ready to make his way toward the exit.

I stepped toward him and pointed my index finger first at him then myself. "That was my decision to make and my consequences to pay for."

Footsteps coming toward us caused me to jump back, and I stepped away from him. In the hallway outside the library, the sound got louder as they approached us. The mood was interrupted in the intimate space. Yolanda had returned. "Miss Rebecca, I didn't know you were here. I just returned from picking my husband up from his dialysis appointment, I wanted to close up once Mr. Chance finished."

He nodded toward Yolanda and picked up his notebook,

walking toward the library's exit. "Don't worry, I finished up here. I got what I needed. Rebecca, nice seeing you again."

Yolanda followed him out of the room, leaving me to wonder if his answer gave me the closure I needed or not. I plopped myself down on a plastic-covered chair and dropped my head into my hands.

Dale had reminded me that a broken heart doesn't always mend. That was good, right? I needed to focus on making the show a success. Getting wrapped up in his scent and his touch and his—

Rebecca. Stop. He's just a man.

And yet it took my last ounce of strength not to follow Dale for one last breath of him.

This was bad. And likely to get worse.

Chapter Three
Dale

I walked into Mom's house and placed the IPA beer as my contribution on the kitchen's butcher-block table. Gone over seven months now, the battle with cancer lost. My brother's and I kept her ritual alive of getting together for dinner at least once a week, catching up over a meal was important to her and it became important to us. Her bullmastiff Kira sat at attention and oversaw all the activity in the entire house. Patting her head and rubbing her ample chest and belly, I cooed. "Who's a good girl? You are. Aren't you?"

Marcos was laying chunks of mozzarella over sheets of pasta and sauce in the rectangular lasagna pan. The menu was Mom's. Living here, we'd eaten plenty of it. Garlic, tomatoes, and beef scented the air as I opened the oven door and saw the garlic bread toasting. "Hmm ... I hope you didn't forget the fennel and sweet Italian sausage. That was the secret to mom's recipe."

Eyebrows lifted, he said, "Duh, of course. You're not the guardian of ma's recipes. She made sure we all knew them."

I shook my head before taking a sip of my beer. "Just asking? Wouldn't want the foodies out there trashing your lasagna."

Said foodies—Carlos, Noah, and Jeremy—were on the sofa playing some game, and from the name-calling and yells, Noah was losing big time.

Marcos smiled back at me. "Count on me to never do that. Kidding aside, Mom taught me that recipe to the T. Mondays were my day in the kitchen with her."

"Yeah, I know, I was Wednesday."

We'd all had an assigned day for cooking, cleaning, and other chores around the house.

Levi walked in from the outside and came to stand by me, a troubled look in his eyes. "Did you meet up with Rebecca today?"

I cocked my head, wondering where the conversation was heading. "Yeah, why?"

"Marisa's coming over with her friends, and asked Rebecca to join us. She mentioned Rebecca sounded off. Was there any problem?"

"Of course, there wasn't a problem," I said. None of that mattered to anyone but me.

He didn't look convinced. "We started another project for the network. We begin next week. Do I have to worry?"

"No."

He gave a slow nod, but there was doubt in his eyes. "Anyway, Rebecca gave an excuse for being exhausted, but Marisa refused to take no for an answer. Strong-armed her into coming for dinner."

Noah had walked in, catching the tail end of our conversation, opened the fridge to get a soda, then joined us at the kitchen table. "I never doubted her for a second. She's probably the only person who could stand up to Rebecca and walk away from it victorious. Just look at how she has you wrapped around her finger."

Smacking Noah on the back of his head, Levi turned to him and said, "My girl can wrap me however she wants. Asswipe."

Noah rubbed his head. "Hey, no need to get physical. Just saying, who would have thought you... Mister Do Everything By The Book would hook up with a coworker."

He pushed back from the table and moved out of Levi's reach, as tempting an offer to live and let live as to invite Noah's playful revenge.

"Don't think I haven't noticed you conveniently show up when Sophia is around. Didn't think you had it in you, liking just one woman. Remember she works for Marisa, you hurt her, and my girl will twist your nuts."

Noah cupped his balls. "Thanks for the visual," Then he winked at me as he moved farther away from us. "Now you've got me imagining Marisa's hand on my balls." His laughter could be heard as he walked away from us.

Levi growled, "One day that mouth of his is going to get him in trouble."

Once Noah left, I found Levi giving me a pointed stare, "I'm working some things out, but don't worry, we're not letting the past stop us from doing our job." No fucking way was I going to tell my brother how badly I'd fucked up.

* * *

Rebecca entered with Marisa's girl squad half an hour later, dressed in jeans and a T-shirt this time. She could have worn a bag, and I would still have found her the hottest woman in the room. Ever helpful, my brothers tripped over themselves, offering them drinks and seats at the kitchen island. The women all offered to help prepare the salad and prep the food. Marcos, who never refused help in the kitchen, soon had four assistants cutting vegetables for the salad and preparing the vinaigrette.

Levi sidled up to Marisa and placed a possessive hand around her waist. She leaned into him, turning her head to place a kiss on his cheek. A person would believe they hadn't seen each other in forever based on the vibe they were putting out, when I knew for a fact that the Home Network had them doing promo shots just this afternoon. They had already started with a new client and were getting to know the homeowners and visiting the property today. "I expect this much help from all of you the next time it's my turn to cook." Levi said as he placed a kiss on her neck.

Corinne looked up from slicing cucumbers. "You guys, I hate to interrupt the lovefest, but we're going to OD on the PDA."

Marisa stuck her tongue out at her best friend and pulled out of Levi's arms, but not before saying, "You can always count on our help. I'll bring the dessert. I make a delicious *flan de queso.*"

Corinne and Sophia nodded in agreement as they continued cutting vegetables for the salad. "Her custard is a slice of heaven. It's to die for," Sophia added. Noah, ever the attention hound, stood beside Marisa's friends. Solemnly, he directed his comments toward Sophia. "The last time I performed was an awful experience for you, but I'll be playing again at Fran's next Friday. We have some new songs, and I expect my groupies to show up to give me some love." Pointing toward all of us.

Sophia peered up from where she was cutting red peppers and said, "No, thank you."

Marcos laughed as Noah's eyes widened, and his chin drew in, not accustomed to outright rejection. "Strike!" Marcos yelled for everyone to hear.

We all understood Sophia's hesitation. Some asshole had doctored her bottle of water, and she'd ended up in the ER. The experience had left her wary of the dive bar and pretty much all places.

I didn't blame her. We were all a little more careful these days to watch our friends' drinks as much as our own.

Her friends exchanged concerned looks as Marisa moved closer to her, putting an arm around her shoulder and pulling her closer. "Sophia, I promise none of us will leave you alone this time. I still feel awful that I was nowhere near you when it happened."

"I don't blame any of you. Just not sure I can go there and not relive some sort of PTSD." Sophia pinched her eyes with her fingers, as if just talking about it was causing her to relive the moment.

"Sophia, I give you, my word. You come, no one is getting near you. Plus, I'll have the bouncer watch your back if I'm not around. No one is messing with you."

I blinked, surprised by Noah's earnest plea.

Corinne, the flirt among them, quickly nodded. "Lucky girl, having the singer in the band be your personal guard all evening. All the actual groupies are going to hate you. What could be better than that? I promised you and I won't break it. This time, I won't leave your side. If I need a bathroom break, you're going with me."

Sophia hesitated. Her eyes full of doubt. "I'll think about it."

Noah changed tactics. By now, Carlos joined them at the kitchen island. "Rebecca, I expect you to be there as well. You're now one of the crew. I'm counting on you to cheer me on." I stepped closer to Rebecca and made her aware of my presence. I loved my brother but watching him flirt with her was not part of the deal.

Her gaze lifted from the romaine leaves she was shredding and placing in the large salad bowl. Her eyes fixed on mine. If I had any desire to leave, it was gone now. I was rooted to the floor.

As if she just noticed I was standing there for the first time, I saluted her with my beer bottle. "Long time no see. If I'd known you were coming over, I would have offered you a ride."

"Waste of time, waste of gas," she said and walked away.

She wasn't going to make this easy.

The worst part? I didn't want her to.

* * *

Marcos was making a move to sit next to Rebecca, but I grabbed the chair before he could sit down and gave him a look that said everything. His eyebrows lifted as he took a step back, moving farther down to a seat by Corinne.

"What is wrong with you? Are you marking territory?"

she hissed through a forced smile as she glanced around the table.

I whispered lightly enough that only she could hear. "What, and miss sitting next to you all evening? No way. Didn't we agree to play nice when in public?"

Her face beamed as if accepting an award. She said under her breath, "Don't push it."

She didn't clarify whether "it" meant the subject...or her. *Only one way to find out.*

I pressed my thigh against hers as we moved our chairs under the table, and she jumped at the contact.

She swiveled her head toward me. "Do you need more space? I can move to another chair if I'm crowding you?"

I placed my hand on Rebecca's upper arm to hold her in place. Goose bumps broke out on her silky skin as my fingers lingered on her before releasing it. If there was any doubt that we were uneasy allies in this game together, she warned me with a look not to back down.

Which made that exactly what I would do.

"No, don't move," I said. "I'll move a bit to make it more comfortable for you."

Her eyes followed my hand, her bottom teeth biting her lips. I held back a groan as her tongue snuck out to lick her lower lip. The tightening in my jeans became more uncomfortable by the second.

"What did you think about the Sutter family's property?" Levi said.

We both turned to him, then looked at each other.

"I'm sure you both saw tons of potential," Levi said.

I'd forgotten that while I was working on the Walton's library, *Renovated* started taping again. In our weekly business meeting, Levi had explained that Home Design required a series of at least six shows for the season. Once the pilot had done so well, the advertisers all signed on.

Levi had a fantastic nose for drama, sometimes so good he didn't even know he was provoking it. Because between me and Rebecca, we could be an atom bomb. And he was very close to pressing the detonator.

"Sure," I said, treading carefully.

"We have more work to do in that kitchen than in the last job. At least it entailed only the primary living spaces. In five weeks, we would never get everything done. The good thing is the couple were open to ideas. We took measurements, and a prototype floor plan is in the works as we speak to present it to them," Marisa added.

Being around Rebecca again was a magnet to iron shavings, the pull and attraction beyond anything I could resist. I stole glances her way throughout the meal, watched her laugh, and make conversation with everyone at the table except me.

Her eyebrows lifted with curiosity when she caught me staring at her, but she said nothing. We'd played cat and mouse the last five weeks, her avoiding me, me staying silent, but no longer. I let her go once before, and it broke me. This time, I was going to stick around and figure this out. I was no longer that nineteen-year-old kid who had nothing to offer a woman.

If she told me to stay away, I would. I'd spent too long hoping for redemption to give up now. I just needed a sign. Anything.

I glanced over at her, as ready to get that sign now as ever. When I finally caught her eyes, she glared at me. I held on.

Come on, Becca.

She could tell me no. Just shake her head, mouth the word, anything would be better than feeling like a fish on a hook. But that's what I was with her. Inescapably hooked.

"When's your next project?" Jeremy asked Rebecca.

She turned away from me. "Me and my assistant are discussing that right—"

"It's not finalized yet?" he said as though this might be a distressing surprise. "Because I need to know if I can book work for some clients we had put on hold while doing Renovated." His job was to schedule, budget, and fulfill work orders, but this didn't feel like business. This suddenly felt like an interrogation.

Marcos then turned to her and signaled both Marisa and Levi. "Yeah, now that the network loves our couple here, what's the timeline?"

Rebecca took a deep breath and expelled it. "None of this is official, but I planned to introduce you to another couple that I feel would be an excellent fit for Renovated. And off the record, they've talked about expanding the budget so that we can get six more shows this season. This means if we get the go-ahead, we're going to be extremely busy. My assistant Sarah flies down Monday to help me with the scheduling and vetting the clients we will choose in the Florida area. Marisa had commented to me you were planning to go on vacation."

"We can just plan our trip to Puerto Rico sooner than later," Levi said to Marisa as they both turned to pay attention to the conversation.

Marisa held her finger to her chin. "Does this mean we have more input to choose the clients we will take on for the new episodes of Renovated?"

Rebecca paused, letting out a breath. "Yes and no, the clients have to go through the vetting process. It's a rigorous list that needs to be approved, but it comes down to budget and marketability."

Jeremy opened his mouth, and more out of instinct than anything else, I kicked him under the table. He started to turn whatever had grabbed him toward me, but then he saw my face.

I glanced at Rebecca, back at him.

Come on, man. She's on the same team.

I don't know if he agreed, but he nodded, and we both turned back to Rebecca answering Marisa's next question.

"They must have the money to complete the project," Rebecca was saying. "And we need to have proof of it. Sarah's job will be to bring us the client's dossiers with the financial proof, from that we then choose the most interesting cases. We need to sell an interesting story. That's our number one priority. We can never forget this is entertainment."

"Or that anything can go wrong," Marisa added. "But I'm sure you'll make your family proud."

She said it with such sincerity that it took someone who knew Rebecca—someone like me—to understand the faraway look in her eyes.

She rose from the table. "Where is the bathroom?"

Marisa pointed in the direction. "Down the hall."

If ever there was a time to give her some space, this was it. My quest for forgiveness could wait for another time.

But as she got up from the table, her eyes met mine. And her lips mouthed two words I thought I might never hear from her again.

Thank you.

I sat there for thirty or so seconds. I couldn't make it *too* conspicuous, right? But by then I'd made up my mind.

"Need a refill. I'll be right back," I said out loud to no one as I got up from the table.

* * *

Knowing she walked toward the bathroom, I headed in that direction. I wanted to grab her without an audience. Yolanda's arrival earlier didn't let us finish what we had started at her house.

Rebecca jumped when she swung open the door to see me waiting for her. "Jesus Christ, Dale, you scared the shit out of me. You might think of walking around with bells on, so I know you're on the prowl. What are you doing here in the dark?"

Inches separated us, but it might as well have been a mile from her distant face. The heat from her body and the notes of her perfume reached me. I kept my arms at my sides. I didn't want to startle her. "I'm sorry about what I said today. I didn't mean to bring up old wounds."

Her eyes looked past me toward the picture frames on the table. Her stare fixed on the one of me with my brothers and Dad. I looked to be about nineteen in it, of course Marcos, Carlos and I looked nothing like Jack Chance. We'd been adopted by the Chance's after being fostered by them, God gave us the parent's we weren't born with. Her voice brought me back to the conversation. "It's the past. I want to keep it there. No good can come of rehashing it. Let's stick to our lanes, you in yours, and me in mine."

Every word she said cut like a dull knife to my heart. "I'm

sorry. I was a coward. I couldn't face letting you down. That's why I told your brother to pick you up at our spot and take you back to New York."

She pinched her eyes with her thumb and forefinger, her voice steely now. "Dale, we've both moved on. I guess you were right. I accomplished quite a few things." Sarcasm dripped from her words as smooth as honey. "I finished my studies, even did a master's in communication. My trust fund kicked in as soon as I turned twenty-four and completed college. All's well that ends well."

I reached out to grab her soft hand against my rough, calloused palm, eager for a simple gesture of what was once between us. "Is there any way we can start over as friends?"

Her shoulders slumped inward, and then, as if remembering her posture, she zipped up to stand ramrod straight. "I don't know if that's even possible, but we're adults. We also are going to be seeing more of each other, so we might as well try."

Once she said those words, I released a tight breath I hadn't even realized I was holding.

"Thank you," I said.

And if that had been the end of it, that would have been the end of it. I would have let go of her hand, gone back to my home away from home, and let it go.

But as I started to pull away, I felt a tug on my hand. Her hand was still on mine.

She looked down at our intermingled hands. "I can't let...*this*...ruin the show."

I'd made too many assumptions before. Let her make too many along with me. "This?"

"Dale." She narrowed her eyes at me as much with

longing as pain. She started to say something—maybe what I'd waited this whole time to hear her say—but then she shook her head. "We've got a show to do. Let's keep our focus, okay?"

Yeah. Focused. When I was around her? Easier said than done, but I didn't have to let her know that.

* * *

I couldn't sleep. My eyes traveled to the letter that sat on my night table. It had arrived last Monday. The return address was from a prison and was still unopened on Friday —fate's ironic way of reminding me why Rebecca and I could never be.

I kept replaying what it was like to be so close to Rebecca after all these years. The dormant feelings for her surfaced like a geyser watching her walk in her house, unbuttoning her blouse. I'd approached her when we started taping the show a month ago, and she'd brushed me off. Making it clear to me she only wanted to deal with me if the subject was about the business.

I picked up my laptop and searched her name for the first time in eight years. I'd fought the urge to look her up so many times. Out of sight, out of mind. But now various images popped up on the screen. Her Instagram was public. She seemed happy. Guys appeared in some of them, but no one stood out, no declarations of love from or to anybody.

You deserve someone who will.

I'd once hoped that would be me, but if what she wanted now was distance, so be it. My cowardice had done a number on her. The reasons I'd given her today were the truth, and those hadn't changed all that much.

I hesitated to open the letter. Dread filled me, knowing deep down that it would not be good news no matter what I read.

Son,

I know we haven't spoken since that summer years ago. We cut ties long ago, don't blame you. I wouldn't have given me the time of day, either. You might ask why I'm writing now. I won't bore you with the details. I have pancreatic cancer. The doctors have told me I have only a couple of months left, but I wanted to make peace with those I did wrong. Dale, if you can find it in your heart to forgive a man, I would like to see you before I go. You know where I am. Please let this old man leave this life with some peace.

Abbot Marlow

I couldn't quite name the emotion that filled me when I finally found sleep. But I could imagine my face. It looked a lot like Rebecca's had when she'd started out answering a harmless question and quickly found herself under fire.

Chapter Four
Rebecca

I finally had the house to myself. Yolanda had the day off, and I refused to have an entire staff while residing on the property. I enjoyed the privacy—especially when I remembered to make sure infuriatingly hot ex-boyfriends weren't wandering uninvited on the property. Accustomed to having staff surrounding them and expected to be served was my parents' life, but I relished alone time. I guess this apple fell far from the tree.

I sat with my laptop in the breakfast nook off the kitchen to catch up on my emails. The one that caught my eye was one from my brother. It read that they would expand Renovated past the original three episodes agreed upon in the contract to ten shows this season.

I couldn't help the grin that split my face as I thought about how my brother Charles could suck it. I was going to make Renovated a household name. I'd show them I had more to contribute to our family legacy than arm candy at a party. Father would have to recognize that I also counted, that I wasn't just a daddy's girl waiting for prince charming to take care of me. But first things first, I needed to call my TV hosts and give them the news.

Lucky for me, I only had one call to make. Marisa answered on the first ring. After they came out as a couple, the news rags ate it up and embraced them as the new reality TV couple.

"Rebecca, anything wrong?"

"Hi Mari, are you with Levi?"

"Yes, he's right here by my side. Is there a problem? I'll put you on speaker." I heard Marisa call Levi over.

"Hi, Rebecca," Levi greeted.

"Hi, I didn't want to interrupt. This may be the only free weekend we'll have in some time, but I have glorious news to tell both of you. The official numbers came in and the advertisers loved the concept. They've doubled the number of episodes, so now we're going to do six more renovations. That means a second season for us."

There was a whoop and laughing on the other side of the call.

"I just wanted to congratulate and thank both of you for your work on the project. I hope you're ready to double down to get this thing going."

I would have thought being closer to success would fill me with confidence. It did, really, but like my high school physics teacher taught me: every action has an equal and opposite reaction.

Good news? Yes.

A reminder of what failure would cost me? Also, yes.

* * *

I walked past gated entrances and high walls of homes in my neighborhood, realizing I had never met the neighbors. Each home is an enclave. There's little movement on the main street that bisects the island at ten a.m. Sea air filled my lungs. The Miami heat beat down on my head. When I reached the three-mile marker, I turned back, making my way toward Villa Tranquila.

Yes, my house has a name, and I'm hoping to have some of that tranquility it promised.

I entered through a side gate that took me straight to the pool house. The rectangular infinity pool called to me with an unobstructed view of the ocean. The Brazilian bikini I had left out here for this exact purpose was waiting for me to work on my tan rather than to look my usual pasty white.

If I wanted my pallor to avoid screaming tourist, I needed to add some color to my skin. I couldn't help posting the self-indulgent selfie poolside.

I finally came out of the pool a half hour later. There were messages from friends I'd tagged in my post. The one that caught my eye was one from Ken. We'd studied at Columbia together, having met when we were neighbors in the same dorm building. Once he graduated, he left for Miami for a job, met Sandro, a Brazilian architect, and stayed. A smile reached my lips as I read his post to me. We hadn't seen each other in over two years. He was now working for the affiliate news channel that was part owner of Home Network.

Ken: Becca is out of NYC! Do you have plans tonight?

**Rebecca: Nope, finally have some time
off work
Ken: New club opening in the Miami
Design District called Club Rain. Come.
Ken: Just added you to the invite list.
Sandro worked on the project.
Rebecca: God bless Sandro <3. See you
guys tonight.**

* * *

Dale's words replayed over and over in my mind; they'd burst from him like a water balloon that couldn't take the pressure of being filled anymore. It opened a wound that I thought healed over. I guess some injuries just scar but never fully close.

I had no energy to play these mental games with him. We all had our truths. He thought his truth justified the actions of leaving me on a bench, waiting for an hour before my brother came to take me home.

I would never forget the look of pity in his eyes. One of the few times my brother never said a word, just held me and let me cry. Was being friends, as Dale insisted, so naively easy for him. No friend had ever broken me into so many pieces that I wondered how I was ever going to function again. I had other things to focus on, so I guess being civil and letting bygones be bygones was the only way we were ever going to learn to be around each other. Plus, I was a grown-ass woman. I refused to hide and cower.

I had hours before meeting my friends, so reading the

novel I'd started was precisely the type of relaxing I wanted to do. I never thought I would love a historical romance, but after binge-watching one on Netflix, I couldn't stop. I lay on my stomach and placed the book on the floor beneath me, then I untied my bikini strings to get some rays. No unsightly tan lines for me. My outfit was going to be a backless number, perfect for the nightclub scene.

* * *

"Rebecca, wake up." An enormous shadow fell across my body as a warm hand shook me awake. I'd know Dale blindfolded.

I squinted as the sun hit my eyes. "Wh... What? I'm awake."

Dale's hand once again shook me. "Becca, you fell asleep." The alarm in his voice didn't sound good. "Your back is lobster red."

I bolted up straight, lack of bikini top forgotten, and pressed my hands to my face. "Shit, shit, shit..."

My heart pounded hard as I tried to gain composure, why was it only this man who witnessed my most embarrassing situations. "I guess I was more tired than I thought."

A breeze hit my chest and I scrambled for the towel beneath me. I'd given Dale an eyeful of boobs again. They perked right up at his staring. But I wrapped the surrounding towel around myself, gingerly aware of the tenderness on my back and side of my face. Heat suffused my cheeks but with the state of my sunburn I'm sure he never noticed.

Now covered and with whatever dignity I could muster, I

met his eyes. "Wait, what are you doing here? Isn't it Saturday?"

Flustered, his gaze went from me to the jet skis and motorboats in the blue waters in front of us. His eyes once again came back to find mine. "In my rush to leave yesterday, I left some tools in the library. I needed them to complete a job. I didn't want to bother you, but no one answered the main door. Now I'm glad I did."

An odd twinge of disappointment filled me, I should have felt relief that it wasn't me he'd come for, but I didn't. I cringed—the towel on my sunburned skin was sandpaper on my flesh. The sun had done a number on my back. Gingerly, I touched the side of my face that had taken the brunt of the rays. I'm sure it was lobster red at this moment, but what was I going to do? I couldn't let him see me squirm.

There was concern in his eyes. "You need to put something on your back and the side of your face. If not, you're going to peel, and the pain will be worse. There must be some aloe or something around this enormous house somewhere."

I nodded in agreement. "Yeah, I think there's some in the fridge for when my dad spends too much time outside. He always forgets to use sunscreen and then slathers the stuff on after playing golf." I stood up, gripping the surrounding towel, and walked past Dale, more than a little grateful for the sunburn for hiding my blush. "Follow me in, and you can retrieve your stuff."

"Thanks, but we are dealing with you first."

He followed me in silence as we walked toward the French doors that lead from the terrace to the kitchen. Walking around the two mega islands in the middle, one meant for entertaining and the other for food prep.

I opened the industrial-sized fridge and sitting on the door among the ketchup and mayo was a tall bottle of aloe. I pulled it out with a flourish, as if I were a hostess presenting on a TV show. "Ta-Da, we're always prepared."

He stepped around the kitchen island and took the bottle from my hands. His voice detached, almost clinical.

"Here, let me. You can't reach where it needs to go."

I took a step back from him, staring at him tongue-tied. Having those hands on me would not be all right with me. Trying to reconcile so we could have a professional relationship was one thing. Being physically close was another. "Ah... no. I'll be fine."

His body stiffened as if I'd struck him. "Okay, I understand." he placed the bottle in his hands. "Put out your hands so that you can put this on your face. You could double as Two-Face right now."

I did as he said. His firm hands pumped the cold gel into my cupped palms. Dipping my index and middle finger in the gelatinous goop that lay in my palm and applied it to my cheek. The sensation brought chills throughout my body.

"Oh jeez, it's freezing. I don't think I can handle doing this right now. I'll just take a cold shower."

Exasperation showed in his face, "Becca, that's not the solution, you know that." He took my palm in his larger one and, with a paper towel, wiped off the excess product on my hand. "I'll take care of this for you."

My breath quickened, having his eyes on me was one thing his hands another. My upper teeth bit down on my lip to contain the groan that was building deep in my chest and wanted release. Big girl panties, Rebecca, you can be in the half naked presence with this man and not want to climb him like a tree.

"Um, I don't think that's a good idea. I'll tough it out."

He lifted his hand to his heart. "You can't possibly apply this to anywhere other than your face and upper shoulders," his hands signaling with the bottle to my body. "You seriously need to put something on that. Those are first-degree burns."

I lifted my hands, palms facing him, "Okay... okay, you win," my finger now pointing into his face, "but don't get any ideas."

He smirked before saying in a deep voice. "You can turn your back around now."

My hands clutched the towel across my front as I swiveled and lowered the towel. I exposed my back till the towel reached the top of my bathing suit bottom. In the privacy of my room, I would take care of applying it to my butt. "I cannot believe you just compared me to a Batman villain?"

I tilted my head up towards him. Our bodies are only inches apart. My eyes fixed on the wall in front of me, a surreal feeling overwhelming me. "Let's get this over with. We've barely spoken to each other in the last month, and now we're in each other's space."

Shut up, shut up, diarrhea of the mouth.

"Maybe it's fate. But I'm glad it was me that found you and not some creep."

I held up the towel in front of my chest. "I don't know why I'm making such a production of covering my boobs; it's not like you haven't gotten an eyeful in the last two days."

Which was true, but then I also had noticed how he'd turned away from me last time while I got dressed. He'd been as surprised as me for us to run into each other like that, but he was still the same gentleman underneath it all.

That's what scared me. That gentleman had broken my heart.

I shrugged my shoulders and turned my face to glance up at him, his eyes glued to my back and bottom. Although covered by my towel, the Brazilian bikini bottom I had on was only a glorified thong tied with two strings on the side. "What's happening back there? Are you going to do this or not?"

He shook his head as if woken up from a stupor and placed the refrigerated bottle that he'd picked up on the counter beside him. His voice rough and hoarse, as if he needed all his concentration to create a rational thought. "Sorry, got distracted. The gel's going to be cold."

He pumped the aloe twice and started with a generous amount on my shoulders. His fingers moved to my neck and slid them down my arms. Goose bumps trailed in its place. I will not survive this. His hands exquisite on my skin. I fought the need to lean into him.

The silence was too intimate. We were alone and no longer teenagers. I had to say something to break this tension. I looked over my shoulder as he continued touching me. "So other than this library, what have you been working on?" I hoped I sounded casual rather than strained.

He pumped the dispenser once again. "This and that, but what's taking the most time is getting my house move-in ready."

My head fell forward as he placed the cool gel on my upper back, letting it drip down in rivulets as it made its way toward my bikini bottom.

Dear God, I'm only human. My resolve was being tested as the butterflies in my stomach were doing back flips.

His hands smoothed the aloe in a thick coat on my lower back. He didn't utter a sound, the silence deafening, but I felt his breath on my body. Shivers traveled up and down my spine. How long could I last with his hands on me? My legs became rubber, and I bit my lip to stifle a moan. The sound of Dale's breath ragged behind me. My chest tightened, and desire pooled between my thighs. It's been so long since someone was between them. But it would not be with him. Been there, done that.

He lifted himself off the floor and took a step back from my body. His well-muscled body moved with effortless grace. I shook myself to avoid staring at him.

My lack of clothing had me self-conscious. My voice was stilted. "Um... thank you, I needed that."

He smiled down at me. "You don't need to thank me. I'm at your service whenever or wherever."

"What a smart ass." I looked down, his desire clear, complex, and lengthy. "That doesn't look too comfortable."

He smirked before saying. "It's not, but it'll go down."

Like I said, still the same gentleman. That was the problem.

Chapter Five
Dale

She stiffened and tightened the towel above her breasts. As if I could forget what hid beneath the bath sheet, the softness of her skin over those hills and valleys. She picked up her phone and texted a response.

I tried to go for casual before asking, "Have plans?"

"I might." Her eyes evaded mine before looking back up at me. "Yeah, I plan to go out tonight. Reconnected with an old friend from Columbia that lives in Miami." She walked toward the service entrance, and I got the hint that this conversation was over.

A change in tactics was necessary if I wanted to have any type of relationship with this Rebecca. She's not the go-with-the-flow nineteen-year-old anymore. "Where?"

Her eyebrows raised as she let out a laugh. "Why should I tell you?"

I threw my hands up in surrender. "I'm a concerned citizen looking out for your safety. Things have changed since the last time you lived here." I said following her.

She walked toward an under-counter beverage center

near her and grabbed two water bottles, tossing me one. Unscrewed the cap, taking a long drink of water as she leaned her hip against the white marble. "Don't worry, I lived in New York for six years. I'm no stranger to living alone in a big city, but thanks for the concern."

I folded my arms, my hip mimicking her stance. "I'm aware of that, still, things have changed from when you were eighteen."

She tilted her head, and suspicion reflected in her eyes. "A place called Club Rain. Why? You plan to go?"

"Just curious."

"Just curious. Might work for some people, Dale Chance. But you forget we're not strangers. I'm a competent woman that can decide for herself and quite capable of going out on her own."

"I know you're accomplished, and you have nothing to prove to me. You faced a network, stood by, and fought for Marisa when they wanted to dump her and the show. So yeah, this Becca has steel in her spine and is not a pushover."

She sighed. "With the show and all, I've just been a mountain of stress. I don't want to complicate things with the past. I have to keep my focus on what's important to me right now."

Now I stiffened. Rebecca just called me a complication. "Well, you have plans. I better leave you to them."

She gripped my arm. "Sorry, my words came out wrong. I meant to say that it was only yesterday that you asked us to have a civil relationship. I need some time to acclimate to that —I mean, us being friends."

Her phone rang and her mother's picture came up on the screen. "I have to take this call."

She walked a few feet away from me as she answered the phone. "Hi, Mother. Ugh yeah."

Her face scrunched up before answering whatever her mother was saying. Her fingers played with some paper napkins on the counter, tearing them to shreds. "Yes, I did, but I've been busy. Remember — my job as producer of a home improvement show."

Her teeth bit down on her lower lip as she continued listening to the Walton household's unofficial leader. God knows what Susan Walton wanted of her daughter. "I'll get on it. Mother, if I agreed to do that, I will. I'll take care of it. I planned to contact the committee chair on Monday."

She paced around the kitchen island. "Love you too, Mother. I'll fly to Nashville when and if it's necessary." I heard the lull in the conversation, and I assumed Mrs. Walton was talking, before the exasperation was back in Rebecca's voice.

She stopped in front of the freezer, opened it up, and grabbed a pint of coconut gelato. Then pulled a spoon out of the drawer and started eating straight from the container.

My eyes widened, as she muted the phone between her and her mother, to say to me, "I'm stress eating," then unmuted as she continued the conversation.

She walked across the room and continued talking to her mother. "Don't you dare. I'll get my date and if I go solo, that's perfectly fine as well. Don't even think of setting me up with anyone. If you do, I swear, I won't go."

She became engrossed with the pint in front of her. Another spoonful of gelato lifted to her lips. Her tongue slipped out and dipped into the tropical concoction. I leaned into the counter to hide the hard-on that was growing with every lick. Damn.

"Mom, I have to go now. Someone's at the door." The lid of her container was on the counter. She retrieved it and threw it out with the now empty container. She paused in her movement while she listened to her mother. "No, Yolanda is not here to answer it. I gave her the day off. I'm going to hang up now. Bye, Mother."

She placed the phone on the white marble of the kitchen island before grabbing her head and pulling at her hair. "Geez, I could scream, but I can't backtrack now. I made a deal with the devil, and she's come to collect."

My curiosity got the better of me. "Can I ask? What do you need to do that has you so stressed and has your mother calling in the marker?"

"It's not really a secret. I needed her influence with the CEO, aka my brother, for the go-ahead of *Renovated*. He'd refused my various presentations of viable options for new network programs, with the excuse that I already had a job at Home Design, and it wasn't as a show runner. Mother handled me getting the program approved, but only if I agreed to chair on the Black and White Ball committee. A gala event for a charity dear to her. When I went over his head, it made him angry."

I nodded because I'd dealt with the force of nature that was Susan Walton. "I can imagine."

"Yeah, last thing Charles wants to deal with Mother again. Well, I had to agree to chair the committee of the Black and White Ball if I wanted her help." A heavy sigh escaped her before she continued. "The organizers must have mentioned to Mother that they have sent me the details and what my responsibilities are going to be. Susan Walton takes her role as chair of these charities seriously." Her cell pinged, and we both glanced down at the phone in front of her. There was a text from someone called Ken.

Ken...

Was that a boyfriend? Marisa hadn't mentioned her seeing anyone. I also had made sure not to ask.

My jaw clenched, and my heart thumped uncomfortably. Was there already someone else in her life now?

Was I too late?

* * *

I arrived at my house forty minutes later. The drive home cooled my desire for the near-naked Rebecca and the Southern drawl that occurred when she was pissed. I wanted more and needed to prove to her she did, too. I approached with pride the modern one-story house I'd built to be my future home. The lot had a water view and was next to a preserve that no one could ever construct on. I liked the privacy it offered me. I'd already built my workshop on my property. It was a third of the size of the main house. There, I worked on special projects and custom pieces for my clients. I'd been able to create a name for myself among decorators and architects.

My brothers were pitching in and installing the finishing touches, which was always what took the most time in construction. They had expected me back over an hour ago. When I returned to my truck, I read all the missed texts on my phone. They ranged from where did you go to, WTF, do you plan to come back? Parked in the driveway were my brothers' trucks. I should have known they wouldn't leave without me coming back. I had started construction over a year ago, and now I was a month away from moving in. I had been in no rush at the time to move out on my own, but since Mom's death, the need to finish my home had been more critical than ever. The land had passed to me on my twenty-fifth birthday, as it did to each of my brothers. And I'd started breaking ground and working with building the home on the two-acre lot before Mom's diagnosis. Carlos and Jeremy had finished installing the high hats for the recessed lighting in the central room ceiling and connected the wiring for the electricity to the switch plates. Marcos was with Noah installing appliances, and Levi had installed the faucets in the bathroom and kitchen.

Marcos stopped what he was doing in the family room and waved me over. "Look who's returned and blessed us with his presence."

Levi came out from the master bedroom with a wrench in one hand and a faucet spout in the other. "Hey, what happened to you?" he asked. "I thought it was a simple grab and go."

Two minutes to come up with an excuse that my brothers would buy. If not, they'd be in my business from now till dawn. "When I arrived at the Walton's there was a problem in the kitchen and I needed to take care of it, before it got any worse."

Plus, I knew my brother wouldn't appreciate me getting involved with our boss and client. Levi would only worry about the bottom line if things went south again. He wouldn't care that I wanted to make amends. He'd remind me I screwed that up eight years ago. No need to screw it up again.

So no, not touching the Rebecca topic with a ten-foot pole.

I plastered what I hoped was a bored expression on my face

Noah elbowed Carlos, who was standing next to him and said, "I wonder if Rebecca was around? Have you noticed how helpful he gets when it's anything to do with her?"

Carlos, not to be left out, turned to Levi. "You should have seen the hours he put in to cover for you when you left for New York. He made sure that the Ortega's house got finished on schedule."

"Hey, shitheads. I made sure Chance Construction looked good for the Network." I placed the tools I'd retrieved from the Walton's residence on a table. "Plus, it helped Levi get the house finished, and that's what we get paid to do."

Jeremy came over to me then, his voice low so only I could hear him. "Bro, you can lie to them, but I remember how crazy you were for her when we were kids. I know how hard it was for you to let her go. You shut down for months, would just do your work and then isolate yourself from everyone."

"I'd been that obvious back then?"

"You weren't. We just thought it was you being an asshole. Mom worried you weren't yourself and asked me to keep an eye on you."

Levi's cell phone rang. He smiled as he looked down at the caller and answered. "Babe, I have some steaks for later on."

Levi was on his phone, speaking with Marisa. "Put her on speaker. I need to ask her something?"

Levi said something to Marisa before pressing the

47

speaker function on the phone. "Hi Marisa, have you heard of a new place called Club Rain?"

"Hi. I haven't. I can ask around. If it's trendy, I'm sure someone will know about it."

Levi's head shook. If there was one thing I could count on, it was my grumpy brother not wanting to go out. He was already seeking to interrupt the conversation when I blurted out. "You'd be doing your future brother a solid. I need to get in there tonight."

There's silence on the other side before she asked, "Can I ask why? What's the urgency?"

"I'd rather not," I answered. "That way you have deniability in case you get questioned."

Noah and Carlos both approach the phone.

"If she can wrangle an entrance for us, we'd go," said Carlos.

Levi decided this was the moment to give his opinion. "I don't want to go to a club. I've been working here all day. I just want to chill with you and Netflix." he grumbled, the big baby.

Her laugh comes across the line. "Levi, how can we not help Dale? He wants to meet someone at a club. I can go with him by myself if you're exhausted. I'll understand."

Levi's eyes pierced right through me. If his glare could kill, I'd be a dead man. "Babe, there is no way on this earth you're going to that meat market without me."

I could hear the glee in Marisa's voice. "I just texted Teresa. She's going to see how she can get us on the list, since we're semi-celebrities. She just needs to contact the party organizers or someone who knows them. But it's not written in stone yet."

"Have I told you lately how lucky my oldest brother is to have you?"

"No, you haven't. I remind Levi all the time. Meet you tonight. I'll get the details from Teresa. Remember no promises."

I handed Levi his phone. "Thanks, I owe you."

His eyebrows went up, a question on his tongue. "So, bro."

He didn't have to say it for me to know what he was going to ask, but you know how it is. He wouldn't be happy unless he got to say the words.

"Just ask," I said.

"Does she know you're interested in her?"

"Not yet."

"Yet?"

I let out a slow breath. "I'm working on it."

Chapter Six
Rebecca

I had a party to go to and was determined to have fun. The feeling of Dale's hands on my body had left me realizing how much I'd missed a man's touch. I hoped deep down inside it was that, and not that I missed Dale in particular. I left the kitchen a woman on a mission. I would meet someone that would rock my world. I would not trip over the same stone twice. This time, I was the one walking away.

* * *

Two hours and an Uber drive later, I was in the warehouse district, standing in front of Club Rain. Electronic music blasted from huge-ass speakers, state-of-the-art lighting, and visual effects played on the buildings alongside the club. Graffiti in psychedelic colors and street art installations peppered the entrance.

Ken had texted that he would wait for me at the entrance. My eyes scoured the area for him, watching beautiful couples as they walked past me—the women in micro dresses, five-inch heels, with flawless makeup and hair. Men dressed to impress in five-hundred-dollar designer T-shirts with the latest expensive sneakers on their feet. Ken was greeting someone near the entrance of the club when he saw me and waved me over. My old study buddy excused himself from whoever he was talking to and met me halfway. Wrapping me in his arms as he lifted me in a hug that left me without breath. We both had changed in appearance. I had lost those freshmen fifteen and he had done a total overhaul.

"Rebecca, wow, that dress is stunning. And you wearing it, oof. If I played for your team, I'd be all over you."

"You've always been good for my ego. You're not doing too bad yourself. Are you working out? I don't remember you ever being this buff." He'd hated exercise of any shape or form in college. His idea of a workout was meeting me at the corner Starbucks for coffee.

"Spinning, Pilates, CrossFit. I wasn't going to find a man in this city without stepping up my game."

"Well, it worked, didn't it? I saw your latest update."

Those baby blues gave me a sheepish smile. "I met Sandro last year. It was instant love." He laughed. "Not true. We had some issues to figure out. But it worked out in the end."

I took in his appearance from head to toe. "It must have. You look radiant."

He hugged me to his side once again. The old camaraderie we'd always shared coming back. "Let's go inside. Sandro's waiting to meet you. I haven't stopped talking about you since you agreed to come tonight. This club has been one of Sandro's significant projects this year."

I couldn't help but be a tad envious of his happiness. "Well, lead the way. I'm excited to meet the man who won your heart."

Then he laughed as he lifted his left hand to his face and wiggled the ring on his finger. "We put a ring on it."

I stopped mid-stride, like a screech on a record, and stared at him, dumbfounded. "When did this happen? Can't believe I missed this. Ken, this is huge."

His eyes wrinkled at the corners with happiness. "A month ago, he proposed, I accepted."

Contentment filled me as I smirked up at my friend, who had sworn against monogamy and had played the field for the four years we studied together.

"Who would have guessed? You settled down before I did. I remember all those conversations about how you didn't believe in the bonds of matrimony. Thought it was all an archaic middle-class invention."

His cheeks turned red under his suntan-kissed skin. "When you find the one, you know it. You don't let him slip away. You grab onto that sucker as if your life depended on it, sister to another mister. Sandro is my one, and I was not letting him go."

He pulled me along with him toward the entrance, looking back at me. "How about you? Last time I was in New York, you were dating that lawyer—what happened to that?"

I cringed at the reminder of my ex. "Nothing. I wanted to explore moving back to Nashville, work in the family business. My career in New York was not going in the direction I wanted. The concrete jungle had lost its allure."

"Well, let's see if the Florida lifestyle suits you like it did me." He winked.

Once we made it to the club door's entrance, a hostess plus two very intimidating bouncers let us through after Ken identified me on the list.

"Is it me, or is security beefed up to get into this event?" I commented to Ken as we did another security check entering the central area of the club.

"That's because the owner of Club Rain is here tonight, performing for opening night. The crazies come out with events like these."

I nodded as we continued our way through the crowds of beautiful people in our search for Ken's partner.

Ken looked fitter and happier than I'd ever seen him. I didn't realize how much I'd missed him till now. "Married life agrees with you. I can't wait to tell Karina. She'll be pissed that I found out before she did."

Guilt riddled his face at the mention of my best friend. "Sorry, but she already knows. In my defense, I flew into New York for meetings with the bosses and we had dinner together."

"What, how? You were my friend first. Hell, you were in my dorm room more than your own." Stopping in midstep, my hands anchored at my waist before deciding to let it be. "Whatever, I'm happy for you. Next time she comes in, we're going to celebrate. I'm going to host a party in your honor."

The noise drowned out whatever conversation we could have had as we entered through the doors. The darkness of a hallway with only mirrors reflected us on both sides, lit throughout with neon and white lights on the floors and ceiling leading us to the premier club.

Once inside, I was amazed at the various levels that made up the club. High above us was a celebrity DJ at the turntables. Bodies packed the dance floor. Lights from the dance floor moved to the beats of the DJ's music. The club's theme was an Amazonian rain forest. There was a thirty-foot water-fall to my left as we entered the cavernous space. From the main club floor, a fog-like effect rose among the dancing bodies. The crowd went wild, the noise deafening as it hid everyone inside the theatrical smoke and fog.

I took it all in as we walked toward the second floor, where I assumed we would meet up with Ken's partner. There, another bouncer let us pass through once he saw and recognized Ken. Impressed, I say, "Is this area the VIP section?"

I could feel the vibration of the pounding music below my feet, but the acoustics here allowed us to speak without yelling.

"Yes, when this place opens to the public, the bottle service in this space alone starts at a thousand a table, and a skybox is twenty-five hundred. They'll fill up with no problem."

"I need to get out more," I said.

We made our way through the crowded box. Pausing every so often to let someone pass us. I saw a group of people that looked extremely familiar to me. I stopped and squinted my eyes to make sure. The only lighting came from the strobe lights on the dance floor. Marisa and Levi were standing less than ten feet from where we were and standing close to them was Dale. This was too convenient. He'd done this on purpose. I made a beeline over to them, my hand in Ken's as I dragged him toward my friends.

Levi stood with a possessive arm around Marisa's waist, with a watchful eye on his surroundings, not appearing at all comfortable. Dressed in a sexy, backless deep-red mini and heels stood Marisa. She seemed very much in her environment. I kissed them both on the cheeks as soon as I reached them. Introducing them to Ken.

"What a coincidence that we are both at the same party."

The best actress award goes to Marisa. Her eyes widened with complete and utter innocence. "I know. Can you believe that? Such a small world."

I smirked. "I agree. Six degrees of separation and all."

"Absolutely," she said, then turned to Levi and pulled him toward the dance floor. "Babe, our song. Excuse us, Rebecca, I have to grab this one while I can."

"Of course, have fun." I turned to Dale. He'd been standing next to his brothers. I noticed his eyes on me since I'd arrived at the area. I walked up to greet him, hissing in his ear, "How did you arrange an invitation on such brief notice?"

An electric current traveled throughout my body as his mouth grazed my earlobe. The smell of sandalwood teased my senses. "I just asked. Guess it pays to be related to a local celebrity." Then he stepped away.

Ken approached us, curiosity in his eyes as he put out his hand to shake Dale's. "Ahem... I'm Ken, Rebecca's old college buddy. A pleasure to meet you."

I politely interrupted, "I'm sorry, Ken. Let me introduce you. This is Dale, Levi's brother and partner in Chance Construction. Dale, this is my friend Ken. We were neighbors at Columbia. His husband is Sandro, the architect that designed the club."

Dale put out his hand to shake Ken's. I watched the play of emotions on his face when he realized this was the Ken that had sent me the text that had him leaving my house in a huff. "Nice to meet you, as well."

Ken glanced back and forth between us. "Rebecca, I'm going to find Sandro and bring him over. I want you to meet him. He should be around here somewhere. I'll be right back."

"I can go with you to search him out."

"No, stay here with your friends. I don't want to drag you around this club in those heels. He could be anywhere. I'll be right back."

Dale sidled up to me, "Don't worry. I'll keep her company till you get back."

"Great, wait for me here," Ken said.

I smiled and nodded. Once Ken left, I moved out of Dale's space. "Are you here to sabotage my social life?"

"No. Marisa happened to have a friend that, had a friend, that was coming and could get her and her friends in. Now that they are reality TV celebs, the doors to so many places are open."

I turn to face him, my back to everyone we know. "Come on Dale, kind of smarmy of you, showing up here."

"Becca, the world does not revolve around you. Maybe I wanted to be part of the Miami social scene." He said this with all innocence, if only I believed him.

My eyebrows lifted at his words as I pointed to his brother who was sitting on the sofa reading off his phone. "Oh, come on, Levi looks like he'd rather get a root canal than be here. How did you ever convince him to show up?"

He signaled over to where Marisa was doing tequila shots with her girlfriends, "She decided to come, and Levi wasn't going to lose sight of her. Believe me he's not happy, but he's crazy about Marisa."

"They make each other happy, it's not one sided. They're truly a great couple, hopefully they'll make it."

He grimaced at my words. "Is that a dig at us?"

"Dale, there's no us."

Chapter Seven
Dale

I wanted to make peace with her. Not only because working with her this last month had been hell on my conscience, but because I never got over having left her. She'd refused to make eye contact with me at all costs this last month. Making it clear to my brothers she avoided being alone with me. You can imagine the curious raised eyebrows my brothers would send me. Leaving any room I was working on and our conversations were always awkward. Now she saw me as smarmy— a total stalker in her eyes. How was I going to change her mind at this point?

More than a few men's eyes lingered on her as she walked toward us. The pink minidress showed off her every curve with its deep *V* plunging neckline, finishing with those very toned and long legs in four-inch heels. She might not be mine, but I planned to make sure no one else laid their hands on her tonight.

Levi, who stood close to me, butted me with his shoulder. "Hey, you had enough? Because I can leave anytime you want to. Nightclubs aren't my scene."

I pointed across from us to where Ken was having a conversation with the girls. "We arrived only ten minutes ago. Marisa will not want to leave." Levi grimaced at the truth of my words.

"Damn, you're lucky she likes you," as he gestured to Marisa, "I wanted to kill you when you brought this idea up. I should be in front of the TV after a barbecued N.Y. strip. But no, my brother had the bright idea of stalking his ex-girlfriend."

My eyebrows lifted, and I shook my head. "Not stalking her, making sure that nothing happens to the boss. You should be thanking me, not riding my ass."

He smirked as he said, "Yeah, right?"

Ken walked over to Rebecca and the girls with some guy in tow. I overheard the exchange of introductions and congratulations to the newlywed couple.

The DJ announced something over the speakers, interrupting all conversation. I couldn't make out what it was, but the entire club roared in applause, whoops, and screams. The women applauded in excitement and beelined toward the balcony that overlooked the dance floor. A stage lifted from the middle of the dance floor. Above the crowd stood the Reggaeton singer, the club's money partner. My construction crew blasted his music at the jobsites all the time. More smoke and lighting effects lit the cavernous rooms while he performed his latest hit. Barely clothed dancers gyrated and moved to a choreographed mix on the stage and tables across the club, causing more sensation from the onlookers.

Levi's eyes rolled up in his head. He leaned over and said close to my ear, "Fuck, never getting out of here now!" He made his way toward Marisa. "Watching my girl ogle some other guy isn't my idea of fun."

"You might as well enjoy the show, dude. Marisa will be more than happy to celebrate with you later. Bet it will be worth your Netflix sacrifice."

Soon after his performance, the famous Puerto Rican singer appeared to be making the rounds and congratulated Ken's husband on his work at the club. *The man must think he was a babe magnet by the way he strutted around like he owned the place... wait, he did own this place.* Sandro made introductions to whoever was standing by him. Figures the in-house talent zoned in on Rebecca.

My fists clenched at my side when the performer placed an arm around Rebecca possessively, as if she were a groupie who wanted a selfie. With a polite step back, she extricated herself from his grasp as she continued talking to him.

Marisa was standing in front of me within seconds. "Hey, if you had any intention of laying claim to her, you better make a move sooner than later. Chago's hot." Levi walked up to us with a drink in his hand for her, "But he doesn't hold a candle to you and your brothers."

Levi gazed to where we both watched as the famous performer poured on the charm. "Bro, you plan to sit here with puppy dog eyes and watch someone hit on Rebecca? Looks cozy to me."

Levi practically had a doctorate in pushing my buttons, but either way, I was already two steps ahead. Every time she laughed at whatever inane comment the performer directed to her, my insides churned with dread. Was I too late to salvage any part of our relationship? No way she was leaving with that guy. I was going to make sure of that.

A server with an entire tray of champagne glasses filled to the brim passed me. I signaled him to stop and grabbed two flutes off the tray. "Thanks, I need to rescue a lady."

I approached them from the side, both glasses in my hands, one of them outstretched for Rebecca. Chago's security detail hovered close to them. I guess to keep the batshit crazy away. "Here, I brought you a refill. Marisa thought you might need a fresh drink. I hope you don't mind."

"Of course not, how could I. But you really shouldn't have." Her eyes shot back at me glittering with anger.

"How could I not, you haven't had anything to drink since you arrived. You must be parched."

"I didn't realize you were monitoring my consumption." Confusion filled Rebecca's face as she took the champagne flute. Then her eyes squinted with suspicion. "Thank you. I appreciate Marisa thinking about me, but again it wasn't necessary."

Once my hand was free, I offered my hand to the singer to shake. "Mr. Chago, can I say, huge fan. When I heard you would be performing tonight, I hounded everyone I knew to get an invitation."

Chago stopped mid-sentence to face me, his English heavily accented in Spanish. "Thank you, so glad you came. I wanted everyone to experience a great time tonight, then come back and repeat it...of course, as paying customers."

Rebecca watched us, taking a sip from the flute I'd brought her. When I interrupted their conversation, she hadn't looked happy with me. I guess now she wanted to have fun at my expense, a sparkle in her eyes as she asked, "Dale, I'm surprised. When did you become a fan of Reggaeton?

Especially Chago's?" The dig was there. I had five brothers. I could bullshit with the best of them.

While the singer was oblivious to where she was going with this, I certainly was not. "Most of my construction crew are Spanish speakers. What music do you think they listen to when they work?" I grinned back at her. There was a ball-buster side to Rebecca, and I'd almost forgotten how unexpected it could be.

She was quick to answer, "But please tell us, what are your favorite Chago songs?"

Chago was silent, clueless to what was going on between us. His head moved back and forth between us. A look passed over his face as if he realized there was history, and he was the odd man out.

He signaled to someone behind me, and a security guard approached him. "I need to make my excuses. There are many people who attended tonight I need to greet. Nice to meet you both. Please return." He turned to Rebecca, took her hand in his, "Rebecca, my pleasure."

Rebecca gave him a radiant smile. "Thank you. I wish your club every success. Sandro did a fabulous job. I'm predicting this is going to be one of the top nightclub venues in Miami soon."

Once he moved on, Rebecca swiveled her eyes sharply and assessed me, hand at hips. "Did you cockblock me?"

I rolled my shoulders like a boxer in a ring, preparing for the next punch she might deliver, ready to defend my title. "Rebecca, how can you say that about me? My intentions were completely well-intended. Marisa suggested I check on you. See if you were okay, needed anything?"

Her upper teeth bit her lower lip. She was holding back a

smirk as she moved. "Oh, really, Marisa's involved in this now?"

From the corner of my eye, I saw the back of the Spanish singer leave the area. Relief flooded through me. For all that she was accusing me of sabotaging her, she didn't look to upset with me having crashed her conversation with the famous guy.

I put on my innocent face. The one Mom said would get me out of detention every time. "Why would I do that to you? Do you honestly think I would have pulled something like that on you? Plus, I didn't peg you for a groupie or of the one-and-done type. Have things changed that much in eight years?"

She lifted her chin at that. "Dale Chance, you did not just go there. Things have changed, you shouldn't assume. You think I want a relationship — you know that thing about girls just wanting to have fun? That concept is alive and kicking nowadays."

I merely stared, tongue-tied, and then totally turned on. I took Rebecca's hand to pull her towards another area rather than standing where everyone would witness our conversation. There were plenty of people ogling us from the couches and chairs. As it was, I felt the eyes of my brother, Marisa, and Ken giving us conspicuous looks. Once I reached a dark alcove, literally a hallway away, I placed her in front of me, hidden from the busybodies that were my family and friends. "Dale, hands-off, space." She demanded in a shrill voice.

"Sorry, I didn't want an audience. Becca, I know you're still pissed at me. I've asked for your forgiveness countless times. Don't get back at me by going off with some random dude you barely know."

Her perfume was doing a number on me in such close quarters. I had her backed into the small alcove, my chest inches from hers. Her eyes never left mine. She pressed her lips in anger. With her index finger pointed into my chest with each sentence, like an exclamation point, before she said, "It's always about you. Looking back, the best thing that happened to us was we didn't elope that night. We had a lot of growing up to do."

I placed my hand on hers, the one that jackhammered into my solar plexus, pressed it into my chest, so she could feel my heartbeat and hopefully the honesty. "Wait, hear me out."

Eyes narrowed on my hand she tried to pull her hand back. But I kept it anchored to me. "What, Dale? We've gone around in circles with this topic. Can I trust you again? Do I want to? You want to pick up where we left off all those years ago. Clean slate it. Then you accuse me of trying to make you jealous. It's always about you, not me. Does what I felt that day not even count, since we never spoke of the subject?" She was hot when mad, but she was also right.

The thought of her writing me out of her life was making me ill. It electrified the surrounding air with the words that hadn't but needed to be said, "You're right, I was a complete coward. How can I earn your trust back? That summer was a whirlwind for both of us. Maybe if we had been older. If I'd been the man, you needed me to be. Becca, what can I say? How often do I need to say I'm sorry for not living up to your high expectations? Can we start over? We're different people than those kids. Give us another chance to begin again. I know I said friends, but don't close the door on us."

Sadness reflected at me from her expressive stormy gray

eyes. "Dale, again...there's no us. You were the one that let me go, remember."

I shook my head. "And I've regretted it every day since. I know it sounds like a lame-ass apology for hurting you."

The music blasted and flashed all around us, but we were oblivious to the people walking past us. Maybe this wasn't my brightest idea. The club scene proved not to be conducive to talking about relationships or deciding the fate of your future. My heart paused a beat as I waited for her decision, we stood motionless in that dark alcove.

Her lower lip trembled as she said, "Dale, you want bygones to be bygones, and me to let go of all my pent-up resentment? Why should I? Just because you bat those long ass lashes of yours."

I placed my hand on her upper arm. "That's not why at all. Because even though I don't deserve a second chance, I'm asking for one. We can make this work. I won't take your friendship or trust for granted again. "

She said nothing. I assumed she was processing, and if there was something my mother taught me was to give a woman space to think.

She stared up at me, shook her head, then said, "I've warned you, don't mess this up because I'm not giving you another chance to hurt me."

"I won't. Cross my heart." Lifting my hand to my chest.

"Becca, you look exhausted. The sun has done a number on you. I hope you reapplied the aloe."

Rebecca gave me a sheepish smile. "I got a bit carried away reading after you left."

"Why don't I take you home? Levi and I came in separate cars. I'll take you to your house."

"Thanks. The sun I took today took a toll on me. What I want is two ibuprofen and to take off all the makeup covering it."

"Then your chariot awaits, let's get the hell out of here."

As we waited for the valet, I sent a text to Levi.

Me: Got to go, giving Rebecca a ride home
Levi: Are you for real? You left? Marisa's on the
dance floor with Corinne and Sophia. I HATE YOU.
Me: You are the MVP, thanks for taking one for
the team

Chapter Eight
Rebecca

Dale had made a fool out of me. Again. The pull I felt toward him made me want to say yes to anything he offered. My resolve around him dissolved, no matter how hard I tried to remain distant. His presence was too hard for me to ignore. But if I was honest with myself, it had been an uphill battle with him always being around. His footprint was everywhere on the set of production. His brothers counted with him in all facets of the build. My father's words repeated in my head. Fool me once, shame on you, fool me twice, shame on me. I found it hard to focus on anyone else in the room when Dale was in my vicinity. He was a vacuum that sucked all my attention.

I wanted to trust him again, but I feared falling for the gorgeous man once again. This time love could break me where I might not return from the abyss —I went through eight years ago. I never loved someone the way I did him, and then he betrayed my faith in him. Dale destroyed my ability to trust and believe anyone else. My therapist in New York had made me aware of my various issues. I tried to work through them. Unfortunately, it was easier said than done. But one thing about all that therapy was clear, I had to forgive and let go if I wanted to get on with my life.

There were other boyfriends after Dale, but none could break the rigid barrier that protected my heart. Exhausted and having drunk a bit too much champagne, all I wanted was to go home and collapse in bed. Ken called out my name as we made our way towards the club's exit. I turned to find him jogging to catch up with me.

"Rebecca, you're leaving so soon?"

I nodded as I pulled him into a hug. "I promise to call. Karina's coming in soon. We'll do something together. I'm exhausted from sunstroke if you haven't noticed how two-toned I look tonight."

He knowingly looked from Dale back to me before pulling me away to talk in private.

He nudged his head in Dale's direction, who had walked toward the valet. Ken turned his attention. "I remembered where I saw him. It was that summer I stayed at your house after our freshman year. I also didn't forget how devastated you were when you returned to campus that semester." He glanced toward where Dale was standing.

I didn't want to reminisce or confront my true feelings for Dale with my old friend. Since I was unsure precisely what feelings I still had for him, I planned to give myself the space to figure it out. Having to be around him, was a constant reminder of why I fell for him.

"Ken, the keeper of all my darkest moments. I thought it was time to extend the olive branch and move on with our lives, nothing more."

Ken's eyebrows flew up in disbelief. "Keep telling yourself that. The magnetism between you guys is off the charts. His eyes didn't leave you all night."

Could Dale's feelings be as Ken claimed, or was this just him romanticizing reality?

What is it about married couples?

Once you took the plunge, you wanted everyone as paired up as you?

"Don't worry. Older and wiser here." I pointed to myself. "Dale was not the only fish in my ocean. You were a witness to my extensive dating."

He scratched his brow as if giving it thought. "Yes. I was there for the revolving door of men that fell head over heels in love with you, and you never gave them the time of day. So maybe he meant little, but no one's stuck after him either." He pulled me into a long hug.

How could I admit to my friend what I didn't admit to myself? That I couldn't shake my feelings for Dale. He indeed was my kryptonite. I had to be careful that no one got the wrong idea about us. We were starting over as friends this time. Of course, we were friends with a severe case of attraction to each other. That was genuinely inconvenient.

* * *

Seeing Dale in the club tonight reminded me of when we'd met at my parents' house. He'd been a complete fish out of the water then, as he was now. And I'm even more attracted to him now than I was then. The first time I caught sight of him eight years ago, he'd been reading the spines of the books in my parent's library. I'd run into the library looking to hide from another shopping trip with my mother. What I'd wanted to do was meet friends at the beach. His cheeks had turned red when I noticed it was where my mother kept her collection of romance novels. I thought it was cute and quickly made a point of introducing myself to him. He was a hunk at nineteen, tall, and built from helping his father in construction.

After that, I always wanted to be conveniently around whenever the cute guy assisted his dad on the job. He fetched wood and tools for his dad and seemed uncomfortable as he walked around the mansion. Now he was this sexy, handsome man and stood out among many wannabes in this club.

The valet brought Dale's truck to where we waited out in front of Club Rain. He grinned as he opened my door and helped me into the high cab. Once I buckled up, he started toward my home. I looked out the window as he drove. Soft music ran in the background.

I leaned back into the leather of my seat, and I twisted my neck to inspect him. "After all these years, some things never change. Still listening to country."

"Yup, there were some things that never changed, well some do. The truck's new, not one of my father's leftover cars."

I nodded. "True, but you know that never bothered me."

With only inches separating us, one from the other, I realized how intimate this dark enclosed space was. Like an old sweater, we sat in comfortable silence. It still fit and gave me all the good feelings. The interior cab smelled of Dale, a combination of leather, sandalwood, and clean male. Dale's eyes traveled toward me, drinking me in possessively before turning back toward the road.

I swiveled in my seat to face him. "You never answered me. Which of Chago's songs is your favorite?"

His face went blank before turning to me, lips quirking into a grin. "None, but you already knew that."

A shiver traveled down my spine. "Yeah, I figured it was a ploy to interrupt us."

He nodded his head while answering. "Yup, he looked a bit too comfortable talking to you. Didn't want you making a mistake and falling for a sophisticated, successful singer."

I sat up straighter in my seat. I knew Dale had been sabotaging the one guy that had hit on me tonight.

"Why a mistake? He was very charming, even polite," I said. "Made a point of inviting me to his next performance."

His lips pursed in a way that I wanted to laugh at but didn't. "Of course, he would. You're a beautiful and smart woman."

I swallowed hard, repeating the words in my mind: beautiful and smart. My ovaries were doing jumping jacks.

I pivoted towards him. The car seat belt dug into my sunburned shoulder. "Shit... are you kidding me? I don't remember you ever being the jealous type."

He shrugged, "I'm sorry it's hard not being that way around you, believe me I've tried."

The lights of the buildings that dotted the Miami skyline held my attention as he drove. There was no traffic at this hour. "Dale, I swear that the number of high-rises tripled since I was last here."

He looked over at me and smirked. "What's the national bird of Miami?"

I lifted my brows in question. No clue what the answer was.

Finally, he said, "The crane."

Understanding filled me, and I couldn't stop the laugh that escaped, "That was so cheesy."

"Yeah, the joke is old, but it's new to you."

"You're like the TV networks advertising that if we didn't see the series during the season we could watch them again during the summer, and they were new to us."

* * *

There was a lull in the conversation, and we drove in silence before Dale leaned over and turned off the radio. "You're right. I was an asshole. Who you choose to hang out with is your business. It's just been hard to be around you the past month because every time I see you I'm filled with regret about how I handled everything."

My fingers played with the edge of my short dress as I looked at the lights from the high-rise buildings. "You know how many times I replayed that night in my mind? And all the excuses I made for your behavior." I made air quotes with every accusation. *"My tire blew out. I got a ticket. The coast wasn't clear. I can't make it out tonight.* I would have taken any excuse. Just telling me you weren't ready or having second thoughts would have been the right thing to do."

He rubbed at his eyes before glancing over to me. "Becca, you have no idea how many times I thought of how things could have played out better. If I'd only done this or that, how we could have come back from what I did. I was so ashamed of my own behavior. I ended up convincing myself that I didn't deserve you in the end."

The weight of his guilt wasn't getting him or me

anywhere. And it seemed we were both stuck in the past and hadn't been able to move on from it. We needed to make peace with this if either of us was going to move forward with our lives, regardless of whether it was with each other. It was time to let it go, I was going to tell him what we both needed to hear to shelve it and start over.

"But I don't have the energy to keep replaying the past. I'm willing to put this in my rearview mirror. No more conversations about this. Let it go."

He reached across the armrest that divided us, placed his hand on mine, taking my fingers in his. Heat transferred to my digits. "Thank you. I'll respect your wishes and not bring it up anymore. I'm sure coming back here was difficult, but I'm glad you did."

My stomach muscles fluttered at his touch as I watched his hand envelop mine, "Blaming someone else for any unhappiness I have in my life is a waste of time. Ultimately, I'm responsible for myself and my decisions. Happiness in one's life is never to be upset or angry about something you can't change. And it's not like we can avoid each other, as it is we're tripping over each other." I said, a sorry attempt to lighten the mood.

Dale nodded at my words but stayed silent. I hoped he agreed.

"To be honest, I'm glad I came back." I said looking out the window, hoping the darkness hid the blush creeping up my cheeks.

He smiled over at me, sending my heart leaping. "What's the next project for *Renovated?* Do you know when it starts?"

"We've already started. Marisa and Levi are starting the vetting process. Sarah, my assistant, is coming out here. Much easier to work on potential clients if we're both together. Plus, I needed her help with getting our satellite office up and ready. She arrives Monday, so I'll have a clearer picture then." At least someone was interested in my work. My family acted as if they were indulging in my current hobby.

A twitch curled the corner of his lips. "Never expected you to enjoy working so much. You seem passionate about what you do."

"Why? Did you expect a wedding band, two point five children, a large house, and a dog?" Sarcasm dripped from my voice. "I expect that from Father, not from you."

He gripped the wheel tight, his focus on the road. "That's not it at all. You never mentioned being interested in production or TV that summer."

"When we dated, I was studying journalism. When I returned after that summer and had to declare a major, I decided on communications. It made the most sense to me, and I found I loved working behind-the-scenes, got internships, worked at a TV station in the city. I never wanted to be the center of attention. They tried to convince me to be a news reporter or correspondent. Being in front of the camera's not my jam."

We passed the private gate for the island and drove through the quiet streets to reach my home.

"You'll be seeing a lot of me come Monday. I'm looking forward to hearing from you about the trials and tribulations of producing a show. We have a lot of catching up to do." He said the words tentatively, as if testing the idea.

I turned in my seat once again to face him. "Well, then you start first. What have I missed in these eight years that we haven't spoken?"

"I believe I'd like to answer that in the coming days, wouldn't want to hit you with all-in-one sitting. But I can tell you I've moved on to furniture design, and I'm pretty good at it." There was pride in his voice though subtle.

"Oh... really?" I knew he was playing his accomplishments down. I had stalked him myself and was aware that he had collectors vying for the pieces he created. He'd made a name for himself among new furniture designers, regardless of not having a formal education in the field. It had been innate and once discovered had placed him on the lips of big-time home decorators and magazines.

"Yeah ... really." he said, his mouth crinkling into a smile.

He stopped the car in front of the main entrance of the house. We sat in the darkness. The splashing seawater against the artificial barriers of the island, and vehicles that traveled across the intercostal were the only sounds around us.

Before I even opened the truck door, Dale jumped out on his side and ran around to help me down. I gave him a questioning look, and he stared back at me. "I wasn't born in a barn, you know. I'm walking you to the door. I know how to treat a lady. Plus, you're all alone in this big house. I want to make sure you're safe." He stepped forward, extending a hand.

I lifted my gaze from his extended hand, hesitating at first, but then laying my fingers in his. The rough calluses sent shivers straight to my lower regions. "What a gentleman." A new and unexpected warmth surged through me.

Once out of his truck, he kept my hand in his as we took the five steps to the front door. When we reached the heavy wooden double doors, he let go. "Do you have your keys?" His aqua eyes riveted me to the spot. "Becca, the keys?"

I pretended not to be affected by our closeness. "Yeah, sorry, got lost in my thoughts." Fishing them out of my evening clutch.

His nearness was overwhelming. "Thank you, once again, for bringing me home."

Inches apart, a look of tired sadness passed over his features. "You're welcome. I'm just sorry it took me so long to talk with you again." His finger brushed a strand of hair that had fallen from my face behind my ear. Shivers traveled straight to my core at his touch, and I gravitated into his space wanting more of the sensation. The pull was strong to throw myself at him, but I fought it, reminding myself to take baby steps.

I was not blind to his attraction—even less my own—but I forced myself to wish him good night as I closed the door on him.

Silence would have been merciful, but as I turned the lock, I heard his voice.

"Night, Becca."

Chapter Nine
Dale

The Walton project was the only thing on my agenda for this week. My brothers were helping me with the finishing touches on my home, and we were down to the last stretch. I didn't want to be hammering at seven in the morning, knowing that Rebecca wouldn't take too kindly to the noise. We'd turned a corner in our relationship, and I felt lighter than I had in years. At least now, we moved in a more positive direction and could maintain a conversation without her finding a reason to avoid me.

Jimmy, my carpenter apprentice, had come along with me to remove the old cabinetry. He'd started working with me over two years ago, when his mom had asked me to take him under my wing. Saying no to Jimmy's mother had never been possible, with Mom standing behind her, nodding her head at me. Later, Jimmy's mom had been Mom's hospice caretaker, our saving grace. Jimmy was working with the county vocational rehabilitation program, but they didn't have an employer available to guide him in his love of carpentry. When he'd continued showing up every day to work with me, I offered him the apprentice position. I knew how important it was to allow someone to do what they loved—demonstrating a natural talent for woodwork and a willingness to learn. I'd kept him on. Now he was my number one assistant.

"Hey Dale, is it true, that you worked on the Star Island house with your dad?"

A ball of emotion clogged my throat as I remembered those days. Dad had decided it was time to take me on a job with him like he'd done with Levi and Marcos. I'd been so proud that he'd chosen me to accompany him this time. As we arrived at the sprawling mansion, he'd looked over at me and said, "Boy, these types of jobs can either make or break you, let's see what you're made of." Little did he know how it almost had.

Glancing over to Jimmy, who waited for an answer, I said, "Yep, I worked with Dad on its first renovation eight years ago. We worked in the closets, library, even the kitchen."

Jimmy grinned, "I'll be able to say I worked on an original Chance project."

Lowering the volume of the radio, "You're right."

I missed Dad. His death had hit us all hard. He'd shown us what it was to be a husband, father, and provider. He'd adored Mom, would do anything to make her happy, had opened his house and heart to three abandoned kids that weren't his blood.

As we passed the gatehouse, Jimmy whistled, "Damn." His head swiveled from side to side. "These are some enormous houses. I've never worked in a house this big."

"Well, Jimmy, always a first time for everything. Today is yours."

* * *

"Buenos días, Yolanda," I said as she opened the kitchen entrance for us. "Let me introduce you to Jimmy. He works with me."

"Morning, ma'am," said Jimmy.

"Good day to you, too. I have a carafe of coffee ready, and there are homemade banana muffins on a plate in the kitchen. Help yourselves."

The aroma of fresh-brewed coffee and freshly baked goods permeated the air. "Yolanda, you're a godsend."

Jimmy went straight for the kitchen island and stood before the plate, waiting for me to give the okay before he could pick one up. I nodded to him. "Go ahead Jimmy, Yolanda has been kind enough to prepare this for us. How can we say no?"

He grabbed one for himself and passed one to me as I served us two mugs of coffee.

Yolanda was already sipping from her cup. "Mrs. Rebecca hasn't come down yet, but she should be down soon."

"If she's not awake now, she will be soon enough between the noise of the saw and the nail gun. We're going to get started, we have a schedule to keep. Thank you, we appreciate the coffee and muffins."

"My pleasure. I miss cooking for a full house. This place is very lonely without the family around."

* * *

Jimmy and I started working in the library. True to my word, between the hammering and the sawing, a not-too-happy Rebecca appeared at the entrance dressed in a silk robe that did little to hide her curves, her hair held back from her face with a headband, and her feet bare.

She had a mug in her hand. The aroma of coffee drifted toward me. "Till you finish, is this going to be my wake-up call every morning?"

I walked over to where she was. I didn't want her stepping on a splinter. There were inches between us. I kept my eyes from traveling her body like I wanted to. "Sadly, yes. Until I finish this project, you will wake up to this every morning." Bed head and all, she was still the best thing I'd seen this morning. My eyes traveled from her feet to her face. I was looking forward to seeing that every day for the next month.

A red tinge touched the fair skin of her cheeks, and her bottom teeth chewed on her lip. Her eyes met mine as she took one step closer to me. The light floral scent of her perfume reached me. I had to fight myself from closing my eyes and breathing her in.

"Hmm ... we'll see about that." She lifted her cup to bring the steaming brew to her mouth.

I took a step closer to her, lowering my head as I whispered in her ear my lips grazing her lobe. There was a slight shiver and her nipples perked up beneath the soft silk of her robe, making standing so close very uncomfortable. "Babe, you look beautiful in that robe this morning, but you need to wear shoes if you're going to walk into this room."

Her eyes moved to the covered parquet on the floor. Strewn around the base were pieces of wood and shavings from the project. She took a step back toward the entrance. "You are planning to clean-up this mess, aren't you?"

"Of course, we clean-up after ourselves." I use my body to block Jimmy's view. "Becca, as much as I'm delighted at seeing you in such a sexy cover-up, I don't want to share that with my crew."

She looked past me to where Jimmy was placing the wood on a workbench. "Oh right, hadn't realized there was someone else with you." But if she noticed my jealousy, she didn't mind it. From the smile on her face, she liked it.

Which was why I kept egging her on. That playful antagonism was what made us so good together. But now that she was playing back, I ought to remind myself how well this worked out for me in the past.

"I need to get changed," she said with a smile at me that was half fun, half try me.

Jimmy saw her and waved shyly. "I'm Jimmy. You must be Rebecca."

She did a small wave back, leaning her body so that it wasn't mostly hidden by mine.

"Hi Jimmy, you're right. I'm Rebecca. Nice to meet you, too."

Finally, we were back on firm ground. Which was when fate always wanted to deliver a surprise.

Yolanda walked toward us, a phone to her ear. "Yes, Mrs. Walton. I will let Ms. Rebecca know."

Both Rebecca and I stilled, not uttering a word. Rebecca tightened her robe, playing with the sash that kept it closed, while she waited for Yolanda to hang up.

Yolanda peered up from the phone in her hand. "Sorry to interrupt, but that was your mother. The car service is picking her up from the hangar. She just arrived in Miami and should be here within the hour."

Rebecca's eyes widened in panic. She turned toward the room's exit. She passed her mug to Yolanda, saying out loud, more to herself than to us. "I need to get ready. This drive-by is not a good omen."

Shit, this didn't sound promising. The mere thought of her mother showing up by surprise had Rebecca running to get ready to receive her. No hanging around in your pajamas to receive good old mom.

* * *

I knew precisely when Mrs. Susan Walton arrived at her home. She seemed to electrify the surrounding air with tension. Yolanda was a ball of energy running up and down the main stairway. Jimmy and I continued with the bookcases when the sound of car doors slamming and a female voice ordering someone to carry her bags pulled me from the job.

Yolanda opened the heavy wood entrance door outside of the library to allow Mrs. Walton inside the house. After greeting the homeowner warmly, she directed the chauffeur to follow her toward the master suite.

Rebecca's mother walked over to where I was working, and I greeted her, "Hello Mrs. Walton, come to check up on the progress of your library?"

Her smile, just like Rebecca's, lit up her entire face. Hair and makeup flawless, dressed in a white linen jump-suit, looking fresh, which seems hardly possible if you've been traveling. Maybe the difference was that it was a private charter. She walked around the room scrutinizing the work in progress, "You're one of the Chance brothers, aren't you?"

"Yes, Dale Chance at your service."

She stopped and recognition flickered in her eyes as she fixed her gaze on me. "I've met you before, haven't I? I mean, I've watched *Renovated* and have seen you on our shows in the background. But I also remember you coming with your father."

There was lead in my belly as I gulped and wondered how much she knew of what went on between Rebecca and me that summer. "Yes, I worked with my dad at your home years ago."

Her expression stilled and grew serious. "I was sorry to hear about both your parents. Your father was a delight to work with, and I remember hearing that your mother passed away also not too long ago."

"Thank you, Mrs. Walton. I like to believe they're together now. I plan to have your library ready for you within the month."

"Fabulous, we probably could have left it as it was, but Charles insisted that this room needed a redo. How could I complain? Charles has never taken an interest in matters of decor, so I agreed."

We heard Rebecca's voice throughout the house calling out for her mother. "Rebecca, I've been chatting with this charming young man. Did you know he and his father worked in our library years ago?"

Rebecca's eyes became saucers. "Yes, I remember. I was here for a summer break from my first year at Columbia."

Mrs. Walton nodded in response. "You're correct. You have an excellent memory."

She winked at me before saying to her daughter, "I probably would have remembered him, too, if he looked like this all those years ago."

I hid my smirk by biting my lower lip as Rebecca's cheeks stained red and she said, "Mother, have you no shame."

Deadpan Susan Walton said, "No dear, I go after what I want in life. There is no shame in that." And she winked at me.

Rebecca coughed before saying out loud, "Let's go, you're impossible. Yolanda has prepared us breakfast, and I'm starving. Dale's busy, I don't want to occupy any more of his time." I held in a laugh. Rebecca's flushed face gave away her discomfort at her mother's blatant flirting.

She tugged at her mother's arm. "Mother, why didn't you call me to tell me you were coming in?"

"It was a last-minute decision. I told your father I wanted to see my daughter, not FaceTime with her—that way we can do the charity ball Zoom meeting together. And if you must go back, we can do it together."

Rebecca looked back at me, her eyes rolling upward as she walked with her mother toward the kitchen.

Jimmy, who'd been busy taking down shelves, looked back at me. "I think Mrs. Walton likes you."

I grinned back at him, "I'm more worried about getting the daughter to like me." But I already felt lighter. Rebecca had stayed in the same room with me for over ten minutes. Now if I could only make her stay for good. Could she see past just being friends to us having more? Moments like this made a man hopeful. I didn't want to lose her again.

Chapter Ten
Rebecca

Whew —thank God for the advanced warning. If Mother walked in on me dressed in my robe, she would correctly assume that my lack of attire would entice Dale, and she would not have been wrong. When I woke to the hammering and shuffling going on downstairs, a smile came to my lips. All because of the man making all the racket. A lightness filled me, and I still couldn't wait to see him. Hence, I showed up downstairs in my robe and watched Dale's eyes get as big as saucers as he took me in.

The camel dress pants, white silk blouse, and ballet flats were the perfect armor to greet Mother. Yolanda had set up a small breakfast on the covered verandah. She had covered the table with linens, china, and silverware. The summer heat was still not in full force, and the sea breeze made it tolerable to sit outside without melting.

We sat in silence as we admired the breathtaking view of the water from our chairs. This was so typical of Miami. Music blasted from the nearby motor crafts and racing jet skis created waves in the blue water. There was a selection of croissants, muffins, and brioche to choose from, which was a total waste of time since Mother watched her carb intake all the time. We each had a slice of bacon quiche and sliced fruit on our plate. Mother poured coffee from the carafe into our cups.

I cornered my mother again because there was no way she was here just to zoom a charity meeting with me. I noticed her fidgeting with the napkin ring and realized for the first time that she was evading me.

What's on her mind?

"Mother, what a surprise to see you. No call, not even a text in the last two weeks. And suddenly you 're visiting me." I took a sip of the coffee in front of me, then placed the cup down. "A pleasant surprise, to be sure."

"Can't a mother visit her daughter in her own house?" Taking a small bite of her quiche, "Mm ... Yolanda's such an excellent cook, her crust is flaky, and the eggs and bacon mixture are firm. You do not know how much I've missed us coming here together as a family."

Now she's obsessing over quiche.

There was something wrong with this picture.

"Of course, you can visit me." I squinted my eyes to focus on her. "What are you not telling me?"

Mother lifted the napkin placed on her lap to her lips to clean her mouth of crumbs. "Rebecca, you're as bad as your brother, seeing conspiracies everywhere."

Pursing my lips, I said, "I just find it hard to imagine you would be here in person because you wanted to appear on Zoom with me for the meeting of the Black and White Gala."

She avoided any direct eye contact as I spoke, her gaze

fixed on the horizon. When she turned back to me, her gray eyes had a pained expression in them. Her lips trembled. "Rebecca, I came because I wanted to tell you something important face to face and not over the phone. You know, your father's been the love of my life for over thirty-five years."

Icy fingers crawled up my spine. Starting a conversation making a point of the length of your relationship never ended well. "Yes, Mother, I'm aware of your mutual obsession with each other. Charles and I joked about it all the time. Most of our friends had parents that were going in separate directions, and you two never were apart."

That was once my goal, too.

My parents had made it seem that I could have that as well. And before that horrible incident eight years ago, I thought I already had it.

Her wistful smile was her response to my comment.

"Mother, what's happened? You have me imagining the worst."

"Well, we had our annual physical around April. They did various exams as part of the wellness check-up. It's all part of the key man insurance policy the network insisted we maintain. Well, they found something in your father's results."

"What? Don't keep me in the dark. You're making me nervous." My appetite left me entirely as my stomach turned on me.

She exhaled a deep sigh, worry reflected in her eyes. "Prostate cancer. They discovered it while doing the tests. The doctors assured us all would be all right. They've assured that once treated. The results should be favorable. That doesn't mean I'm not worried, but I put on a brave face for your father."

My heart stopped in my chest, and my voice sounded shrill even to me. "Why didn't you tell me? Who's treating him and where?"

She put her fork on her plate as she lifted her palms. "Calm down. Your father wanted to handle this without making it a big deal. It was a strategic move on his part. He wanted to make sure Charles was in place. That way, no one on the board would override him. I'm sorry we waited to say anything."

My appetite was all but gone. My body vibrated with the hurt of feeling excluded. "Are you telling me that Charles was aware all along, and you all withheld this from me?"

Mother looked uncomfortable. She realized it upset me, the news she'd given me. "Your father sat Charles down to prepare him for the role of CEO and the responsibilities he would face. More so, he had to know why your father was moving up the time clock on his takeover."

Once again, my family didn't believe me capable of handling the realities of life. Their persistence in protecting me from the truth, hit me the wrong way.

I might have understood their motivation to keep this under wraps from the board and stockholders. But me, when did I fall into that category?

"Mother, did you or Father ever think how I would have felt if he had taken a turn for the worse? I would have found out when it was too late. Why does Charles count more than I do?"

"Dear, don't take it that way. You know we love you both

equally, no favorites." Her hand covered mine, and she squeezed. I pulled my hand from beneath hers.

My jaw dropped because deep down, she believed what she was saying. But that didn't stop me from the pain of the metaphysical knife plunged into my back. "Mother, that's not true. Charles was always going to take over the network, and what they expected of me was what? Father's expectations for me are to marry, chair charities, and be a figurehead on the board of Home Network someday."

My mother shook her head at me. "Yes, Charles knew. Your father didn't want to talk about it. You know how he is. He's the personification of avoidance."

"I'm aware of how he is, but that's still no excuse for not telling me."

She was already speaking over me. "He's already started the treatment, and fortunately, he came out fine with the procedure he had done. The prognosis is excellent, and your father has always been in perfect health till now."

I couldn't hold the sarcasm back, nor the hurt from my voice as I crossed my arms in front of me. "I'm ecstatic Father is doing well. But you left me out of the loop. Did any of you think at any moment how I would take the news?"

"Why make this about you, Rebecca? It happened to your father. This was how he wanted to deal with it."

My mouth fell open as usual. They did not take my feelings into account. I might as well be invisible in my family. I'd gone into this show thinking if it was a success, a ratings giant, they would see me. They would respect me. They would love me.

But none of that was a guarantee. Especially when even having a shot at that kind of success depended on Mom's support. Which was, despite my pleas, going to my brother. As usual.

She continued talking over me. "This only reinforced our desire to travel and enjoy what's left of our time together. Father stepped down as CEO. We've placed your brother to run the network. Life's too short. Illness puts things into perspective."

I just nodded numbly at her words. There were no words that I could say that would make her nor me feel better about the predicament. Mother continued her rambling, and I just kept nodding in futility.

"I told him I wanted to come out here more often, and he agreed. That is why your brother was pushing you to take on my role at Home Design Network. That way, I can also take a step back and not focus on the charities. I don't have to remind you how much we give back to the community surrounding us."

Now I understood the real reason for her impromptu visit. Susan Walton had a plan. Her goal was to guilt me into taking on her role at the Network, not what I wanted to do. She always felt she knew what was best for me. Forget the fact that Renovated was a brilliant concept, and I would make it profitable for the advertisers and us.

I relaxed my face into a reassuring smile. I'd fought her one way or another for years. This close to victory, I needed to remind her we weren't enemies. In the end, we wanted the same thing. "Mom, we'd agreed I was dipping my toe in the charitable foundations that Home Design works with, but I'm not ready to go that route yet. I want to develop my career first in ways that will fulfill me, not take over your responsibilities."

Mother cupped my hand with hers. "Of course, dear, you must do what makes you happy, but keep an open mind, don't close off all your options. But I don't understand why you are making life so hard for yourself. How many women would love to be in your shoes, presiding over gala events, and being heads of charities. You've been fortunate and don't know what it's like to struggle to get what you want out of life. But then again, why should you, you were born a Walton. You have no idea what the world can really be like."

My stomach plummeted. The tightening in my chest had me zoning out of the rest of the conversation. Mother was judging me with the same measuring stick of her own humble beginnings. It was beyond her comprehension, my desire for a career of my own and forging my own destiny, rather than seeking a man to complete me. I needed an excuse to walk away from the table before I said something that I would regret. My phone pinged with a message, and it gave me the perfect reason to change the conversation. There was a message from the administrator of the new rental site. He was confirming the rescheduled appointment to meet and discuss the details of what Home Design required. With my mother's impromptu arrival, I had emailed Sarah to free up my day.

I pushed back from the table and stood up. "Mother, I have a minor emergency with my new assistant. Can you excuse me while I deal with it?"

She smiled up at me, oblivious of how her words had hit me like a cannonball. "Of course, work comes first. The Zoom conference isn't till this afternoon."

I picked up my phone from the table and made my way into the house. Frustration with my family had reached its peak. I needed to get as far away as possible. I refused to break down and reveal how cut up I was by my parents' actions. My chest was tight, and there was suddenly a lack of air in this house. Luckily for me, I had left my purse in the kitchen.

I made my way to the service entrance. The sight of Dale with his protective glasses on standing behind an electric saw table, the whir of the blade as he mitered a piece of wood greeted me. He shut off the machine as soon as I walked up to him.

He searched my face, then asked. "Leaving?"

With lips pursed, I nodded. Anything more might make me scream in frustration as I continued to the separate garage area. Dale followed beside me, placing a gentle grip on my upper arm to stop me. I stopped, then looked down at his hand on my arm. He continued to hold on to me, but the concern was written all over his face, as he loosened his grip but still held on.

My eyes burned with unshed tears. You'd think at twenty-six I'd get a grip on my emotions and the way my mother saw me.

"Becca, wait. What's wrong? Did something happen?"

I lifted my face. When our eyes met, I had a hard time maintaining eye contact. I had been told frequently growing up that I wore my feelings on my sleeve, and with Dale I'd always been transparent. That's why I'd distanced myself from him when I first came back to Miami, he'd been my safe place, someone who I could be myself with and we had lost that.

"What could be wrong? My father had cancer, and everyone in my family kept it from me till now. My mother is making it her mission to mold me into a version of herself.

She had her agenda to fulfill, regardless of what I might have to say about it. I proved to Charles that I could run with a TV program, despite that, he is not backing me up." I let out a deep, pent-up breath at the end of my tirade, my eyes moving to my next goal—getting to the garage.

His hand moved from my arm to cup my face. I shifted my gaze up to meet his.

"We'll go for a ride. You're not driving in that state of mind."

I didn't fight him on this. Road rage was not my thing. "Fine."

He pulled me along to his truck. His assistant came out of the house at that moment. "Jimmy, going for a drive, do me a favor, finish removing the old shelves of the library. I'll be back later."

He opened the truck door and gave me his hand to help me get in. Once buckled up, he glanced back at me and said, "Where to now?"

Chapter Eleven
Dale

When Rebecca stormed out of the house through the service entrance with such a flustered expression, I ran after her on autopilot. I don't think she even noticed me. She was so lost in thought. The table-saw had been at full power, but she walked past me without even acknowledging the sound. She was heading toward the carport. I couldn't let her drive being that upset. If something had happened to her, I'd never forgive myself.

I couldn't fix the past, but maybe I could be there for her in the now.

For over a month and a half, all I wanted to do was reconnect with her. When she entered the library in that pale-lilac, silky robe, her curves highlighted by the drape of the fabric, the outline of her breasts with its deep V made my mouth water at her stiff nipples. All I wanted to do was untie that delicate bow and bury myself in her body. As I stood close to her in the library, the light floral scent coming off her body, her hair still mussed from waking up, I was hard in seconds. Thank God my back was to Jimmy, and she never looked down at my waist. All it took was Yolanda announcing that Mrs. Walton was on her way to the house to deflate.

"Hey, if you want to talk about whatever is bothering you, I'm all ears. If you don't, we can sit in silence, and I'll keep you company. But I'll tell you something my dad told me a long time ago and holds today. Things only rot if you don't deal with them. It will get full of purulent and become infected, by the time you are ready to deal with the problem, it's too late and you just need to amputate the limb."

After about five seconds, she twisted in her seat, "Okay— no more talk about festering wounds. You're grossing me out. I barely got in two bites of my quiche when my mom dropped the cancer bomb on me, and my stomach was turning. I'm just pissed at my family's continuous desire to make all my important decisions. All in the name of knowing what's best for my career."

She looked over at me and groaned, throwing her head back against the seat. "Sorry, you're probably thinking poor little rich girl with champagne problems."

I took my eyes off the road for a second to give her my full attention. "Hey, don't put words in my mouth. I never thought or said that. You are the only one who knows your own emotions, no judgment here."

"My parents are the best … I truly love them. But they still treat me as a child, deciding for me, and expecting me to agree with them. This overprotection makes me crazy and it's only gotten worse since I returned to Nashville. Now they have me rambling like an idiot." A tear traveled down the side of her face, and she wiped it away with the back of her hand.

Nothing I could say would fix her family drama, and there was a heavy churning in my stomach that at one time I caused her to doubt herself. I had even been a conspirator by deciding on her behalf, all because I believed I was doing the right thing.

I let a deep breath out. My goal right now was to get her out of the funk she was in. "Let's see if you're game. You didn't finish your breakfast, and I only ate a muffin. I'm still a growing boy. Let's have a do-over."

Her shoulders shook as she smirked, "A what?"

"Do-over, like we act as though right after seeing you in that sexy robe this morning, things happened differently."

"Like a multiverse?"

I smiled. "Like time travel. I took you to breakfast, and you said yes. This place is famous for its house specialty, which are the blueberry pancakes. Plus, I wanted to show you somewhere important to me since you arrived back in town but hadn't gotten around to doing it."

Her eyes brightened, her head tilted to the side, and there was a softness to her voice. "You remembered."

"Of course." I shrugged like it was nothing. But really, it was everything. How could I ever forget? It was the first and only time I had ever told a woman I loved her. I mean someone that was not my mother. I turned my truck around and headed toward US1 and Saltview, where my family had lived since they established roots in 1925.

Taking her here for breakfast had been something I regretted never having done with Rebecca when we dated.

Where did you take a woman, you wanted to impress and who'd traveled the world and eaten at the best restaurants? Sam's Diner had the best breakfast known to man. Well, maybe for this man.

Once parked, she swung open the truck door and waited

till I made my way over to her to help her down from it. I took her soft hand in my work-roughened one and was reluctant to let go when she was safely on street level. My chest tightened when she smiled up at me as we walked toward the entrance. That smile she aimed in my direction took my breath away.

My hand went to the small of her back when we entered Sam's. I watched her face as she took in the blue retro vinyl booths, shiny chrome, and the stools that lined the counter. I led her to the back of the diner, away from prying eyes.

Large gray eyes looked up at me with delight. "Oh my God, this is fabulous. This is so 1950's, I love it. This alone was worth the drive to Saltview."

Esther came with two menus and placed them in front of us. "Dale, we've missed you this week. Are you two-timing me?"

"Never in a million years, I'm working on a job that takes me out of town early." I pause and put my hand out. "Rebecca, this is Esther. Esther... Rebecca. Esther knows everyone and everything that is happening in Saltview, we practically grew up eating here." Esther nodded to her in greeting and gave her a warm smile.

Esther took out a little pad from the skirt pocket of her uniform. "Hello. You must be special because I have worked here my entire life, and this boy only comes here with his family to eat."

Rebecca's cheeks flushed a light pink, and her back was ramrod straight as she replied, "Thank you, a pleasure to meet you as well." She signaled with her thumb at me. "He promised me the best blueberry pancakes I'm ever going to eat. So, how could I refuse such an offer?"

I shrugged and nodded, getting comfortable in the

padded seats of the booth. "My goal was to impress her with our town's authentic diner. Sam's is an institution here. My parents' first date was a malted at the counter over there. Every time we'd come as a family, they would tell us the story."

"They were such a wonderful couple, so in love with each other," Esther said in a reflective tone. She shook herself slightly. "What can I serve you both?"

"We'll have two tall stacks but add to our order, sides of bacon and sausage. Oh, and chocolate malts with a glass of water." I signaled over to Rebecca with a raise of my eyebrow, who had been eyeing the menu before her.

"Becca, do you want something else?" She was fidgeting in her chair since we'd arrived, her expression clouded."

"Sorry...." She leaned forward, her elbows bent on the table, and nodded. "The same, thank you."

Once Esther left to put in our order, I sat back and admired the view in front of me. My staring must have made her self-conscious. She started squirming and fidgeted with her hair, pushing it behind her ear twice. Her eyes widened as she stared back at me. "What? Do I have spinach between my teeth or something?"

I smirked as I shook my head. "I can't believe I'm here with you. During that summer, we went out. I never brought you close to town. I was afraid that someone would have told my parents. If Dad even suspected what was going on between us, he would have taken me off the job. Now I feel like I let you both down."

She reached out and clutched my hand, squeezing it, interrupting my guilty thoughts. "Don't put that on you. We were kids. Who wants to get into trouble with your parents when you still live with them? I wasn't honest with my parents either. If you need me to give you absolution, let it go."

I nodded.

The lunch crowd was meandering in, people coming up to us to say hello, everyone getting introduced to the beautiful lady with me.

She turned to me when the last couple that came in had stopped by to say hello as they moved toward their table. "Everyone so nice. What fascinates me the most is the way everyone greets each other like old friends as soon they enter the place."

Those silver-gray eyes sparkled. I could sit here and watch her all day. "What can I say about small towns for you? You either studied with their kids or have done a job for them."

Her eyes met mine. "Yeah." And this time, she didn't look away. "You're staring at me again."

"You're staring right back," I said.

"You started it."

"Just admiring the view."

Now she did look away, just for a second, then met my eyes again. "You sure that's all?"

I knew better than to go in that direction, but I'd waited years for this moment. I couldn't just waste it. "I screwed up long ago. I see that I've been just as guilty as your parents."

She shrugged before giving me a breathtaking smile. "I guess with age comes maturity, apology accepted. I never said thank you for taking me away from my house. To be honest, this is just the same old, same old. They will not change."

"Never?"

She ran her hands nervously through her shoulder-length bob. "When I wanted her support with the network, she helped, but honestly, it was a means to her end. Mother wanted my cooperation with her pet project and would only agree if I said yes. She must have expected *Renovated* to be a colossal flop, and I would go crawling back with my tail between my legs. This trip was her ploy to have me back on track with what she wanted. Now you know why it's so important for me that *Renovated* succeeds."

I shook my head as the pieces fell into place. I'd seen the dynamic between them, but I didn't know it was that bad. Or how much it had hurt her. Although she was very accomplished, she still saw herself as unseen in her own family. It broke my heart.

Shaking my head, I said, "Your mom may be many things, but I doubt she wanted you to fail. She's a woman who's prided herself on her family and their well-being. Mrs. Walton would destroy anybody that so much as touched her children, she would not help them dig your grave."

Her hands shredded the paper placemat in front of her. "It's just..." she said but cut off her thought process to continue shredding the paper like it was a job. I took her hands gently into mine to make her stop and come back to the present.

Her eyes went from our hands to my face, then she moved them out from beneath mine to move her hair once again behind her ear. "You're right. Just sometimes I feel powerless. I don't like the sensation. No one thought to clue me in that my father had cancer, regardless of if it was serious. She's probably only told me now to guilt me into it since she wants to pass the baton on to me as the next in line."

The imperial march from *Star Wars* resonated from her bag. She fished it out and as she picked it up; she mouthed her brother's name, Charles. "Hi."

I couldn't decipher what her brother was telling her, but I got the gist of it by her one-sided conversation.

"Mother called you, didn't she? Did she tell you that the cat's out of the bag about Father? When did I become someone you have to keep shit from, Charles? Answer that?" she demanded, her voice filled with a mix of hurt and rage.

There was silence as she listened to him.

She said, "I don't care that there was a reason for keeping it a secret till you took over. When did I become the odd man out in our little family? When did you decide that you couldn't trust me with the truth?"

She again waited for him to respond, and I waited for her response to tell me how bad his had been. Her eyes rolled back as her eyebrows lifted, whatever he was saying must be quite a load of shit, because her lips tightened in response.

"Mother thinks I left the house to solve a work emergency," she said. "If I stayed one more minute in her company, I was going to lose it. She came to Miami with the excuse that we would sit at a Zoom meeting together to discuss the gala. Then when she saw how unenthusiastic I sounded about the party, she came out and told me about Father."

While she spoke to him, I texted Carlos to make sure he was at the Walton's and Jimmy got home. My fingers paused over my phone at her next words.

"Don't worry about me. I'm with Dale. He offered to drive me wherever I needed to go."

I could imagine what was being said on the other side of the line.

Her face scrunched in response to a comment that Charles said. "I'm an adult. No. You can't tell me what to do or who to be with." She placed the phone back in her bag, just as Esther arrived with our food.

I wanted to say something, anything. I hadn't heard her brother's exact words, but I'd seen her face.

"Rebecca..."

She eyed the malted and eagerly placed it in front of herself. "Drinking these feels so sinful, it's like eating dessert first."

"Hey, you okay? I didn't hear what your brother said, but just from your face I could tell you weren't happy."

She shook her head as if dismissing the conversation, she had with her older brother and boss, "Charles being Charles, pay him no mind. He knew about us years ago and warned me that being with you maybe wasn't such a bright idea."

I gritted my teeth but kept my opinion to myself. I was more than aware of what Charles knew and how much he'd had to do with me not showing up eight years ago. But we weren't here to rehash old wounds, much less to talk about her overprotective brother, so when her attention went back to the malt in front of her, I let the topic go. My eyes laser beamed on her lips as she placed them around the straw and started sipping, her eyes closed in pleasure, then opened in delight. My imagination went to other places those lips could be and an electric current traveled down my lower spine. I forced my eyes away from her mouth. "Mm, delicious. You remembered what a chocoholic I was. Didn't you?"

I was transfixed. Her eyes shoot up to mine. "Aren't you

going to try yours? This is a dream in a glass. I didn't know what I was missing in life."

I cough and take a sip of my chocolate malt. "Yeah, this is good." Then I saw her wave toward the entrance of Sam's. Who the hell does she know in Saltview. Confused, I look at what had distracted her from her chocolate liquid orgasm and the pancakes sitting in front of her.

Jeremy and Marcos waved back to her and started walking in our direction past empty booths and tables. Once they arrived, neither bothered to ask if they could join us. Just sat their big asses down. I gave Marcos the evil eye as he gave me a shit-eating grin.

"Scoot over, bro. Great timing, you got a table before the lunch rush. Rebecca, hi. Do you mind if we join you?" said Marcos, not even bothering to wait for an answer, just made himself comfortable.

I look up at both, my head tilted looking them squarely in the eyes. "What rush? There are plenty of tables available. Go pick one."

Rebecca quickly scooted over to accommodate Jeremy. Marcos slid right next to me. Both of my brothers ignored my scowl. "What are you guys doing here? Don't you have work?"

Marcos laughed and Jeremy answered, "You mean are we done working on your home while you're here wining and dining our best client?"

"Yeah, again, why are you here? I left you finishing stuff at my home."

"Wow, and we thought Levi was bossy. We were hungry, dude. Your fridge is a desert." Marcos then turned to Rebecca as he grabbed the daily specials menu off the table. "So..., my brother, the big spender, brought you all the way to Saltview for pancakes. Hmm, what's the story?"

Her cheeks turned a pretty shade of pink as she took a small bite of the blueberry pancake, chewed, and swallowed. "Your brother wished to impress me with the culinary genius that is Sam's. He was right, these are delicious." Her smile was brilliant. "Remind me never to doubt your food recommendations."

Jeremy turned to her, a questioning expression on his face. "Okay, you guys know why we're here. But the real question is, why are you both in Saltview? Weren't you going to be working on the library project at Rebecca's?"

Rebecca was fast with an excuse as she responded, "Dale promised to show me something important, and I forced him to bring me to see it."

Recognition dawned on my brother's face and Marcos smiled.

"Well try not to tear each other's throats out," Jeremy said.

"Yeah." Marcus grinned. "I'd hate for you to come in tomorrow wearing turtlenecks."

I coughed. "Marcus—"

"Then we'd all think you were a couple of teenagers."

"We're not—"

He waved his hand to shut down any defense. "You're not kids. We can trust you."

After lunch they walked away without another word, leaving me and Rebecca to wonder how much we would deserve that trust by the end of the night.

Chapter Twelve
Rebecca

Dale taking me to this little jewel box of a diner was precisely what I needed to escape my current reality. The silliness of his brothers was a blessing because soon after sitting down with us, stories of their misspent youth started and didn't stop until we stood up to leave. Laughter was the best medicine. Being with the brothers for the last hour made me forget this morning's fiasco with my mother. Dale, the image of a Scottish highlander, Marcos, who could play a role in a Spanish telenovela, and Jeremy's model good looks hidden behind a scruffy beard didn't hurt, either. Just watching these men interact among themselves was better than any reality TV show. My stomach literally hurt from laughing at their stories.

"Your poor parents, you must have given them gray hairs."

Marcos then turned to me, all laughter leaving his face, his tone solemn as he spoke of them. "The only thing we didn't do was ever give our parents a moment to regret ever adopting us. They were the best parents a kid could hope for. They gave us a home and opened up their hearts to us."

Dale nodded. "Yeah, true. A handful and a half were what we were, but we brought no trouble home. It was the unspoken rule."

Was this why he never showed up that night? He didn't want to let his parents down.

Was there guilt in his eyes as he said this, or was I projecting? I knew why we never made it to Saltview when we dated. That he might disappoint them must have weighed heavily on his conscience. I was a fool to not realize how he battled the guilt of keeping us a secret. A sinking feeling lay in the pit of my stomach at how careless we had been, believing we were the center of the universe. Not thinking of the repercussions of our actions might have had on others.

Esther came with the bill and placed it on the table, shaking me out of my thoughts. "No rush."

Dale took it from her and handed over his card. "It's on me today."

Jeremy winked at her. "Esther, no pity party for him. We're the suckers working on his house for free while he's entertaining a girl." My mouth fell open as I saw him charming our server, who could have been his mother. Jeremy was normally not that sociable.

She laughed as she pointed to me. "Watch out for these Romeos. They'll charm the pants off any girl. But if Dale brought you here, then you're family."

I nodded because she was no doubt telling the truth from my experience. My chest puffed up with the sensation that I passed some critical test that I had no clue I had taken. I just wished that it hadn't taken so long to get to this place. "Thank you, Esther. I'll keep that in mind."

* * *

Once sitting in his truck, parting with his brothers, there was a comfortable silence in the car. He looked over at me and winked. "I fed you. My brothers even entertained you. Now you're going to see a bit of Saltview. There's something been meaning to show you if I got the opportunity."

I looked at my phone. Three text messages, all from my mother. Shit— now I'll never hear the end of it. She came here to do that damn Zoom meeting and I'm blowing her off. What does that say about me? My eyelids pressed together as I slowly breathed out letting my lungs empty before looking down to read what she wrote.

Mothership: Don't forget our meeting.
Mothership: Remember our agreement,
parties don't organize themselves
Mothership: Rebecca, let me know every-
thing's alright.
Me: Mother, everything's fine. Please
make my excuses to the other members.
Tell them I'll take on any task to help them
with the activity.
Mothership: Waltons do not take on
menial tasks.
Me: God forbid. Sorry, but I can't make it.

Mothership: Dinner tonight. I'll make reservations. We'll talk then.

I missed part of the scenic route because of my texting. But I was appreciating it now as he drove with our windows lowered, the smell of salt air and the sound of the waves crashing as the wind blew in our faces. We were approaching the Chance property according to the sign-posts placed every so often. I read them and looked over at him.

Pointing at the signs, I said, "I don't remember seeing those the other day when I came over."

He let out a heavy sigh. "We've had trouble with the government trying to take over some of the family lands, something about wanting to appropriate it for easements. Some developers also have been making offers. We want to make it clear this land belongs to us."

"Good luck, lawyers charge by the hour, and they can be persistent."

"Yeah, we've realized that. Levi feels it gives us more clout. They're not picking a fight with some backwater nobodies. We can defend ourselves if we need to."

"This is beautiful over here. No wonder none of you want to leave it." My gaze lifting from the phone message to the surrounding area.

He nodded, then noticed me looking down at my phone. "Something wrong? You've been frowning at your phone."

A sigh left my lips, the weight of the world heavy on my shoulders. "I'm sure I'm on my mother's shit list. She flew in today to make sure I didn't do a disappearing act for her precious charity ball. Which I did. Plus, regardless of how well *Renovated's* done, her focus is on me taking over her role on the different boards."

His fingers interlocked with mine where they lay on the armrest, pulling my attention from the phone to my hand in his. His rough and calloused fingers caressed my fingers, my eyes lift from them to his face, not expecting this open affection from him.

I knew I was fishing, but I still needed answers, and though we had decided to let lying dogs lie. That niggling feeling was in the back of my mind and caused old fears and uncertainties to make an appearance.

"Was what Marcos said about the unspoken rule of not doing anything to disappoint your parents' was the reason you didn't show up?"

"Becca, I understand not letting anyone down. I snuck around with you behind my parents' backs that summer. All I thought about was how I was doing exactly the opposite of the principles that my parents had tried to teach us. Sneaking behind their backs like a dirty secret, while exciting at first the more serious we became, the worse I felt about it. I should have been proud and able to show up with the girl I loved by my side. Also, being the client's daughter, so out of my league, didn't help the situation either."

Once again, so much water had gone under that bridge, so much pain that I didn't want to revisit. My voice was low, almost a whisper. "You've never been less than me."

He gave me a warm smile that didn't reach his eyes. Did I want to change what tenuous relationship we'd reestablished? What I wanted from the man in front of me changed. The more time I spent in his presence, the weaker my resolve became to keep my distance.

I reminded myself that I'd been there and done that — before the urge to reach across the console and take his hand won over. I clenched my hands into fists till the skin broke in my palm. I would only get hurt looking in that direction. Plus, I had bigger challenges to focus on, like a meddling mother whom I loved and adored, but believed she knew what was best for me.

We drove into Dale's family property, past his mother's Victorian and Levi's Spanish revival. "Where are we heading?"

We drove for ten minutes, then I saw two structures. Painted in a dark gray, and next to it, a single-story house of very modern design. It had a coastal look, with wood shingles, painted a stark white, and lots of glass and steel. Then it hit me like a Mack truck, but I still had to ask, "This is breathtaking. Who does it belong to?" I turned my head to look over at Dale when he parked right by the big barnlike structure.

Pride filled his complete demeanor. "All mine. This is my house. Come, I want to show you something."

"Okay." It was gorgeous, a visual personification of what my dream house would look like.

If I kept one secret from him, I had to keep that one. I wanted a home of my own. I wanted one that *felt* like home as much as looked like it. To have it all—and the man who was showing it to me—was almost too big a temptation.

We had to finish the show and put an end to this.

Why was it important that I see this now? Was he trying to convince me he had made it as a businessperson and artisan? I was aware of his success. I had not been above cyberstalking the man I once loved. When I'd needed a reminder of why I didn't trust men with my heart, I'd find Dale on social media, and all was right in my world again.

We walked to the shed entrance at the large door. He inputted the numbers at the keypad entry. The door slid open on tracks to a workspace. My jaw dropped, but I closed it as my eyes fell on the beautiful tables and chairs at different stages of completion.

"Dale, are all these your creations? They're stunning, all of them. Who knew you were so talented?" The admiration in my voice was apparent.

I walked farther into the workspace. The left side had finished pieces ready for new homes. Live edge wood tables from complete slabs of walnut and maple, smooth to the touch, polished, and varnished to pick up the natural beauty of the wood, were in different stages of creation. Combinations of epoxy and reclaimed wood made beautiful cocktail tables worthy of any fine furniture store. My hand touched the pieces of craftmanship with reverence. This was an artist's studio, and I was getting a glimpse of the soul of the man who ran it.

"You like them?" His eyes never left my face as he asked. He wasn't fishing for compliments. He wanted to know my opinion.

My eyes traveled across the wall filled with the tools of his craft and back to him. "How can you even ask? Your pieces are beautiful. When did you do this? You weren't making furniture when we were together."

He took a step closer to me. His hand lifted to move a lock of hair off my face and push it behind my ear, his finger trailing softly down my neck. A delicious shiver went through me where his fingers touched. My breath stopped for a few seconds. It would be so easy to fall into his arms, hug the firm body in front of me, bask in his warmth. I never had this attraction to anyone but Dale and being around him only reminded me of the void I had in my life.

"After working at your parents' house that summer. Dad thought I had a talent for working with wood, had me apprentice with wood masters." he said as he walked farther away from me toward another original design of his. "After that, I started experimenting on my own. After we had done a client's house, and they'd paid ridiculous amounts of money for some custom-made tables, I decided I could do better, and I did." His chest expanded with pride.

I fully appreciated the ninety-inch dining table that would sell for a pretty penny. The quality and craftsmanship were apparent, and the design was nothing short of brilliant. My fingers traveled over the grain of the wood, sanded to perfection, varnished with a clear gloss to emphasize its beauty.

"Do you have customers for these pieces?"

He stepped closer to me. His fingers came near mine but didn't touch them. I couldn't help but fixate on the hands that had crafted such beautiful pieces. "Well, this table and that cocktail table already have a designated place assigned to them inside my house. But yeah, I usually work on commissioned pieces. The waiting list is a year, I'm so busy. I have to do this on my downtime from the construction gig."

There was pride in his expression as he walked into his workspace before I said, "Congratulations, and thank you for showing me this side of you."

He took my hand as if it were the most natural thing in

the world as he pulled me with him toward the main house. "Come."

I stopped in mid-stride as we made our way toward the entrance. Once again, words failed me.

"You're home's lovely. What influenced your choice of design? This is nothing like your brothers' or parents'."

My thoughts went to a conversation we had long ago as I had laid in his arms watching the sunset. How naive we were, believing the world rotated around us and our desires.

Taken aback by what was right before my eyes. He'd never forgotten. Every detail of what I wanted for my dream home was in front of me, coastal modern architecture with lots of windows within a streamlined design. When he'd asked me what I wanted our future home to look like, I'd been so adamant about it being a complete opposite to what I'd grown up with. No damask heavy curtains, nor antique fit for a wing at a museum or a home that looked straight out of a magazine. I wanted something that reflected us and nobody else. Not giving me time to articulate my thoughts, he pulled me toward the entrance, punched in the code again at the lock, and the large door pivoted from the middle on an axis.

He stepped aside to let me pass. "Come into my humble abode. It's still a work in progress. In about two weeks, I should be living here full time. My brothers are helping me get it finished."

I walked into the open concept floor plan. The main living area shared a kitchen, dining, and family room, all open to a covered terrace with a water view.

He stood by the island in a kitchen fit for a chef, stainless steel top-of-the-line appliances, quartz countertops in white and white lacquered cabinets. "Do you like it? I haven't furnished it yet, other than the pieces in my shed that I've yet to finish. These stools were the first things I made for my house."

"Wow, this is fabulous. You should be so proud of yourself. You said you were going to do it and you did." I walked toward him, pulling out a stool and sitting across from where he was standing.

He seemed almost shy with the praise. "Yeah, after Mom died, I picked up where I'd left off in the construction. My first investment on the property had been to do the large shed. I needed a workspace all my own."

"Do you have a lot of jobs that you need to complete? Because the craftsmanship is on the same level of some serious furniture designers. Levi mentioned the waitlist of clients that want your pieces. Congratulations, you've made quite a name for yourself."

A smile teased at his mouth, "I don't lack for work if that's what you're asking? Between the construction company and this, I keep busy." he stepped closer to me. "What are you going to do about your mother? We never finished the conversation we started at the diner before my brothers made themselves at home at our table."

A deep sigh escaped me because I'd been able to forget for a while the confrontation I needed to have with my family. There was a reason I had left for New York and hadn't returned. Once I was in the same zip code as everyone in my family, they all had opinions about what was best for Rebecca.

Shrugging in mock resignation. "Well, I have a few hours to figure it out since Mother expects me to meet her for dinner. I'm sure this will be a major topic of conversation. I'm just going to break the news that my career path is way different from what she wants for me. What's ironic is I came back. I had received an offer to work for an affiliate station in Europe, but I wanted to work for the family." Leaning my elbow on the table, I rested my chin in my hand.

His eyes widened a bit at that bit of news. "Well, I for one am glad you came here."

"I must look like such a wimp to you." Biting my lip, I looked away from him.

He touched my hand, his face inches from mine. "Becca, please look at me." His calloused hand moved to cup my cheek. I met his eyes, but he didn't give me a chance to say anything. "You're many things, impetuous, brave, daring, but wimp would never be a word I'd used to describe you." His gaze came to rest on my lips, desire reflected in the deep green of his eyes.

At that moment, all the bottled-up anger I'd kept as a shield fell away like a cape drifting to the floor. He'd dropped everything to be at my side and, for that, my shriveled-up heart plumped up with every action and conversation we'd shared. His body still turned me weak in the knees, didn't matter how much time had passed. My vow not to become involved with him was breaking down as I lifted my face to stare at his lips as he lowered his mouth to mine.

His lips were tentative at first, waiting for permission to continue the kiss, then deepened as I opened my mouth and tangled my tongue with his. I let the flurry of sensations erupt from my belly and spread warmth between my thighs. Butterflies fluttered in my stomach at every brief touch between us today. Now I was in his arms, and it felt so right. My heart swelled with a fullness I'd thought long dead. His touch thrilled me as air fled my lungs. How could I still resent him, when neither of us were those kids that fell in love as teenagers? There had been so much growing up to do. Could we honestly say we were the same people that we met eight years ago?

My hands traveled to his waist to pull him closer to me, as his lips covered mine, claiming and possessing me as he crushed me to him. His mouth covered mine, the kiss urgent and exploring, making up for the lost time. His tongue slipped between my lips and tangled with mine. I tasted chocolate malt and the mint he'd picked up before leaving the diner. His hands caressed my throat and traveled to the back of my head, keeping me still as his tongue explored the recesses of my mouth.

He groaned while saying my name like a chant. "Becca ... Becca."

"Yes... don't stop." I said, my voice sounding like a plea.

My stomach did a little flip. Being in his arms again just seemed right. My body still craved his hands on me. A moan escaped my lips as his mouth traveled from my cheeks to my neck as he breathed me in. His mouth ate me up, my breaths shallow. This was what I'd been missing for so long, but it felt so natural to be back in his arms again. Some things only got better, like the man holding me against his hard body. His attraction was apparent from the hard evidence in his pants that brushed against my abdomen. All these sensations I've fought were me punishing myself rather than him, because of my pride getting hurt.

His touch sent tingles throughout my body, his mouth against mine as he spoke. "Becca, you still taste the same to me. I've missed this so much and what I want is to be inside that beautiful body of yours. But I don't want just a fuck buddy, this time I want to do right by you."

A bucket of ice would have been less shocking to me. Furious at myself for the vulnerability I'd shown toward him. I pushed away from the table, needing to put space between us. That's right, being around him always made me lose brain cells.

Fortunately, I had just enough to put together what he'd said.

"Sorry, do right by me? Is this your guilt talking, for having shattered my heart? This," I pointed to him and me, "will not be a repeat of our teen years. You don't owe me a do-over."

He looked at me as if I'd sprouted another head. He didn't get me at all. The spark of hope had quickly extinguished in his eyes. He took a step toward me, but I stepped out of his reach.

Then he had the gall to say, "Becca, your head might say one thing, and to protect your heart, you feel the need to warn me off. What we did right now wasn't fake, or you are getting your rocks off. That kiss, those moans, your body doesn't lie."

I chose my words carefully. "You're right. My body will probably always want yours. I can't help that I find you hot. Why deny it? But I can only fight one battle." I turned away so he couldn't see how much it hurt me to say it. "And whatever this is between us? You already lost."

Chapter Thirteen
Dale

If she thought that was the end of it, she was wrong. Losing the battle didn't mean I'd lost the war, not as long as she kept looking at me with that fire in her eyes. There was a hollowness in the pit of my stomach, I was going to lose her if she wasn't willing to give us a chance.

"Don't you think there might be something worth salvaging? Aren't you the slightest bit curious about what we could be?"

"You had my number. If you had wanted to make amends, why didn't you?"

"I fucked up. I burned the bridge and didn't believe you would forgive me. I thought you hated me for letting you down, and you were better off without me."

I raked a hand through my hair, yet again I was considered a distraction from her principal focus, which was the success of her show. She wanted to keep me at arm's length, use me at her convenience, and put me back on the shelf when she didn't need me.

I sighed. My previous comment had us going to the door instead of the bedroom. "Look, I'm aware that I gave up the right to call you mine a long time ago. Doesn't change how I feel about you, and you've always had this effect on me."

I covered her hand with mine and trailed my fingers softly up her arm to cup her shoulder.

"Dale..." she whispered.

"Do you want me to stop?"

She swallowed. "Making it awful hard to want you to."

"I'll be who you need me to be at this moment. I don't like the fact you seem to see me as derailing your goal. You've made it clear I'm not what you want now. But I may be what you need and if that's all you have to offer, I'll take it. Till you realize you have more to give."

She shrugged off my hand from her arm. Her mouth opened and closed words didn't come out, but when they did, the pitch broke crystal. "Are you seriously proposing we be fuck buddies?"

Shit, this conversation is going downhill fast.

Had I only moments ago declared winning the battle didn't mean I'd lost the war?

"Strangers have worked with less, at least we're attracted to each other."

Her hands went to her waist with indignation. Even pissed as she was, she still turned me on. "I'm not sure what to think. You don't believe someone other than you would want to have sex with me?"

Foot in mouth, doesn't matter what I said to her. I need to fix this before another ice age passes without her talking to me.

"Not a chance. They'd kill for a chance with you."

"Are you're saying sex is the only reason they'd talk to me?"

Damn, I'm contradicting myself, but this might be the only way she'll ever let me this close to her, what with our past. "I don't doubt you'd find tons of men to have sex with you. But do you want a total stranger? What's better, you need to focus on getting *Renovated* off the ground and you're too busy to get involved with anyone. This would be an arrangement of convenience for you. Think of it this way, any other man's going to want you to dedicate time to them, be in a relationship. We're being clear about our intentions, no expectations."

"That's what you say now. Then feelings get hurt and hearts get broken. I have allowed no one to get close since you." She folded her arms in front of herself.

It was killing me to have to settle for less than I wanted with the woman I never stopped loving, but I'd brought this on myself. I'd lost her trust and if I was going to earn it back, I had to play by the rules she set.

"You're the one who gets to decide," I said. "Not your mom. Not me."

"And you know what I want?"

"Not what." I tasted the heat between us. "Who."

Her brows furrowed, and she gave a small smirk before saying. "Assuming much, aren't you? Time has just given you the biggest ego. Does this work with all the girls?"

"There've been no other women."

She stepped closer. Her eyes fixed on mine. "You honestly want me to believe no one replaced me in your affections?" Sarcasm dripped from her words. "Because you know... eight years is not I'm leaving for a business trip and I'll be right back."

A lock of hair held up by a clip fell into her face. I couldn't help myself. Taking the silky strands between my fingers, rubbing them between my fingers. Her breath hitched at my nearness and touch. There was vulnerability reflecting at me from the depths of her eyes.

I moved even closer. "Honey, I didn't say I was a saint. There were plenty of hookups, but no one was serious and few repeats. I didn't want commitments or the complications that came with them. Then Mom got ill three years ago. I wanted to be there for her. I occupied my time between construction projects, custom orders and taking her to the chemo appointments."

Rebecca's face fell, her voice soft, the wind out of her fight. "Sorry about your mother."

"Thank you."

We faced each other, and she placed a hand on my upper arm. "Getting back to your generous offer of being my orgasm provider, as tempting as it might be. For the moment, I'll pass. I refuse to use you because of convenience."

"I wouldn't feel used..." She lifted her finger and placed it lightly on my lips. I kissed that digit before she removed it, her breath hitching.

Her cheeks were flushed as she continued, "It wouldn't be fair to either of us."

"I can take it."

"I know you can...but there's this thing I call self-preservation. I'm a powerful advocate for it."

She leaned against the door that led to the outside of the house facing me, her head raised toward mine. My arm extended above her head, careful to give her strong arms to fall into without leaving her no space to escape.

"I don't see it that way. You were the best thing that ever happened to me, and I let you go. I've regretted that more than anything else that has happened to me."

Her hand lifted to trace the open vee of my shirt with her index finger. Her lips pursed, giving serious consideration to my words. I could almost hear the gears in her brain doing the computations.

"If we are to do this, we need to set boundaries. Someone might get hurt, and I don't mean you." She smiled. "Well, maybe you."

My heart filled with hope, her admitting that she possibly entertained the idea of us at least pretending to be together once again. For however short a time. My skin tingled at her touch, and I craved it. Hope burned in me.

If we could love each other again for a minute, could I convince her we could love each other again for forever?

I covered her hand, that was now over my heart. My heartbeat pulsed against her fingers, the heat of her hand transmitting itself to me. "Rebecca, no way will I ever hurt you again. Believe me. I won't fuck up, give us a chance to start over again. We'll work this however you need it to be."

Her pocket was buzzing, interrupting the moment. Her eyes sparkled with mischief. "I really need to get home. My mother is expecting me, but I think we should revisit this starting over between us."

"I'm glad because I like the idea of giving us an opportunity."

"I'm willing to give this a trail run because you're right. I don't want to live with what-ifs in my life and you're still my biggest road not taken."

She straightened out, brought herself closer to me, her touch tentative as she caressed the tendons of my neck, tracing a light path over my skin. "We need to keep this between us. Your brothers can overpower any situation, and it would be awkward if things don't work out. Too many questions I'm not willing to answer."

"Hon, we'll take this slow if that will make you happier. This is our life, and this is between us and only us. You don't need to warn me about my brothers. I'm aware of what busybodies they can be."

Warm fingers cupped my cheek. "Thank you. I don't mean to be a party pooper. It's just that I don't want to confuse everyone with what our status is as a couple, when I'm not sure myself what I want." Her upper teeth caught her lower lip as she avoided eye contact.

I shriveled internally. Rejected again. She wanted to keep us under wraps in case things didn't work out. That rubbed me the wrong way. But I could understand where she was coming from. I would take this one step at a time till I proved I could be her one and only, and then maybe we would make it to the other side. She could have asked me for anything, and I would have given it to her or made it possible. I wanted another opportunity with this woman. The girl she was at eighteen had turned my world upside down, even made me willing to throw away all my parents had taught me. The woman she'd become kept me on my toes, didn't take crap from anyone, and was hot as hell.

"If that's what you want, I'll agree to keep whatever this is between us. But don't think I won't do my damnedest to convince you to believe in me and what we could be." I hoped she understood how earnest I was and willing to put in the work to make it up to her. I held out my hand, palm upward, so she could place hers in mine.

Her smile was tentative. "Okay, let's do this."

* * *

When I returned from taking Rebecca home, I returned to my workshop. Nothing eased my mind more than working on my creations. I got busy sanding the table that Rebecca had admired in my workshop. This piece was certainly going in my house. I'd been at it for over an hour when I received a call from Levi inviting me over to eat dinner. I never refused a home-cooked meal, and he insisted Marisa wanted to feed me.

When I parked in front of Levi's house, it was to find him outside throwing a tennis ball to Kira, "Hey grab a drink and come out and join me."

I waved at him and continued toward the entrance of his house. He'd been slowly renovating and rebuilding the house that had once belonged to his great-grandfather and was over a hundred years old. The job was a work in progress, and he'd been at it for the last two years.

"Okay, I'll get my beer and be out in a sec."

Caramelized peppers, onions, spices, and beef scented the air. My taste buds were paying attention. My mouth was watering by the time I reached the open kitchen where Marisa was plating the food in serving dishes.

"I was going to join my brother outside, but the aroma in this kitchen is delicious. What can I do to help you?"

Marisa jumped when she heard me. "Oh my God, I almost dropped the plate. You scared me, next time make more noise or announce yourself."

"Sorry, thought you heard me pull up when I arrived. I didn't realize how hungry I was, till I walked through the door."

"You're forgiven. My grandmother prepared this dish for us, one of my favorite Cuban recipes. The name of it is *ropa vieja*, which translates to old clothes if you can believe that." She pulls a fork out of the drawer and serves me a bit of the meat for me to try.

"Levi's going to want your nana to prepare dinner every night."

She smiled as she said, "The secret is boiling the beef till tender, then she shredded it and added to it a sofrito of peppers, onions, garlic, and tomato sauce. She also sent along with it the rice and frijoles negros to go with it. You do like black beans, don't you?"

"If Nana made them, of course I'll love it," There was no way my brother would share such a bounty with me if he didn't want something, or maybe it was Marisa behind the invite after all.

"I'm surprised Levi is sharing this feast with me." My eyes dared her to contradict me.

She bit her bottom lip and then grinned. "You know your brother so well. You're right, I invited you. But I had an ulterior motive, and I'm not above using my grandmother's cooking as the perfect bribe to get information from you. I witnessed a lot of flirtation between you and Rebecca at the club, even your attempt at diversion when the owner paid attention to her. Was she the girl you were interested in, and why we went to the club in the first place?"

I scratched my scalp with my hand while trying to figure out if I should let the cat out of the bag. I'd kept this a secret from my family for so long, that sharing it was foreign to me. "My story has an unhappy ending. Are you sure you want to hear it? It may ruin your appetite."

She nodded before saying, "I'd ask Levi, but I know he would never share a secret that wasn't his to tell."

I owed her an explanation. She was extremely perceptive. She'd gotten us into Club Rain with her connections, and if anything happened between Rebecca and me there could be blow back on the program.

I wasn't sure if I wanted to look at the pity in her eyes as I told her our backstory. I grabbed another beer from the fridge, took off the cap, and took a swig of beer. "Rebecca and I dated a long time ago. We'd fallen hard for each other that summer eight years ago when I worked with my dad at her parents' home. You know they talk about love at first sight. She was my one, she still is that one. Had even planned to elope. We were that in love."

Her jaw dropped before recovering and snapped closed with the news I'd just dropped in her lap. "Whoa—hold up. We're talking about our fearless leader. She loved you enough to leave her family to marry you. I mean no insult, but how old were you? Nineteen—twenty?"

My head fell into my hands, then lifted to peek up at her. "Yeah, around that age. As hard as you may believe that to be true, we were very in love, extremely naive and too young." I took a deep swig of my beer.

Transfixed by my story, Marisa stayed quiet, internalizing

what she hadn't expected to hear. "What happened? You didn't elope. If not, this story would be very different."

I jumped up from my stool and paced, uncomfortable with my part in Rebecca and my history. I didn't want Marisa to think I was a scum bucket also, but I just let the word vomit flow.

"I didn't make it to the meeting point. I failed her and never confronted her to ask for forgiveness. Rebecca has hated me for the last eight years."

Marisa stopped stirring the pot on the stove to sit on a kitchen stool. "What happened to you? It's hard for me to believe you would do something like that, if you loved her like you said you did."

"Love doesn't make you perfect."

She shook her head. "Well, it should."

"Well, I fucked up anyway, okay? When she first arrived in Miami, she only spoke to me when necessary. I'd made countless approaches when we were taping, but she evaded me."

Her tone was sympathetic. "Well, I can understand her being pissed at you. If you had left me high and dry without an explanation, I wouldn't want to speak to you either."

"Thanks. I knew I could count on you for sympathy," I said wryly.

"I'm sorry, but if I felt the rejection she did, I wouldn't be so forgiving either. Continue, I promise to be impartial. Why didn't you elope? I mean, I couldn't imagine doing that, especially with the baggage I was carrying."

"What happened was her brother. The day before we were to elope, he came up to me. He convinced me she would end up resenting me... something about a tragedy in the making. She'd lose her trust fund and wouldn't be able to finish at Columbia. I don't know— what he said made sense. My birth mother hated being saddled with a kid she never wanted."

Marisa placed a hand over mine and squeezed it, giving me the strength to continue my story. "My birth mother OD'd in front of me. I couldn't be witness to another woman resenting the shit out of me for ruining her life. My birth parents were exactly what I didn't want to become. I would not take away her opportunities. At first, I argued we loved each other, money wasn't important. I could take care of her. But then I realized I was only lying to myself."

She kept her hand on mine. "I'm sorry. I'm sure that wasn't a simple decision. You had the maturity at that age to make it, then take the blame for it. I'm sure that conversation with Charles Walton wasn't easy either. He's such a *charmer*."

She opened her eyes wider as a thought occurred to her. "Does she know about his involvement?"

"No, I never told her. I didn't want her hating her brother. The most important people in my life are my brothers. I couldn't do that to her. His reasoning made too much sense. He asked that I not elope, not because he found me beneath his sister, but because he didn't want her to resent me in the end. I would alienate her from everything and everyone she knew. I was a coward. I should have sat with her and explained why I didn't show up. But I knew that if I saw her, I would have run away with her and gotten married."

"You know there's this Spanish saying, '*No hay mal que por bien no venga*.'"

I groaned but had to ask. "What does it mean?"

"There's no ill where good doesn't result from it. Maybe it was fate bringing her back into your life, and this time you can make it right between you both. If it is, it will be."

"And if it isn't?"

"Nothing you could do will make it so."

Chapter Fourteen
Rebecca

Dale's gaze was soft as he waved to me goodbye. I leaned against the wrought-iron gate of the entrance, following the headlight of his truck blinking red as he turned onto the main road taking him off the island.

I had to be honest with myself. His nearness made my insides spin, and I feared this would never change. Would I seriously consider his offer? Yes ... I would. Obviously denying the feelings I had for him hadn't been working on the distraction factor. All I could do was think of him, and even if I didn't, he succeeded to further pull my mind away from the reason I came here in the first place. Maybe a friends-with-benefits arrangement could work out between us, if we didn't get messy about it once we parted ways.

I walked past the living room entrance to find my mother reclining on the sofa, which faced the infinity pool and tennis court, and backtracked to enter it. She rocked a long silk leopard print caftan, a romance book in one hand, and a wineglass filled with her favorite white cabernet on the side table next to her. Mother was always the glamorous socialite, even when chilling. My steps faltered as I approached her, pulling my spine straight as I got nearer. What would a mature, competent, and independent twenty-six-year-old woman do? Because that's what I am. A grown-ass woman should be able to sit down and express her desires and wants. I pulled my big girl panties up because this was the moment, if there ever was one. When she looked up from the book that engrossed her, I wiggled my fingers in a wave.

"Mother, we need to talk." I plopped myself down in the chaise across from her and turned my body lengthwise to face her. I was her mirror image except thirty years younger. Not a believer in aging gracefully, she fought that demon unapologetically head-on.

She placed the book on her lap and took a sip from her wineglass. "Mm-hmm, would you like me to serve you a glass? I have some chilling in the beverage center. Something tells me we're going to need this, in vino veritas."

I shook my head, not needing wine to speak the truth. "No, thank you, maybe later."

Mother didn't feel the same inclination and brought the wineglass up for another sip as she waved me to continue. "Okay, go ahead. You need to get something off your chest. There's been too much tension between us today. Don't think I believed even for a second you had an emergency meeting."

My fingers played with the fringe of the decorative pillow close to me. Taking a deep, unsteady breath, I said, "First, I wanted to apologize for leaving you to handle the committee on your own. It was irresponsible of me. I'd promised I would uphold my part of the bargain we'd made and help with the fundraising and whatever else they needed. I'm aware how important this project is to you, and I shouldn't have reacted to Dad's illness like a child and hightailed it out of here. What I should have done was tell you how much it upset me that my family had kept me in the dark."

She placed her hand over mine and squeezed. "Dear, you've made a mountain out of a molehill. You need to remember the most important thing in this equation. Your father has been coming to terms with his mortality. That has been difficult. Ultimately, the decision to tell you was his. It's not been easy for him to process this."

"Yeah, that might be so, but I'm still hurt. You all excluded me from what happened to Father. How could you have hidden this from me?" I blurted as the anger resurfaced once more.

My mother's eyes opened wide at my explosive response.

"It was all under control. Your father had complete faith in the physicians in charge of his health, and he didn't want the focus on him. These situations become wake-up calls, and we plan to take advantage of what's left of our lives and enjoy them together." She sighed with exasperation.

"I might understand up here," I pointed with my index finger to the top of my head, "but it still was cancer, no matter how you explain this to me." My fingers went to my brow and rubbed the frown lines created there.

"Rebecca, I spoke with your father about this last night before I made the trip. He said he would call you and explain it, though he preferred to do this in person. He's fine now. Having to face an illness changed our perspective about what we wanted as a couple. Let's not speak more about this and enjoy our evening together. I missed our late-night conversations. I've gotten spoiled having you back home in Nashville. Tomorrow, I fly back."

This time I sighed. The subject was closed? Not this time. At least not the one that mattered. "Mother, you're ignoring the elephant in the room?" A knot of emotion in my center uncoiled. I was going to get this off my chest.

She picked at a hangnail, then looked up at me. "Dear, what are you talking about?"

My eyes widened in amazement. I was going to need to spell it out.

Her eyebrows arched. "Rebecca, I know you only agreed to help with the gala for your show. But I think you'll be shortchanging yourself by not giving this an opportunity. If you only realized what the moneys received accomplished, you'd understand how important the work we do benefits the foundations we choose to help with these so-called frivolous parties. We reconstructed the autism center into a state-of-the-art facility, with sensory rooms, occupational, speech, and behavioral therapy free for the students attending. You should see the progress the children and young adults have made. There's satisfaction in knowing you worked on something which helps so many."

I took her wineglass from its perch and took a sip while I thought about what to say next. I might not get another shot. "I'm more than aware of what you accomplished as the head of the Home Design Charitable Endowment. But I want to decide for myself what I excel at in life, not be told what to do with it. I will help with anything they assign me, because I know that this is dear to you. I'll make the calls, sell the tables, even help with getting donations for the auctions. Just don't expect me to make that all I do for the network." My voice sounded more like a plea than a declaration.

A long sigh left her lips. "Your father warned me that this would be an act of futility when I told him I was going to Miami. You were always a headstrong child and were proud of your achievements. You know that. It shocked many at the Network at how well you could rebound after the hosts of the last show screwed the pooch."

My eyes widened, and my mouth dropped open. Laughter bubbled out of my mouth. "Mother, how shocking. Slang? I'll never get used to it. When I tell Charles, he won't believe me."

She ignored my banter. "The way you could turn it around when the press hounded Marisa. Smart thinking pulling Karina into the mix. A fine fixer and power to be reckoned with. You can't underestimate that girl. Shame about her parents, but I'm getting off topic. You did well when you aired *Renovated*."

I sat up a little straighter and my chest filled with joy at the recognition. Unusual coming from my perfectionist mother. It was usually my brother Charles, for whom the sun rose and set in our household.

"What are you saying?"

She studied me with narrowed eyes. "Maybe you're right. Do a good job and we'll see what happens."

Was that hope I felt? Maybe. If I could stop thinking about what would happen if my last and biggest shot didn't work.

At least I'd figured out the Dale situation.

* * *

Mother was flying back to Nashville today, and I was driving her toward the small private airport. Charles had the jet waiting for her since she wanted to be back home before dinner with my father.

"Rebecca, my assistant will email you the tasks we discussed last night. Now that you're staying at the house again, your father thought it might be a good idea to stop over and spend some time with you here."

I kept my eyes on the road but couldn't help but turn my attention to her. "You want to come out here? When?"

She lowered the sun visor to look at herself in the mirror and reapplied the light pink lip gloss she'd taken from her purse. "Yes, it would allow us to enjoy the house as a family once again. We've realized we hate the empty nest. Having you back in Nashville once again was nice. Plus, that way, I can oversee the library project."

My head swiveled in her direction for a second before going back to the road. "Since when have you been interested in overseeing anything? Home renovation. I know that's the family business, but that's not your thing."

She flashed a look at me I'd only ever seen in the mirror. My words must have hit a nerve. "I'll have you know I oversaw the first renovation. You were at college and were not interested. Now, I'm curious why the head carpenter left his well-paid job to come to my daughter's rescue. He had no problem leaving the house yesterday to go off with you. Don't think I didn't notice that." She gave me a knowing look.

I let out a breath because now there was no stopping her meddling. "Mother, please don't go there. You don't need to bother supervising the library renovation. I can do that. Plus, Dale's a total perfectionist. He will do the job to your architect's specifications. He was just concerned and didn't want me driving in the condition he saw me in."

She nodded, soothing me but suspicious. "Sure... just friends."

Except her tone left no doubt that she had noticed plenty.

Chapter Fifteen
Rebecca

Now that Mom had returned to Nashville, I could get back to the business of home renovation.

The phone rang, and Sarah's name came up on my car display.

"Hi, Sarah, how's it going? I'm actually on my way over to view the —."

Drilling and who knew what else drowned my voice out.

After the din finally died down a tad, I asked, "Is that a jackhammer?"

She yelled her response over the noise of the construction. "I'm calling from chaos central. They had to break the cement for the plumbing for the private bathroom. But kidding aside, don't worry, I got this under control."

"I'm so psyched you're in Miami to help me. You'll be in the thick of things. It's not the same over the phone. How's the office? Are you taking charge there?"

"As much as I can be in charge, with Jeremy handling all the construction crew. He's promised me a semi-functioning office by next week. You're right. It's been challenging working with a clean slate, but it's taking shape. I'm excited to see the progress develop in stages. Once again, I'm so thankful you gave me this opportunity. If not for you, I would still be doing the rounds of the secretarial pool."

My heart swelled with pride. After all she'd done, she still carried so much self-doubt. I needed to tell her what no one else had told me.

"Remember, you've earned your job," I said. "You deserve this, don't you forget it."

"I appreciate that."

"And I'll be there soon enough to help."

"Rebecca, don't bother coming into this mess," she said. "It would be a waste of your time that you can put to better use. Before leaving headquarters, I had everything requisitioned. There is not much you can do here. It's a madhouse right now. What with the movers bringing in the furniture and equipment, plus Jeremy's crew is hanging the drywall and gypsum."

Even though it was against my nature to dump all the dirty work on Sarah's lap, I had to agree. But I couldn't disagree with her argument. I would not get much done with the racket, plus my computers were at my home. Until there was a decent workspace, my command center would remain on Star Island. "You're right. I won't get much done till they set up our office. Let's do this, send me all the prospective clients' files we're considering for renovations in this area. We need to study each application and the financials. Remember, that's a key component. To start the project, the client must prove and show evidence of the availability of the money needed."

Sarah's voice projected confidence, even though I was

sure there was a shitstorm occurring in our offices. I was more than happy to delegate that responsibility to her so I could focus on the show. "Hey, don't worry, you know me. I thrive under pressure. Plus, Jeremy's told me they should do this in the space of two weeks." Her voice rose when she said Jeremy's name, giving me the impression that she wasn't alone.

In the background, amid the sound of hammering, equipment being dragged across the room, and men speaking loudly to each other. Jeremy's deep voice came across the line. "Rebecca, Jeremy here. Don't worry about this project. It's in the bag. You'll be sitting at your fancy desk before you know it."

A wide smile spread across my face and a thrill zinged in my stomach at the thought that this was all happening because of the success of the show. "Twist my rubber arm, why don't you. I'll be at home, working on the numbers. I must present the proposed budget for the next quarter to headquarters by Friday. Please coordinate a meeting with the director, screenwriter, and production designer."

"I'll send them to you ASAP, plus I'll look into your schedule and make it happen before Friday. Oh, and Rebecca, there've been various messages. A mister Phillip Townsend has been most insistent. When I asked about what, he wouldn't leave a message."

"Good, let's leave it like that, and Sarah, even if he insists, don't tell him anything."

Sarah's concern was understandable when she asked, "Should I call and bring security in on this? I can make the call and report the situation?"

"No, he's harmless but insistent, just say we didn't receive the message the first time." I didn't need another blast from the past haunting me now.

"Okay, if you say so. Remember, the guys you think are harmless are the ones that give you the biggest headaches. I'll email all the files to you once I'm off the phone."

"Well, call me if I'm needed. I'll contact you if there's any problem on my end."

Dale's truck was by the service entrance of the house when I arrived home. An electric current went through me as I replayed everything we did yesterday. The shared kiss in his place had my insides melting with a delicious shudder. I'd almost forgotten what it was like to desire someone the way I did him. Geez, all my initial resolve to remain distant went by the wayside within a month of being around him. I could not repress the heaviness in my thighs and core with just the thought of his deliciously hard body against my soft one. *God, Rebecca, get a grip.* This time, I won't let my heart fall victim again to his easygoing charm, swagger, and hotness. The lawn mowers, leaf blowers, and trimmers pulled me out of my musings as I walked to the house's kitchen entrance, under the canopy of bougainvillea – which connected the main house to the independent garage area.

"Hello." I called out as the aroma of chicken filled the air, and I walked over to where Yolanda was standing by the stove. She was serving a dish with red beans and ham hocks.

"Mm... that smells delicious."

"You arrived just in time for lunch. I made *arroz con pollo,* your favorite from when you were a child. Please sit and eat. You don't eat enough. Where I'm from, a man appreciates a little meat on the bone." Patting her waist.

I placed my purse on the table and took a plate from the

ones she'd set out. "Believe me. There's plenty on my bones, and no one's ever complained about that. And I am starving. No one cooks as you do. You remembered how much I loved eating your chicken with rice."

A pleased look filled Yolanda's face, her head bobbing in agreement. "Sit, please sit. I promised Dale that I would prepare this for him the last time he was here. I will go tell them it's ready now."

I nodded and sat at the banquet table in the kitchen.

I placed the napkin over my lap and took my first bite when Dale sauntered in, followed by Jimmy and Carlos. "Hope you're hungry. Yolanda made food for an army." I extended my arm out toward the kitchen island in front of me.

"Are you kidding? I've been drooling since smelling the caramelized onions. I love this dish," said Carlos.

"Well, help yourselves. Yolanda prides herself on her cooking, and she's been feeling neglected since we're never around. Oh, and Carlos, congrats, Marisa filled me in, med school, huh?"

Dale placed an arm around his younger brother's shoulder and pulled him close. "See, you can't judge a book by its cover. The kids got brains oozing from his pores."

"Thanks, I start in August," Carlos said as he disentangled himself from his brother's headlock, his cheeks a slight pink under his tanned skin, as he served himself a heaping plate of the rice and chicken dish.

When Dale finished filling his plate, he walked over to where we were all sitting and looked down at the seat right next to me, and asked, "Can I sit here?"

I waved my hand to the seat next to me, and he lowered

himself on the banquet seat, the heat of his lithe body moving beside me. He leaned in toward me and whispered in my ear, "Hi again, long time no see. I missed seeing you this morning." There were touches of humor at the corner of his lips and eyes.

I smiled back. "Had to drive Mother to the Opa Locka. They sent her the plane so she could return to Nashville."

I leaned forward and rested my chin on my hand. My knee brushed against his and remained there. He peered at me intently, his eyes registering surprise, but he said nothing as he took a bite of the dish in front of him while I directed my conversation toward his brother. "So, Carlos, will you be working on the future constructions with the show?"

He stopped mid-bite to answer. "I want to. But it all depends on the load of schoolwork I'll be required to do. I've been able to save money all these years, so tuition's covered, no loans for me."

Yolanda was busy cleaning the kitchen and stacking new plates on the counter for a dessert of a chocolate mayonnaise cake, a recipe that belonged to my mother, a favorite with anyone who came to eat at our house. She was pulling out all the stops in the cuisine department. At this pace, Dale would have no problem getting volunteers to assist him.

Yolanda turned toward us and said, "Miguel, that's my son, is a PGY3, that's a post-graduate year three, and he has no time for anything but to study. I tell him we are working hard all the time so that he won't have to one day."

With well-deserved pride, she and her husband both had sacrificed to give him the opportunities they'd never had. I lifted my head and shared a smile with her. "You must be so proud. He'll be a great doctor one day."

Dale interrupted them but directed himself to Carlos. "All you need to do is focus on your studies, we're all behind you, and we'll support you. Plus, you're an owner of the construction company, so if we have work, you make money. You live at Mom's, so there are no housing costs."

Carlos looked down at his plate, and when he looked up, there was gratitude on his face. "Damn, Dale, you're going to make me cry."

"We're all proud of you. How can we not support your dreams?" Dale lifted the glass of water to his mouth. He was uncomfortable with his brother's show of emotion.

His knee knocked mine under the table, drawing my attention as if he didn't have it already. "What are you doing today?"

"Well, Sarah has emailed me all the homeowners that have requested auditions for Home Design Network, and specifically want the services of *Renovated*. I'll have to cull the list, look at possibilities, and then set up interviews to confirm if they fall into the parameters."

"Whew, I'll stick to carpentry," said Jimmy as he scooped another serving of the savory rice dish.

Dale's concerned look was endearing. "You do all that by yourself? It seems like a lot of work."

My brows went up at that. "How do you think this all gets done? Of course, this is a lot of work."

He must have realized the foot-in-mouth situation and pivoted. "But how many people apply?" His leg once again found its way against mine, the connection intimate and ours alone. I couldn't not be aware of the strength and warmth beneath those jeans.

I cleared my thoughts, pretending not to be affected by

his nearness before I tried to make a cohesive thought. "Some competent people at headquarters do the preliminary work of checking the financials, making sure the house is legitimate. Then my crew comes in to verify that they had the prerequisite cash for the show because although we don't charge for the services of Marisa or Levi, the costs of construction need to be covered. Plus, we provide the homeowners with warranties, in case there's a problem, they're covered."

Carlos and Jimmy pushed back from the table to clear their spaces and take the plates over to the sink where Yolanda was standing. Once they did, Dale looked over at me and whispered. "I came in my truck so that I could stay longer. Can we talk later?" I was thrilled. I wanted to continue what we had started at his home. Every glance we shared as we ate, the touches we had indulged in, only made me hunger for him more. I was looking forward to that conversation.

His gaze never left my mouth, and I found it hard to breathe.

"Sure, I'm going to be squirreled away in my father's office. As you already heard, I've got my work cut out for me."

After a bit, he took his plate to the sink. Yolanda was already placing the dirty dishes and silverware into the dishwasher. He looked back at me as if memorizing my every feature, then strode to the door to follow his crew.

I lifted my glass of water, taking a big gulp of the cold liquid to quench the burning inside of me.

Did I really think a FWB arrangement was going to keep him from distracting me?

Don't knock it till you try it.

Famous last words. This man would be the end of me.

Chapter Sixteen
Dale

Yolanda walked in and picked up an empty bottle off the floor as I placed the last of the tools away. I put my hand out to stop her, but she waved away my concern.

"I'll take care of that. I was putting some of my stuff away before getting to the trash."

She placed the trash in the bag that I held out for her.

"Don't worry. I'm used to picking up after my son and husband. I need to leave soon and pick my husband up at the center. My son helps me when he has time, but he had to study for an exam at the med school library."

"As soon as I finish up here, I can let myself out. If you need to leave, I'll close up." I didn't want her staying later than necessary if she had other places to be. I knew what it was like caring for someone and having doctor's appointments. My brothers and I had rotated, getting Mom to chemo.

She smiled, and before she left, she turned toward me and tilted her head in the hallway's direction. "Before you leave, can you let Miss Rebecca know I left her dinner in the refrigerator? Enough for two." She winked as she walked toward the exit of the library.

She left with a wave. "Tomorrow?"

* * *

After I finished cleaning up, I ventured down the long hall toward Mr. Walton's office. The exasperation came through loud and clear from where I stood.

"What do you mean, you don't have the contracts available yet? How can I approach prospective guests for the show if I don't have the paperwork ready?"

I knocked on the wood frame of her father's office door to get her attention. Her body faced the French doors with the view of the Miami skyline. Lost in conversation, she didn't realize I was standing in the room. She was dressed in a pair of cropped black yoga pants and a pink V-neck T-shirt that hugged her curves, hot as hell.

She swiveled at my intrusion and broke into a broad smile as she gestured at the club chairs in front of an immense desk. I was still wary and treaded carefully after being on the receiving end of a cold shoulder for the past month. The room was a smaller version of the library, with the dark wood panels and shelves, but Mr. Walton had a full bar and wall full of high-def TVs, a comfortable-looking couch in front of it. This room was a man cave if there ever was one.

She paced in front of me as she continued her conversation. My eyes traveled from the red toenail polish on her sexy bare feet, the curve of her ass, and the way her breasts rose and fell, with her exasperation with the guy on the phone.

My breath caught at how utterly beautiful she was to me. The flowery scent of her soap surrounded her as she moved around the room, and I breathed her in.

"Neil, please send me those files as soon as possible. There's another couple I plan to consider for the show, but I need the legal mumbo jumbo. So cut and paste from our contracts for previous productions and bring *Renovated's* paperwork on board."

Her hand raked through her scalp in frustration as she leaned her butt against the edge of the desk that faced me. I sat down in the club chair in front of her and made myself comfortable.

I could watch her all day, but that would be weird.

Weird enough not to do it, though?

"Thanks. I'll expect the email by tomorrow. I wanted to approach the clients within the week." She swiped to finish the call and placed the phone on the desk next to her.

As she pinched her eyes with her forefinger and thumb, she said, "Ugh, this happens when they think you're a one-hit-wonder and don't bother preparing the paperwork. No one wants to give me credit."

I pulled her hand gently from her forehead. My thumb rubbed at the crease that had formed between her brows.

She looked up at me from beneath long lashes, "I'm aging myself, aren't I?" Her deep gray eyes closed, and she leaned into me as my thumb continued to move over her forehead, her mouth opening in reaction to my touch. Then her upper teeth bit her plump bottom lip to suppress her response. Man, I so wanted to lick and bite those lips.

"Becca, no one should underestimate you. You'll just come back stronger to make a point." I moved in closer so that our bodies lined up as I lowered my index finger to outline her lips. We were alone. The pounding of my heart was in my ears as I stared once again down at her face.

Am I rushing this?

Should I ask more questions?

Would she even let me know?

I was her past, and maybe she wanted to keep me in that space. My stomach dropped as her face lowered, and I attempted to take a step back when her hand grasped my T-shirt.

Her lips tilted in a smile as her hands traveled up my chest to reach around my neck. She began playing with the hair at the back of my nape. "You're not rushing this. I'm tired of fighting my desire for you. I want you, and I'm not sure how much of that is my body craving connection or the fact that my body craves you."

Please, God, let it be true.

My pulse skyrocketed, air caught in my lungs, and my pulse quickened. Her full lips met mine. Her breath was minty, and her mouth is warm and soft. I breathed more of her into my lungs, and warmth spread through me at having her in my arms. She nipped at my bottom lip before licking it, letting her tongue tangle with mine.

A slight sound escaped her as she grasped my shoulders tighter, bringing me in closer, and she whispered against my lips, "Mm, don't stop."

Her fingers traveled down my back to reach under my shirt, causing a shiver that moved straight to my dick, her fingers tracing below it as she lifted it off me. Our eyes met before I helped her completely remove my T-shirt.

"Babe, you sure you want this?"

"Yes," she said. "I want this, or I wouldn't be climbing your body." Her voice breathy with need, she pulled back to inspect what was before her, her eyes dilated. "I forgot what a masterpiece you are."

Her fingers traveled the planes of my abs and scratched the fine hair of my chest before working their way up. Lowering her mouth to my nipple and flicking her tongue at it. I hissed at the contact. Her mouth had my body burning. It had been so long. I stroked her face as I focused on her movements. Her blond head moved to my other nipple, nipping before soothing it with her tongue, my fingers ran through her silky strands as she looked up at me. But, damn, the heat from her mouth had different parts of my body wanting her attention as well. Her fingers traced my shoulders, while mine found the space between her leggings and fitted shirt, skimming the smooth skin beneath.

"Can I?"

My eyes sought hers. "Say the words, I want to hear them."

A smile shaped her lips. "Yes, that and so much more," she whispered as she lifted her arms so I could pull the shirt over her head, her breasts covered by a lacy bralette. Adrenaline surged through my blood, making its way straight to my cock. Our breaths were the only sound between us. My finger traced the edge of the lacy bra. Her heart pounded beneath it. Both our chests rose and fell to my movement.

I lowered myself to my knees. The delicate scent of vanilla and her flowery body cream reminded me I had been working all day. That just wouldn't do, but this was one problem for which the solution was more than worth the trouble.

Her eyes widened. "Where are you going? What's happening? Did I do something wrong?" There was insecurity reflected in her eyes.

"Becca, no. Just —fuck, being around you has me with a perpetual hard-on." I took her hand and placed it on my cock. Her fingers wrapped around me. Her grip tightened as she closed her eyes for a second and inhaled deeply. I was sure she could feel my pulse through the well-worn jeans. Her eyes widened with a question as she pulled away. "Then, why?"

"It's just...I stink. I've been working all day. I took apart an entire library today."

She shrugged before she smiled slyly down at me, "Good thing we have plenty of bathrooms in this house. Come here, now." Her lips once again found mine as I placed my fingers at the band of her bra and lifted the fabric. I appreciated the view before my mouth latched on her nipple and sucked.

Her nails gripped me as her head tilted back.

"I plan, too." I nipped, then sucked on her nipple. I felt her gasp, her fingers running through my hair, scratching my scalp. I then moved across to her other neglected breast.

My hands, which had been holding her up, moved to her waist and lowered to her yoga pants, pulling them down, taking my time to place light kisses on the areas that I uncovered as I kneeled on the floor.

"Yes." Her voice was low and sultry.

I shook my head, my voice rough and hoarse, as if I needed all my concentration to create a rational thought. "Sorry, got distracted by the view."

"Have I changed much? I mean, my body had to have

changed in eight years." uncertainty weighed down her words.

I lifted my eyes with reverence. "Hon, you're still the most beautiful woman to me."

I groaned as my head lowered to place a light kiss by her navel, moving lower still, my large hands cinched around her waist as I drove down toward the pretty pink lips before me. The zipper of my jeans was branding itself on my cock, but I would not stop.

'Bong—Bong — Bong.' Rebecca squirmed beneath me, pulling at my hair and pushing at my shoulder, her breathing as heavy as mine.

"Dale, Dale, the door. They're not going away."

'Bong — Bong'

"Ignore them. Whoever it is, they'll go away."

That's when the yelling started. "Rebecca!" Bong, Bong. "Rebecca!"

I lifted my gaze and met Becca's eyes. Unease reflected there. Whoever was making that racket out front was persistent.

"What the actual fuck?" I stood up from where I was kneeling in front of her, adjusting my sizable discomfort.

"I'm sorry." Rebecca pushed away, pulling her leggings up in one fell swoop as she moved towards the front entrance.

"Shit, shit, shit... I didn't think he'd show up," she said, more to herself than to me. "Wait, how did he get past the guardhouse?"

"Who? You know who the fuck is making that racket?"

"Just someone I used to date that didn't get the message."

She scrambled to put her bra and T-shirt on. The damn doorbell hadn't stopped sounding throughout the mansion.

She raked her fingers through her hair before she said, "You can stay here while I deal with what's outside."

My eyebrows lifted. Did she think I was just going to sit here and leave her to face a jilted ex? Someone who thought it all right to bang and shout at her door. I don't think so.

As she walked toward the front door with me on her heels, she sighed before saying, "Don't say I didn't warn you."

Chapter Seventeen
Rebecca

I knew exactly who was on the other side of that door, and his timing sucked. And I wasn't looking forward to the conversation. Dale was at my back as I made my way to the foyer, probably thinking that what was behind the door was dangerous, which couldn't be farther from the truth. God knows what's going on in that mind of his. The perma-scowl had become a fixture on his face since we left the room.

Not that I blame him.

Judging by the long and hard outline in those well-worn jeans, Dale was more than a little uncomfortable.

Once I arrived in the foyer, I checked myself in the framed mirrors above the matching console tables. I finger combed my hair into some type of semblance and hoped my flushed cheeks and swollen lips didn't scream that I'd just come from a make-out session.

Pointing my index fingers to my face, I swirled toward Dale and said, "Okay, I don't look like I've just been in a heavy petting session and was seconds from being naked on my father's office floor, do I?"

Dale's lip curled in a heart-stopping smirk as he leaned against the archway with his arms crossed in front of him. "All signs of success." He nodded toward the door. "When you're ready."

I laughed, as ready as I'd ever be for these two men to be in the same room. I tucked my hair behind my ear, took a deep breath, and opened the door.

Standing before me, red-faced and disgruntled at having to wait at the door one more minute than necessary, was my ex. We hadn't seen each other in over five months, and now he was standing before me. My last words to Phillip had been very definitive about the state of the relationship, or better yet, lack of one.

But as usual, he'd dismissed my wants and needs and just thought I was looking for a proposal. Even dared to tell me I was a fool looking for daddy's approval, and once I realized what a catch I'd let go of, I'd be back.

But he wasn't a catch. Not for me. He was a fine enough guy, but almost no one had ever done it for me. Settling for Phillip had been the price I was willing to pay to move past Dale.

When I'd first moved back to Nashville, he wouldn't stop hounding me to come back to New York. After a while, I just sent his messages to voice mail. On the few occasions that I had answered my phone, the conversation ended up in the same place.

Suppose I'd tired of proving to everyone in my family what I could accomplish. When was I returning? It was those drops of sarcasm that had broken this camel's back.

I opened the door and gave him a wide berth to enter. Phillips's face was red and flustered from all the yelling. He gave me a disgruntled look as he swatted at the lovebugs that had swarmed around him.

I waved him into the house with my hand. "Come in... come in, before bugs fly in as well. What a surprise," I said as I moved to the side to let him in.

This was the last thing I needed.

Phillip, dashing in a three-piece suit, was as tall as Dale and prided himself on his runner's physique. As he stepped into the air-conditioned space, he let out a sigh of relief as he brushed off the wings and remaining bugs.

I stifled a small laugh and kept a concerned look on my face. "Sorry about that, it's the season."

"I'd forgotten the heat and humidity in Miami," he said as he took a handkerchief from his back pocket and patted his face. His eyes darted throughout the foyer. It was hard not to be impressed with the understated elegance.

"So, Phillip, what brings you out here? I know this is not your favorite city."

"A client of the firm needed personal attention, and I offered to take care of it, intending to mix business and plea-sure." A movement to his left had him turning to the sound.

That's when he noticed Dale for the first time.

He looked around and froze, narrowing his eyes at Dale. He stood up straighter and snapped his attention back to me. "Who is he? Am I interrupting something?"

"Phillip, this is Dale. Dale let me introduce you to Phillip." Knowing my ex the way I did, he was already taking in Dale's steel-toed boots, his paint-stained jeans, and dismissing Dale as a potential rival for my affection. What would he say if he knew Dale was the only one who'd ever claimed my heart?

Probably the same thing I'd say.

Because there was no way I was admitting that out loud.

Phillip held out his hand to shake Dale's, "Nice to meet you. Has Rebecca told you about us? We used to date when she lived in Manhattan."

The thought that another man, especially one who worked with his hands, could be a potential rival for my affection was incomprehensible to him. I should have known Dale would not let the snub go without a comment.

As he shook Phillip's hand, Dale shook his head as he said, "Sorry, Becca hadn't mentioned you, but nice to meet you too. We were about to have a drink and eat what the housekeeper prepared for us. Would you like to join us?" I had bitten my tongue so as not to laugh, but Phillip's face reddened at the not-so-subtle hint of intimacy.

He shook his head, then looked back at me. "No, thanks. Can we speak? Alone if possible. There's another thing I needed to tell you."

I looked over at Dale, his arms at his waist, not looking too pleased with being sidelined, but he shrugged. "I'll be in the kitchen, checking out what Yolanda left in the fridge. Call me if you need me," he said and lumbered down the hallway toward the kitchen as if he owned the place.

His eyebrow lifted as he followed Dale's movements toward the kitchen and said with a hint of mockery in his voice, "Did you already replace me? Sorry, wrong words, this seems to be a bad time..."

A sense of dread rolled through the pit of my stomach. "Come with me." I signaled for Phillip to follow me in the opposite direction from which Dale was going. His eyes traveled from one beautifully appointed room to another as we made our way to the formal living room. I sat down on the plush, burnt sienna sofa that faced the covered terrace with the view of the ocean. He stood with his back to me, taking in the picture in front of him.

He turned back to face me, dark eyes settling on mine. "Why did we never come here in the year and a half we were together? I wouldn't have been averse to staying here if you'd asked me?"

This was not an enlightening moment. We would not be sharing the details of why I had avoided coming to Florida. It was too personal, and he and I never got close enough to share our pasts. "We were always so busy, and then I decided it was time for me to go back to Nashville."

He walked back to where I was sitting and sat down next to me. "You've been avoiding my calls, haven't you? I really thought we would get back together once you got whatever you needed to, out of your system, but that hasn't happened." His tone deflated.

I knew what it was like to be hurt, and I was the one causing the pain. I tried to be as gentle with my wording as possible. "I'm sorry. When I left, it wasn't to pursue a fancy, like you thought. I just didn't want to give up on pursuing my dreams. Maybe I wasn't clear about my intentions regarding the relationship, but it had run its course." I laid my hand on his shoulder. "We were moving in separate directions."

He gripped my hand a little tighter than was necessary, but he was hurting. "I was always clear about what I wanted with you, Rebecca. It was just convenient for you to keep me at arm's length. You never gave us a chance, did you?"

I pulled away from him, stung by his words, but more-so at wondering if this was how I'd made Dale feel. "I'm sorry,

Phillip. I'm making my life here, for now. I thought we had been clear about our feelings when we parted ways."

"Well, I had another reason to contact you, and getting past the bulldog that's your assistant has been a challenge. If you had answered my calls, I wouldn't have had to show up unannounced." He took my hand in his smooth one, the contrast so apparent compared to Dale's rough and calloused ones and I realized my preference for the latter.

I pulled my hand out of his. After having Dale's all over me, it felt wrong. "Sorry, I've been busy, what with the show and all. Sarah is there to field my calls. It's not personal."

"Well, there's another reason I came to see you. You know my firm is legal counsel to the Home Design Network's competitor." He paused for effect, but I just nodded, staying silent, wondering where Phillip was going with this.

"They want to expand their European division, and you're the candidate for the job. It will be exactly what you were looking to do."

Six months ago, I would have jumped at the chance. But right now, I was different, and I wasn't sure if that was the direction, I wanted to go in.

"Thank you for relaying the offer. Maybe I would have jumped for the opportunity to do something different when I was in New York and unhappy with my career, but for now I'm doing what I dreamed of."

His thumb jerked in the kitchen's direction. "Are you seriously involved with that guy I just met? What could you possibly have in common with him?" His tone was dismissive, as if the possibility was beyond his comprehension. A fire burned in my stomach, and I was trying to hold it in before I lashed out at him.

My body swiveled to face him. "That man in the kitchen was my first boyfriend."

He lifted himself off the sofa, walked to the French doors, and focused on a cruiser passing us by. Knowing him, he was gathering his wits to think of a response to what I'd said. His lawyer's mind was working overtime for the correct answer. "I guess then this is for the best. I was looking for a wife, and you were clearly in a different headspace."

All I wanted to do was be in the kitchen with Dale, not figuring out how to move on from this uncomfortable situation. I was going to take the bull by the horns and be the bad guy. It was so much easier when we were dating in the city. Phillip and I were always so occupied with building our professional lives. There had been nothing left to give of the personal one. It had been convenient. We rarely had time to see each other. "I'm sorry you had any illusions for us ever getting back together. I thought I'd made it clear when I left. Our relationship had no foundation, and we both deserve to be in love one day. And not once have you said you loved me."

He shrugged in agreement. "You can't blame a guy for trying. We would have made a great couple." He looked down at the watch on his wrist. "I better get going then. I have an early meeting tomorrow morning. The offer is on the table till the end of the month. They want you, but they need to fill the job."

This was so typical of our relationship that it only just hit me about why I had left.

Was it nice to be pursued so relentlessly by him? So openly? And for him to do so without me feeling so confused about how I felt in return?

Sure it was. But with Phillip, life rotated around him, his firm's activities, his nights off, and his friends. When I had decided that neither my career nor our relationship was growing and needed a change of scenery, saying goodbye to him had been easy. Unfortunately for Phillip, he thought I would grow out of the novelty of producing my show and come running back to him with my tail between my legs, begging for another chance to be together. It was not happening.

"Of course, I understand. Thank you for coming and making the offer, out of courtesy I'll consider it. Let me walk you to the door." I slumped against the door as soon as I closed it, relief flooded me at putting the past where it belonged for once. All I yearned for now were the confusing emotions that only Dale had ever made me feel.

* * *

Cabinets were being opened and closed, a pan placed on the burners, a knife sawed through a loaf of crusty bread. Unaware of my spying on him, I watched Dale from the kitchen's archway, arms crossed at my chest. He appeared lost in his thoughts. I needed to assure him he had nothing to be concerned about. The only man I wanted stood in front of me.

I ambled over to him. "What did that bread ever do to you? You're butchering it."

His hand flew to his chest. The knife clattered to the board as he swerved to face me. "Fuck, you scared the shit out of me. Is he staying for dinner?"

My eyebrow went up at the question, my arms crossing in front of me. "Did you honestly think he would?"

"Did you love him?" His eyes searched my face for any tell. "Was it serious? Because he came looking for you?"

I took another step closer, our bodies inches apart. "No, I didn't love Phillip. I'm not sure if what I was to him was anything more than someone that would look good on his arm at the firm. I checked a lot of boxes for the perfect wife in his mind," I admitted with a sad smile.

His arms traveled to my hip, bringing me closer, our lower bodies connected. "You would make anyone an amazing wife."

"Would I?"

"Just not his." His mouth lowered once more to nip at my bottom lip before soothing it with another lighter kiss.

"You don't say. And who do you think should have the honor?"

Uncertainty flooding into my system. I'd been on that route with Dale and had paid the price with my heart. Could I afford to be this vulnerable again? Would I be able to survive the ache if I let myself trust him and he betrayed it again? There had been nobody but him for me.

He was the only one who could make me feel like I was home again. But he was also the only one who could hurt me like before.

Say yes to him and I could be whole.

Say yes to him and I might break again. This time for good.

He placed a light kiss on my nose before letting me go, but he did not step away. "Any man would treasure the gift of your heart. Hopefully, I'll earn it back one day."

I hated to admit how much his admiration caused a ripple of excitement to flow through me because, for all that Phillip had been my last boyfriend, there was no passion between us, only convenience. But Dale would always be more than that to me, no matter how hard I had tried to put him in my rearview mirror.

"Thank you. I needed to hear that." I lifted myself on my tippy toes to reach his chin and kiss him there before moving to his neck and breathing him in. His five o'clock shadow rubbing against my face, the scent of wood, warm man, and now the cooked food surrounded us.

But neither of us were thinking about food.

His eyes brimmed with tenderness and passion. His warm hand covered mine. "This is your time, Rebecca. Your moment. I believe you can do this."

"Thanks, it's nice to hear that someone believes in me." Bitterness leaked from my voice.

His gaze traveled over my face and searched my eyes. "I never stopped. You had goals, and you're not afraid of going after them, starting with finishing at Columbia and then continuing for your masters. You achieved what you set out to do." His tone was low and husky. Warmth filled me. Why could he see me for who I was and what I wanted? When Phillip, hell, my family only saw what they wanted me to be?

I leaned into him and placed a gentle kiss on his cheek. My body ached for his touch. He couldn't answer those questions in a single night. And I'd probably regret even asking. But as soon as he had his hands on me, for tonight, I no longer cared.

Chapter Eighteen
Rebecca

Hips and thighs brushed against each other below the counter in the kitchen, but all I wanted was to be close enough for his musky scent to make my head swim with heady intoxication. Now we sat in silence, each lost in our thoughts as we finished what Yolanda had prepared for dinner. My body was on edge.

I was all too willing to continue where we left off before Phillip's untimely arrival. His interruption was a reminder to us of my other life, the one I'd left Miami to pursue when things didn't work out to plan. I wasn't sure if I could trust Dale with my heart again, but I could give him other parts that were famished for attention. It baffled me how right it felt to be close to him again. The rightness of it confused me. Every nerve in my body wanted him, and I wasn't fighting it any longer.

I hadn't realized that I had finished my first glass of Merlot until he was refilling it.

His left eyebrow took a quizzical dip as he asked. "Liquid

courage? Are you regretting what happened between us earlier? Did you change your mind?"

Once again, the flip-flop in my stomach reappeared, and I was afraid that I would lose myself in the depths of his eyes if I allowed it. They appeared to read whatever ran through my mind, and I played out some very sexy scenarios.

"No... not at all, just distracted," I answered.

The wind outside the house was causing an eerie whistle from the palm trees, and the sound of the waves crashing against the rocks was warning us of a storm brewing. I pressed my legs into each other, intending to relieve my need. All it did was heighten it. Though the mood had certainly shifted with Phillip, I wasn't ready to extinguish the fire that Dale had lit.

I turned in his arms to face him, his arms circling my waist. "Becca, I don't know how I could make it through that meal without finishing what we started in the office. But, if your mind is not ready to go there after seeing your ex, let me know." His steady gaze bore into me with silent expectation.

His hard arousal now at my hip height, a prominent reminder of what we had left unresolved. Every nerve strained toward him. An electric current raced through my body at his closeness.

"Who said anything about me not wanting this? Are your intentions to leave me high and dry? Especially after revving my engine."

A self-satisfied smile appeared on his face as he lowered his lips to mine. "You don't have to ask me twice. Sitting next to you has kept me with a semi for the last hour, and I'm ready for dessert." His muscular arms lifted me to the edge of the counter and anchored me there when his fingers gripped my yoga pants and slid them down off my legs. Once done, he stepped between my parted thighs, his gaze a warm caress that sent shivers throughout my limbs.

Naked from the waist down in my parents' kitchen? Didn't think I'd ever go there.

Doubt was making me self-conscious. I was not a stick-thin eighteen-year-old anymore. At twenty-six, there were some curves and dips that hadn't existed back then. Was it possible he would see me and regret wanting me? That his feelings would be so persistent and yet so fickle?

I wrapped my legs around his waist, trying to get as close to his body as possible. His jeans were a physical barrier that prohibited me from getting closer to him. The sensation of being so open to him had me vulnerable.

His eyebrows came together in a thoughtful frown. "Becca, don't hide from me. I've always found you sexy, now even more so." His hand traveled over my soft stomach, slowly moving lower, and opened my knees wider.

"Dale..."

"All I want to do is feast on you. You're so pretty, and it's all I've been thinking about."

My body shivered against the cold granite beneath me, the contrast of his warm breath as he lowered and placed kisses at my navel, trailing down to where I wanted him most.

"Don't make me wait anymore," I said. "You're teasing me with your words."

His mouth lowered to place a kiss just above my pussy, then continued to lick my lips before pushing my legs farther apart. His tongue was licking his lips as if savoring me, while he stared between my legs, and I couldn't take my eyes off his hungry face. It was all for me.

"You're so beautiful, and I'm so damn hard for you," he said. He took my hand in his to place over his erection, my fingers closing around his girth as he moved my hand to stroke him.

I liked this.

"Are you going to make me beg? Because you're doing a superb job of making me wait. And we've waited plenty." His eyes met mine with an intensity that caused me to shudder.

Hands calloused and roughened from working with wood and construction work brought the most delicious tingles to my center when they moved from my knees to my upper waist with a tender touch. My hands reached out to pull him toward where I needed him.

His hands pushed my thighs farther apart as he lowered himself to fit his shoulders between them. "Babe, brace yourself ... I'm going to make this night memorable." My heart jolted, and my pulse pounded at his words. This need and passion had been missing from any other relationship I'd tried to have, but it always came back to him.

My eyes caught his, "Promises, promises." As I widened my legs and Dale's mouth found my clit, his finger moved to find my entrance and touched the fleshy part inside me, massaging me from inside as he suckled, bit, and licked.

He wasn't kidding about making this unforgettable.

He certainly had learned a few things since we'd been together.

"Don't stop. I'm close... so close." I climbed, gasping my pleas, seeking the elusive sensation that was building toward a cliff that I wanted to free fall from, and he kept taking me higher, higher, higher—

Tears leaked from my eyes at the sense of rightness of his mouth and body pressing on mine, I melted beneath his touch. A flush rose to my cheeks and my body clenched when he lifted his head to watch my expression and his eyes held me captive. I reached my release, my body unwinding, my limbs light, a sense of calm washing over me.

"Oh, my." A relieved sigh escaped my lips.

His soft voice penetrated my consciousness as I lost myself to his ministrations. "Becca, you're so wet for me. Your body readying itself for me has me aching." His tongue was at my entrance then, as he penetrated me with it. My head fell back, my breathing sawed in and out of me at the intensity of his touch. "You're made for me. I could eat you forever. Becca, I'm holding on by a thread here."

I lifted myself on my elbows to look up at the only man that ever took me to this state of fulfillment, and I wanted to give him the same satisfaction he'd brought me. I also wanted to take this elsewhere, somewhere with an actual bed or comfortable surface. I grabbed his T-shirt from his shoulders to pull it over his head and off his body. I reached for the button of his well-worn jeans and carefully pulled his zipper down.

His lips were tilting up in a massive grin as he pulled me up so that my core was against his flat stomach, his hands cupping my bare cheeks as he lifted me, my legs around his waist. My pussy rubbed against him, reminding me exactly where I wanted him. "You promised me a shower, and I think we should conserve water..."

I laughed at how carefree and relaxed I felt. "My room, now."

* * *

Lowering my head to nip his lips, soothing it with my tongue. My mouth was trailing down his neck. The delicious scent of wood and man surrounded him. He carried me up the stairs to my wing of the house as if I weighed nothing, and I pointed to the second door on the left once we reached my hallway.

He walked with me in his arms toward the large en suite bathroom, placing me gently on the cold marble surface of my vanity, taking my T-shirt off me in one full swipe. His enormous hands cupping my small breasts, his thumbs outlining my nipples till they were stiff. Tingles of pleasure moved straight to my core as he lowered his head to kiss, lick, and suck my nipples while I held on to his shoulders. He lifted his head, cool air stiffening the tips where his mouth had been. My head lay against the mirror behind me. It was the only thing keeping me upright.

"Don't move," he said. "I'm going to turn on the shower."

Perched on the counter, I smiled as my arms wrapped around my knees. "Where do you think we're going without clothes? Go ahead, turn on the showerheads. If you don't remember, I like my water pretty hot."

"There are some things you never forget," he said with a grin. He peeled his jeans off within seconds. Then he looked at me, his grin growing wider, and said, "I'm a bit under-dressed here. Join me. Let's get wet."

His cock stood out proudly from his body, his hand

wrapped around himself, stroking himself further. I watched his movements as a voyeur, enjoying the show, but not a part of it. His eyes never left mine when he said, "Come here, we're far from done tonight."

I lifted myself off the vanity counter as naked as the day I was born and took hold of his hand, a jolt passing through me at his touch. He pulled me under the oversized rainforest showerheads that had filled the room with steam. I was in the arms of the last person I thought would ever hold me again, and I realized it was precisely where I wanted to be.

I disengaged myself from him to pump the liquid body soap into the palm of my hands. The scent of ginger-lily perfumed the air. "Don't move. I want to do this for you."

"Hon, I won't move an inch if that's what it takes for you to touch my body." His tone was reverent as my hands explored his body again. From the slope of his back and buttocks, strong shoulders, ripped arms, and powerful legs, down his midriff to reach his engorged shaft.

While I got reacquainted with him, his hands were busy covering ground on my body, his fingers moving over every erogenous zone he could reach.

"No wonder I can't get this scent out of my mind."

He groaned as I kneeled before him, my hand stroking him as my mouth lowered to lick, tongue, and suck his hard cock. Above me, he bucked deeper into my mouth and growled an unintelligible sound that I barely understood as the rain shower was falling on us. He stroked a finger down my cheek, nuzzling my hair.

"Becca, I'm so ready to come, but I want to be inside you. Are you ready to go there with me?" He lifted me to my feet, his desire hard between my thighs.

"Yes, I very much want this."

Turning off the water, he reached for the towels that were hanging just outside the glass stall, wrapping one around me as his eyes locked with mine. He lifted me in his arms and carried me to my bed, placing me on the edge. Our chemistry was off the charts. I'd never replicated this with anyone else. Yet, he still held my heart and could consume my body. I was throbbing with need and ached for him.

He reached for his jeans, pulling out from his wallet a condom, and ripped the foil open.

I smiled. "Prepared for anything, aren't you?"

"Prepared." He smiled back at me. "And hopeful." He smirked before placing it on himself and rolling it on. "It's been a long time for me, too."

I moved back to the middle of the bed, my thighs spread wide, and I bent my legs to accommodate both him and his girth, my body prepped and ready. My hand was moving over the curve of my stomach, down to the juncture between my thighs. His eyes were intense. My breath caught in my throat at the intensity. "Don't make me beg. I haven't lost control in so long. It fucking hurts. I've missed having this. I've missed you."

His body slammed into mine, making a point of owner-ship and staking his claim clear. "Becca, there will be no begging from you. My cock was yours and always will be. You're so wet and tight." He grabbed my hips, impaling me with rapid-fire strokes, and I arched to meet his thrusts, move for move. "Honey, just let me know what you need."

My fingers grasped his hard ass, bringing him closer into me, "Don't stop, keep moving, I'm about..."

When I was getting close, his thumb lowered to my clit to

rub as he continued rocking in me. I bucked before my sex clasped him in release, his head burrowed in my neck, kissing me and sucking on it before groaning out loud in release.

Our bodies pressed together, our heartbeats pounding as if we'd run a marathon. His fingers brushed over my face hooking the hair behind my ear, "I don't have words for all I'm feeling at this moment, but you need to know we're repeating this tonight."

After eight years, we were making up for lost time.

Chapter Nineteen
Dale

I held on to her all night, her warm body curled into mine. After a long night of reacquainting ourselves with each other's bodies, I had forgotten to set my alarm. I woke up so many times throughout the night not believing that she was back in my arms, it felt surreal. Her breathing steady and trusting, all seemed perfect in my world. My heart swelled with a feeling I thought long since dead till she came back into my life, because I'd been on fire for her. I was sure that when her ex had shown up, Becca was going to call the whole thing off, and send me packing. It made me want to possess her, to claim her, and to keep her. But this was a different Rebecca and I had to play by her rules if I wanted to be a part of her life.

Her delicate perfume of white flowers surrounded me like her body did mine last night. So many thoughts raced through my head. What if she wanted me gone before anyone came to work on the house? She'd been clear about keeping this on the down-low, and that grated on me, but I guess I needed to earn her trust. *Was her disappearing act this morning a mega hint, her way of hinting at no uncomfortable morning after confrontations?* Having Rebecca's blast from the past pounding on the door, interrupting us, was like a pail of cold water thrown on a campfire. When her ex noticed me in the mansion's entrance, I'd seen him size me up from head to toe and find me lacking. The confusion on his face at Rebecca's apparent choice to stay with me baffled him. It confused me as well. The slick lawyer living a sophisticated city life and I were as different as two men could be. I loved my small town. It was the place where my parents gave me a home, and my brothers surrounded me.

I heard her laughter echoing outside the door of her bedroom and the voice of the housekeeper. "Good morning, Yolanda. I'm expecting a package from Home Design. They were going to send it next day delivery."

"Buenos días, Miss Rebecca. I'll place it on the table in the kitchen as soon as it arrives."

* * *

When the door opened, I covered myself up. After she closed the door, the sheet that covered my torso slipped lower and desire-filled her gaze. Her jaw opened and closed as she stared at my growing erection. I watched as her nipples hardened under the silk of her robe, teasing my desire.

She held two cups of steaming coffee in her hands as she walked toward me. "Morning sleepyhead, for someone in construction, you certainly woke up late."

I lifted my arms, took the mugs from her hands, and took a sip from mine. "Mm... delicious, thanks." I placed the mugs on her night table. "Can you blame me? A certain someone had me up till all hours and put me through the wringer. This man needs eight hours." A smile broke out on my face.

Her grin was mischievous as heat rushed to her face. "I like this. I mean you and me."

"I'm glad, because I like this too." I leaned forward and clasped her by the waist, sliding her across my thighs so that she straddled them. The silk robe opened to reveal a naked Rebecca. Her teeth nipped at my shoulder, and her hands climbed from my biceps to curl around my neck.

I dipped my head down to press a kiss to her lips one more time, and her hands slid to cup my face. She placed light kisses across my stubbled jaw before returning to my mouth, biting on my lower lip, urging me to let her in.

I heard myself moan. Or was that her? I was too lost in the sensation of having her in my arms again.

Her bare core rocked back and forth over my cock, the wet heat driving all blood away from my brain to center at my groin. Her nipples beaded under my gaze, and my thumb stroked across the sore point of one as my lips suckled and nipped the other. She cried as I took her breast in my mouth, gently teasing her nipple with my tongue, making me groan.

I shifted to graze her clit, my cock between her lower lips, her movements causing delicious friction, my balls tightening. Either I said something now, or I'd lose the chance to come where I most wanted.

"Mmm, Dale," she said. "Just like that, keep rocking."

"Becca, I'm going to come. I want inside you, but I don't have condoms on me."

Her eyes glazed with passion—her voice low. "I got tested in my last checkup. I'm clean and on the pill."

"I'm clean, too, nothing but my hand for the last three years."

No point in telling her just how rarely I'd been with anyone in the eight years since her. Those three years I had been clean, and the full eight I may as well have been celibate too. Why bother when they all reminded me of her?

She nodded in agreement as my mouth covered hers, the Sumatra coffee flavor she brought for us on our tongues as I slid into her, it was a tight and wet sheath around my cock.

She impaled herself on my stiff length with every thrust. Her heat surrounded me. I was going to blow, but not before I gave her an orgasm. Carpentry terms and lingo repeated in my mind to help me last longer— dovetail, ceiling moldings, biscuit joiner. I clasped my arms around her as I pumped up as she drew herself down. She arched to meet my thrusts. She was everything to me, and I would not let her go this time.

Her breathing was shallow in my ear, her body squeezing me tight. I shifted my angle to graze her pleasure spot, filling her again and again. My heart hammered in my ears. She sagged into me at her release, her upper body blanketed over mine. Her breath caressed my ear as I marked her as mine from the inside out.

I breathed her in, my nose in her neck, her scent now a combination of us both, and a sense of completeness filled me. I kissed that space between her neck and shoulder one last time. Shivers travel through her body as she shimmied above me.

She laughed before she said, "Stop — I'm ticklish."

"Honey, you keep that up, and we're never getting out of this room." I grasped both sides of her ass and gave a light squeeze.

She chuckled again. "Promises, promises."

* * *

After another shower together with a slight delay, we walked down to the kitchen together. Waiting for us on the kitchen table was a bacon and cheese quiche, crispy bacon, and a carafe of coffee. The table was set for two, and the house-keeper was nowhere in sight, but I was aware of who had prepared everything. We had our in-house matchmaker. Rebecca sat down and patted the chair seat cushion next to her and smiled up at me before saying. "Yolanda must like you because she is making you feel welcome."

I grinned before saying, "My charming personality and looks. It gets them all the time. But if it allows me to eat her food, I'm all for it."

I was getting a laugh out of her while she placed a slice of quiche on the plate in front of me. I brought the egg and bacon mixture with its flaky crust to my mouth and chewed.

"Babe, this is orgasmic."

"Told you she likes you," she said as she poured coffee in the mugs already set out for us.

We ate in comfortable silence, then my phone pinged, and I realized my Brothers Group Chat was in overdrive, and I had placed my cell on do not disturb. My smile slipped off my face, and my stomach did a nosedive knowing the crap they were going to send my way.

Noah: Stopped by your house. Where were you? You didn't come home last night.

Carlos: Hey, where are you? Do you need Jimmy and me today?

Carlos: How come you haven't texted me back?

Levi: He's busy. He'll text when he wants to.

Levi: Dale, text us

I let out a breath I hadn't realized I was holding. Jeez, I'm a grown ass adult. What's with the questions?

Jeremy: I need you to stop by the new HDN offices, need to consult you on something.

Marcos: Hey ASSHOLE, are you alive? You're not answering your calls.

Noah: Don't forget tonight at Fran's. My group is playing. Tell Rebecca we're expecting her as well.

Dale: I'm fine and alive. You guys need to get a life. I'll stop by HDN first thing. Carlos, bring Jimmy with you. I'm going to need you both if I must run out.

Her eyebrows lifted with a questioning look. "Everything okay? You're scowling at the phone."

I leaned over and cupped her cheek before placing a light kiss on her lips, and her eyes fixed on mine. "My nosy brothers. The problem when you live with them, they're always in your business. By the way, Noah wants me to remind you he's performing tonight, and he doesn't take rejection well. So will you go with me?"

She leaned back in her chair. "Sure, I wouldn't want to be the reason behind Noah's ego getting bruised."

"God forbid, my kid brother has an ego problem," he added.

"Plus, I'll be able to take Sarah. She's new and hasn't had time to meet anyone or see much. But if you want to talk about nosy brothers, you might have five, but mine trumps yours any day of the week. "

"I don't doubt it, being the only younger sister." I was more than aware of how protective Charles was of her.

"You've heard of helicopter parents. Well Charles is a helicopter brother. I think he took his role as a big brother too seriously. He can be a total jerk, but what can I say? I love him anyway." She let out an exasperated sigh.

I bit my tongue, not wanting to throw her brother under the bus since stepping away had been the right thing to do. Just not the way I handled myself in the situation.

Well acquainted with her brother's overprotective nature, I shut my mouth, not wanting to sour the moment with my opinion of her interfering brother. I would not knock him off the pedestal she'd placed him on.

Yolanda arrived with a large manila envelope in her hand and placed it on the table in front of us. "This just came for you. Buenos días, Dale."

"Good day to you too."

Rebecca snatched it to open it and read its contents.

"Thank you for the quiche. It reminds me of when my mother would make them for Sunday brunch. Except with seven men, she'd prepare three of them."

She preened under the compliments. "Thank you. It's Mrs. Walton's recipe, with just a few tweaks of my own." With that, she left the room once again.

I turned back to my plate of food to find Rebecca with a scowl on her face. Now it was my turn to ask. "What's the problem?"

She frowned as she looked at the papers that had been in the folder. "I think I'm being set up to fail."

I glanced at the paperwork, but since I had no clue what she was talking about or what she was reading, I just asked, "Why would you think that?"

"They assigned everyone on the committee a target goal for donations. The goal set for me is two hundred thousand."

"Dollars?"

"Equivalent in value. That could be in products or services. I was just given a partial list of some donors from last year. There's just no way I'll ever reach that number. Ugh! I need to sit down, study the contacts, see what strategy I'm going to use. I mean, this year's charity is to help with an autism cluster in a center that's part of an underserved community in Nashville. That type of work requires money and lots of it."

"What options do you have? Can I help you with anything?" I said as I took a sip from my coffee and savored the brew.

Her brow furrowed as she once again looked at the paperwork. "I can't say yet. I will have to sit down and study this, then see what I can add to the mix. But before I start on this, I must make a stop at our future office. I've dumped the whole thing on Sarah, and I'm sure she's overwhelmed."

"I'm headed that way. Do you want a ride? Jeremy asked

me to stop over, had some questions, needed my opinion about some stuff."

She hesitated before answering. "They're all going to speculate about us and I'm not ready for that."

I restrained myself from voicing the other side of that. Was the problem that she wasn't ready to come out as a couple? Or was the problem that she wasn't ready to be a couple?

"You told me you agreed to keep this between us for a while," she said. "Did you change your mind?"

I leaned forward, my hand running up her arm toward her shoulder. "Becca, my brothers all know that I'm crazy about you. I have no problem answering questions they might throw my way. But we'll play it your way. When you're ready to be open about us, you'll let me know, won't you?"

She nibbled on her lower lip, contemplating my words. I understood her hesitation. They could be a handful. She wouldn't trust that quickly again. I wanted to be honest with her this time, more than I ever was when we were kids. If this was going to work, I needed to give her the space she wanted to decide about us.

My insides ran cold, and my heart stopped at the thought of her rejection, but I couldn't force her to love me.

"Why does this matter so much to you?" she said.

"I told you. I hurt you good, and I—"

"But I forgive you. Or whatever," she said. "This is something else."

I guess it was a day for revelations.

"I never told you who my birth parents were," I said. "I mean, they don't matter because my life began the day Jack and Karen Chance fostered my brothers and me. That day they changed our lives forever."

Her eyes never left mine as she held my hand in hers. "Thank God, they came into your life, and you couldn't ask for better brothers, blood-related or not."

My hand raked through my hair. "What I mean is my birth parents were total losers. My birth mother was an addict that OD'd in a shitty motel room. My actual father was not any better. He left me with her while he went out and robbed a gas station, killing an off-hours cop."

She went to speak, but I held my hand up and shook my head. Now that I started, I needed to get it out.

"My legacy was a junkie and an ex-con," I said. "That was one of many reasons, I thought I was never good enough for you. The kicker is that my father got out of jail and didn't last a year before he was back in there. And he's been there ever since."

A ball of emotion clogged my throat, but I said nothing.

"After never hearing from him, he recently sent me a letter asking for forgiveness and wanting to see me. He's dying, and I don't know what he wants from me—absolution, maybe."

I guess that made two of us.

Her eyes held compassion, as much for him as for me. "Maybe it's too late for him to make things right," she said. "But you can still offer him forgiveness, can't you?"

Maybe.

And maybe going to see him was the one way I'd know if it was possible for a person to get both.

Chapter Twenty
Rebecca

We had left in separate cars to go to the Home Network office, regardless of Dale offering me a ride over. Neither of us knew how long it would take to solve our respective jobs, and I didn't want to inconvenience him if he had to leave early to check on his crew. Plus, it gave me time to digest, his heartfelt confession.

There was so much we had never spoken about that summer we had fallen in love. We were kids who thought we discovered the concept of love.

How foolish of us.

He was so sure of my rejection of him. He'd hidden such a crucial part of his past from me. He had been so sure I would have dismissed him for his birth parents' actions. His insecurity was so telling about what made him tick. Another reason that confirmed how ill-prepared we'd been to take a step forward as a couple. We could have solved all these resentments with conversations we didn't have the maturity to deal with eight years ago. My heart broke for us. So much wasted time.

Both of us arrived at the same time at the new office parking lot. My insides tingled with memories of this morning's escapades as his muscular body walked up to my car and opened my door for me.

"Are you going straight in? Do you want to walk in together?" His smile disarmed me, and my knees wobbled a bit.

Pull it together, Rebecca. This is not your first rodeo with this man.

"Sure. Then I'll go and meet Sarah. We need to catch up on some office stuff." I grabbed the tote with the thick file sent to me and my computer from the back seat.

We arrived to witness a flustered and red-faced Sarah having a discussion with Jeremy, who looked like he was one second from losing his shit. Both of us watched the battle of wills with curiosity, but neither of us uttered a word. When he saw Dale he waved him over before turning his back to Sarah and walking away from her.

There were men painting, putting up drywall, installing fixtures, and working with plumbing amid all this. Sarah's eyes threw invisible daggers at Jeremy as she walked over to meet me. I made sure to circumvent the debris strewn over the cement floor as I met her halfway over.

Grimacing, she pointed to the black leggings and T-shirt she had on. "Excuse my appearance, but my luggage went traveling and took a detour via New York. The airline promised me delivery tonight, so I'm living out of the few things in my carry-on and what I could scrounge up here and there."

I dismissed her worried look with a wave of my hands. "Forget about it. With this mess, would you want to come in business attire? What's important is that you're here to help me."

I reached out to touch her hand. There were deep frown lines on her forehead. "Are you okay? If Jeremy is giving you a hard time, I can talk to him. I know he can be prickly, but he knows what he's doing. To be honest, it surprised me as much as the next person when he offered to help you."

Sarah's hands clenched and unclenched. The New Orleans accent became more pronounced as she spoke. "No, I'm fine. We had a slight disagreement, nothing that serious. But that man could try the patience of a saint."

I smirked in agreement, "Don't they all? I'm here to pull you away from this for a while. I need your help in this other project I need to dedicate time to. There's a courtyard café right in front. Let's get coffee."

* * *

We ordered two cappuccinos and selected croissants filled with guava, custard, ham, and cheese. We sat at a round marble table for four, where I set up my computer and files. Once the fragrant coffee and mouthwatering pastries arrived, we got down to business.

Sarah looked over the rim of her cup. "So, Dale. He's better looking in person than on television. He's working at your parents' house, isn't he?" She picked up a croissant and took a bite as she waited for my answer.

I nodded. "Yep, the one and only. Oh, before I forget, the Chance brothers have invited us to see Noah perform in Saltview at Fran's tonight. You would, of course, go with me. That way, you don't walk in alone."

Her eyes widened. "Sure. I'd love to go. Do something other than work for a while." Once again, peering down at her wardrobe, she said, "I have nothing to wear. Is this place fancy?"

"If you have jeans and a T-shirt, you're good to go. Think of it as one of Nashville's honky-tonk bars."

This seemed to calm her, and she got back to the business at hand. "So, what is it you need my help with?"

"I received the list of donors that I'm supposed to approach. Most of them are in Nashville. So, I need you to book my trip to Nashville, but only once you have scheduled appointments with each of the ten donors on this list."

"Okay... it seems like a lot of appointments for one day, are you sure?"

I broke off a piece of the croissant in front of us and took a bite of the flaky pastry. "Yes, super sure. How can I ask potential contributors to donate their products or money over the phone? My mother always said it was harder to reject someone face to face, rather than over the phone. These are tough times and there's a target goal to reach. You don't ask for these types of donations while someone's attention is divided between what they were doing prior to getting on the phone with you and figuring out how to get off the phone with you. Mom has always dealt with them, and few dared say no to her. I want to make sure I don't drop the ball, since the money is funding something vital to the community."

Sarah nodded, writing everything I asked down on the yellow pad she had in front of her. "What else do you need to do? Did you receive the email I sent you with the candidates I with the highest potential to be on the show? I made appointments to visit every one of them before narrowing the list. Jeremy offered to accompany me."

Shock must have reflected on my face because she was quick to defend him. "He's not so bad when he wants to be."

I lifted my face from the screen in front of me when her cough distracted me and met Sarah's eyes. She turned her monitor over to me so I could see the spreadsheet she had created with the prospective donors' names and phone numbers plus rows to input the scheduled appointments and outcome.

I looked up from the screen and met her eyes. "You know I've been allowing an idea to percolate in my brain, and I wanted to know what you thought about it. Mind you, I haven't mentioned anything to my mother or brother, but I've thought of a way to both get a huge donation and get promo for the show."

Sarah's eyes held a puzzled look, but she said, "Okay, I'm all ears. Shoot me with your best shot."

"Well, I'm thinking we could have our Renovated hosts offer their services in a room renovation to the highest bidders at the gala, then we tape the show for Home Network. That would be one stone, two birds. It would give great promo to our show and the network."

Sarah bit her lip as she nodded in agreement, "Wow, I love it. I think you nailed it with that one. How did things go with your mother? Did she bring up the job again?" She watched me warily. She knew that the job they wanted me to handle was a hot button with me.

I sighed. "We spoke about it. Once again, Mother made her wishes known. But I made an argument that Renovated had been a success and my efforts had to focus on that in the meantime. I can schedule the meeting for the end of the week, fly in, coordinating the sessions that require a face-to-face with donors, then fly back. Plus, headquarters needs the projected numbers for the new shows, including payroll, set costs, equipment rentals and incidentals."

Sarah, not one to let the grass grow under her feet, gave me the second-page list of names, and picked up her phone. "I'm going to start scheduling those appointments. Your list contains the names of donors. I'll call the first five, and you can start on the other five."

I nodded and took the page with the names in my hand. "Okay, let's just get this done. The sooner, the better."

I tackled the first name on my list, Mrs. Glori Ann Hutchins, a neighbor of my parents and recent widow. Her husband had died last year and left her the sole heir of over ten blocks of rental property in the heart of Nashville. I wasn't sure if the right approach was outright asking her for a donation, even though last year she was good for ten thousand.

No better time than the present.

I dialed the number.

After an hour, I had arranged four appointments with potential donors, we scheduled to meet at their place of preference. The pleasantries were exhausting, each call I would introduce myself as Susan Walton's daughter and explain my involvement with the charitable activity and the chosen cause. Mom had been right as usual. It was harder to refuse me in person.

Time to flex that power. This close to the finish line, it was time to close the distance.

* * *

A shadow over my screen alerted me to the fact that we were no longer alone. I'd been so involved in getting these calls done, I hadn't seen the one man I couldn't look away from.

Dale sat down next to me, moving so close there was not an inch between us. His heat was comforting against my side after not having much luck getting half the appointments necessary. I smiled at him, putting my hand up so he could wait till I got off the phone.

My current conversation with the owner of a burger franchise in the downtown area was not going in the direction I needed. I'd become a sounding board to all his frustrations with the economy and how things weren't the same this year. I was understanding of the situation and thanked him for giving me his time.

Once I got off, my head fell to Dale's shoulder. "Ugh."

My hands flew up in frustration before me, "I'm so frustrated. This is a lot harder than I thought it would be. Not everyone will part with their money."

Sarah eyes widened but she kept the conversation on topic. "I confirmed five appointments for Monday. I'll book your flight out for Sunday."

"You're leaving?" Dale's voice broke me out of my misery.

My shoulders tensed as my eyes found his. "Um ... yes. I need to get these donations for the silent and open bidding auctions for the gala evening."

"I get it. Just hard to see you go." A frown etched into the side of his mouth.

"If I ask over the phone, do you honestly believe I'll have

the same success? I didn't realize how hard asking people to part with stuff can be."

His hand went to my shoulder in a reassuring touch. "If anyone can do it, it's you. Look at the way you could get Marisa and Levi to work together. But the reason I came over was to let you know I'm heading back to the house. Carlos and Jimmy are already there." He looked at Sarah and put out his hand. "Where are my manners? My mother taught me better. Hi, I'm Dale, you must be Sarah. You've had the pleasure of working with my grumpy brother, Jeremy."

Now I remembered why I hadn't wanted to have distractions. Tunnel vision was what I needed to get through the task at hand, and it didn't help that he was so damn understanding, only making me feel worse. And if I was honest with myself, the last thing I want is to leave for Nashville and the arms that held me so close last night. Life was throwing me a curve ball, because I hadn't seen this coming.

Sarah shook his hand. "Nice to meet you, too. I'm grateful for the help Jeremy has offered me. He's been a lifesaver."

Dale's eyebrows shot up in surprise. "People just don't understand him, so they think he's difficult. He's just a very detailed person and a genius at what he does." He lifted himself out of his chair, but not before placing a light kiss on my forehead."

"See you later. Don't forget tonight."

A little dazed by the attention, I didn't answer right away. "Oh, yes, tonight. See you later."

I couldn't help but watch him leave. I followed the man with my eyes as he strolled to the door, nodding at a few people as he made his way out. I turned back to Sarah, who was staring back at me with the oddest expression on her face. "What?"

She grinned, then said, "You like him, don't you?"

I laughed before answering, "Yeah, I do."

Chapter Twenty-One
Dale

I walked through the glass doors of the new Miami offices of Home Design. The last thing I expected was to find my brother flustered. Few things bothered Jeremy, and even fewer got him in a foul mood. He was always even keeled, and we counted on him to always be the voice of reason among us.

"What's going on?" I looked toward the pretty, petite brunette who was now with Sarah on a FaceTime call with the in-house design department of Home Network.

Jeremy pulled me by the arm, farther away from where the women were standing before he answered me.

"Some bitcoin millionaire came in while we were in full construction mode, started hitting on her, this isn't speed dating." As his hand went out to signal all the workers on task, "I told him this wasn't the time or place, then said he needed to leave. If he wanted to make plans with her, it had to be outside the doors of Home Design."

I whistled under my breath. "Not cool, bro. Last I remember, women don't appreciate being told who and when they can speak to someone. Did she tell you to fuck off?"

My brother bent his arms in front of him, "No, she called me an idiot and told me to mind my business." Then he smirked, causing the silvery scar on the right side of his face from a near-fatal car accident, to crease. "But before the guy left, she told him politely she wasn't interested."

"Good for her. She knows her mind. Hey, I hope it won't be an issue because Rebecca's inviting her to go tonight to see Noah." He shrugged in response to my question, but there was definitely interest in those baby blues of his.

We walked over to the table with the floor plans and Jeremy's work papers. "So, what's the problem? Why'd you need me? You seem to have everything under control."

We filled the three thousand square foot loft with over twenty men in hard hats, each assigned a task. Jeremy had them divided equally, so that some oversaw office partitions, setting up the framework in metal while others worked the drywall. The plumbing contractor we used on projects such as these was laying pipe for the private bathroom. My brother had this under control.

Thank God one of us does.

Rebecca walked over toward us, and I put my hands in my pockets to control the urge I had to pull her against me. She was in control, and this was her stage, and my heart stumbled into my chest before finding its footing again.

"Hey, I'm going next door to sit in the café and work with Sarah in relative quiet. If you need us, just call."

"Sure, I'll stop by there before heading to your house. I'm supposed to meet with the architect to discuss changes I want to make to the original design."

She smiled and nodded, then left us to meet her assistant, who was lugging a tote larger than her.

Now it was my burly brother, who was looking at me with suspicion in his eyes. "Dale, what's happening between the two of you? Do I need to remind you how well things ended the last time you guys were together? It was me that picked your drunk ass up off the floor when she left Miami. Can you survive that again?" Concern lined his eyes, his lips slanting downward.

"Don't worry. We're not teenagers anymore. We know what we're doing this time around." I wasn't sure if I was reassuring him or myself.

Jeremy's brow lifted like he knew which one of us needed to be reassured. "If you say so, I hope you know what you're doing. Anyway, let me show you the real reason I called you. Follow me to the decor center that they want to integrate into the show."

I followed behind him. We entered a twenty by twenty-foot room at the back of the office. My brother walked into the middle of the space, drywall installed and refinished. Everything looked to be under control. I fist-pumped the three guys from our crew hello, before turning to my brother, "Okay, what's the problem?"

Jeremy ran a hand through his hair, scratching at the back of his neck. "This room is to showcase the clients with all the samples. They want to make client presentations in a controlled space in order to control the narrative."

I'm sure my eyes doubled in size. "Did you just say narrative? What the fuck?"

"Yeah, narrative, I'm not an idiot, asshole. I was thinking

of starting a thirty-foot island with a waterfall in Calacatta porcelain, the look of marble without the costs."

"Great — and I'll create a tile display area under half of the island, and the other half can act as storage and stools for clients to sit and discuss their choices."

I waved over to the men installing glass dividers for Rebecca and Sarah's open office concept, which allowed for privacy, although there was none.

He stopped and pointed to the area in front of us. "They've asked us to create something unique here. No fucking clue, not my wheelhouse, if you get my drift." He stood, scratching his chin with an overwhelmed look on his face.

I walked around the floor, imagining what could work in the space. His goal was to impress and make it unique to Rebecca.

"Sure, give me tonight to sleep on it. I'm going to design something that will make *Renovated* pop out. This project means a lot to Rebecca, which means it's important to me."

He placed a heavy hand on my shoulder. "Man, I think my warning came too late. You're already a goner."

My shoulders lifted, then dropped as I pulled the tape measure that hung from my belt off. "You're probably right. Regardless of that, help me measure the wall, so I can sit down and start coming up with ideas."

* * *

I coughed to break up the intimate conversation between Carlos and the architect of the new library. They parted, and I extended my hand to shake hers.

"Ms. Santos, sorry I'm late," I said. "A lot of traffic coming back from the Home Design office that we're setting up as well."

Her fuchsia lips that had seen plenty of fillers gave me a toothy smile. "No worries. Your brother showed me what you have been doing. He's extremely entertaining."

I bit my tongue rather than tell her what would happen to their brief affair within the next two weeks or when Carlos met the next flavor of the week. "Ms. Santos, why don't we sit outside on the terrace? That way, we can talk without all the noise and dust."

She looked agreeable to the idea as she brushed the dust off her hands and slacks. "Please, call me Marta." She gave a backward glance at my brother. With a small wave, she followed me out the French doors.

Our meeting took longer than expected, but there was no way to rush it. She insisted on going through her schematic point by point.

"You know this design is based on the principles of the etagere." A tad condescending as she sat down in front of me.

"Ma'am, I know what open shelving is. This isn't the first bookcase I've tackled. Don't let the appearance fool you." I pulled out the sketches I'd made with the alterations to her design.

Her eyes opened wide at my words, but she said nothing as she grabbed for the sketchbook I'd placed on the table. She sat silent as she took in the changes recommended, they were minor, but the impact would be breathtaking.

She picked up the graph paper, studying the changes I wanted to make, and looked up, nodding her head. "These are spectacular. I can't believe I didn't think of this. Incorporating backlighting will create drama by flanking the centered windows with the ocean view and bring balance to the space. But I'm concerned. I promised Mrs. Walton I would do this before she comes at the end of the month. This means having to connect electrical, and we might need to order more of the shelves."

Casanova walked out and joined us, ready to go in for the kill. She never had a chance. "Marta, don't you worry. Dale's talented that way. If he's suggesting this, then he's got a solution."

I crossed my arms at my chest before agreeing, "He's right. I wouldn't have offered it if I couldn't do it."

Such a small victory, but it made me feel brave.

Or stupid.

There was often so little difference between the two besides the results.

For me, it all depended on how things would end with Rebecca.

* * *

It was close to four p.m., and we had already cleaned up the area for the day when I heard Rebecca's throaty laugh and another female voice coming from the foyer. I took a deep breath in and blew it out, controlling my inner cringe, because Karina's tone of voice was unmistakable. While Rebecca had avoided me like the plague when she first moved back, Karina threatened actual physical harm if I approached her best friend. As if Rebecca needed protection against me, when just the thought of her leaving again paralyzed me.

Rebecca's face brightened once she walked in with her

friend, greeting Carlos and Jimmy. When she walked right up to me, I placed the last tools on the mobile cart we kept at the jobsite. I let Becca set the pace in front of her best friend, but I clenched and unclenched my fists to keep them by my sides instead of pulling her into my arms, like I wanted to.

"Great, you're still here. I wanted to tell you I hired a car service to take us all to Fran's tonight. That way, we can all drink and not worry about drunk driving."

"She's lying. She hired a freaking party bus to take us to Fran's. What are we, fifteen?" Karina was sarcasm with a Southern accent, but then she winked as if it was all for show. "We'll have a blast. Plus, now she has control over everyone coming back in one piece."

Rebecca's eyes rolled up in her head. "Stop being such a party pooper. I got inspired to do something fun when you messaged me that you landed in Miami. Don't be such a shrew. Enjoy the fact that I'm taking care of you for once."

I scratched my head, and I'm sure there was a puzzled look on my face. "You hired a bus for just you two?"

Beaming up at me, she laid a hand on my upper arm, her fingers tightening as they traveled down to my bicep. My skin prickled under the heat of her touch. I cleared my throat pretending not to be affected by her casual nearness.

Her eyebrows arched as she said, "Of course not. There's Sarah. Then Karina texted she flew into Miami, so I called Ken and his husband to join us. He said yes instantly. It's been forever since the three of us partied together. Plus, many of the Renovated crew wanted to watch Noah perform."

"Wow, that was last-minute? When did you find the time?" I asked.

"It was nothing but a phone call. Marisa was the one who gave me the idea."

Carlos stepped up to join the conversation at that. "It doesn't surprise me that the Cuban connection moves mountains in Miami. She does it in mysterious ways, but it gets shit done."

"Well, anyway, they stopped by to see the progress in the office and give me their input. Plus, there were some things I wanted to pass by them regarding the charity event I'm part of. Marisa called a friend who did this for a living and took care of the whole thing. How could I not include her and her besties to come along?"

Carlos placed a hand over Karina's shoulder as if they were close. I wanted to laugh at the letdown he was about to receive. "Hey Karina, you need someone to hang out with tonight? I'm your man. I know all the hot spots."

She shrugged his arm off. "I'll keep that in mind, but don't hold your breath."

Becca's voice lowered, "Kari, put those claws away, be nice."

Yolanda appeared at the library door. She excused herself to go with the housekeeper. Carlos and Jimmy said goodbye to Karina. Carlos, always one to have the last word, turned to Karina. "You know we're only two years apart in age, and I'm going to med school. You're going to regret not giving me the time of day."

She clutched her chest and winked at him. "Be still my heart, maybe you'll get lucky."

I pushed my brother out the door before he said anything more to embarrass himself.

Before I could follow him out, a hand reached out to

grasp my elbow. Karina's whole body came close to mine, her voice low enough that only I could hear her. "Not so quick, sunshine. I will say this fast before the closest thing I have to a sister walks back into the room. You break her heart again? I will destroy you."

I pulled my arm out of her reach. "This is none of your business, but there's more to the story than, you know," I said through clenched teeth. I would not tell Karina that her best friend owned my heart before I'd even told Rebecca.

Karina looked at me with suspicious but perhaps optimistic eyes. "You better not fuck this up."

* * *

Karina and I parted ways in the hallway. She went to freshen up, and I continued toward the kitchen. Rebecca was ready with two champagne flutes in her hand. "We're starting the pregaming early. Dale, would you like a glass?"

After taking the flutes from her hands and placing them on the marble counter, I pulled her close, placing a kiss on her lips. Mutual groans escaped our lips, staking my claim before her friend sought us out. I cupped her cheek with one hand, wrapping her waist with the other, her soft to my hard. When we parted, her eyes were wide, her mouth forming a soft 'O' before she said, "Wow, I could get used to these kisses."

"I've been waiting to do this all day."

She grinned, her hands trailing up around my neck, her fingers playing with the hair at my nape. "Oh yeah?" My thoughts have been replaying what we did also, and it's been distracting. Sarah has had to call my attention to work today."

I let go and placed some space between us before saying,

"I promise not to say anything about us till you're ready to claim me as yours. I won't pressure you."

Rebecca's hand moved to place her hair which had fallen into her face, behind her ear as she lifted a glass of champagne to her lips. "Thank you for giving me time. Are you sure you don't want something to drink?" she said lifting the flute in my direction.

I needed to convince her. This time I wouldn't fail her. This small-town boy wasn't going anywhere. "No thanks. Need to get going. It's been a long day. I'll leave you so you can catch up with your friend. Call me when you're on your way, I'll be waiting for you."

Karina lifted her champagne glass in salute. "What about little old me? Will you be waiting for me, too?"

A warning edge entered Rebecca's tone as she waved away Karina's question. "Don't pay her any attention, she's not acting like the charming best friend everyone loves."

Jimmy walked back into the house through the service entrance, knocking on the door to get my attention. "Hey Dale, Carlos said he's leaving, wanted to let you know."

The interruption couldn't have come at a better time. There was nothing I could say that would redeem me in Karina's eyes besides seeing what we'd started through to the end.

"Thanks. Tell him I'm leaving as well." I turned to Becca. "I'll see you tonight."

This close to the endgame, I couldn't help but wish we had more time.

Chapter Twenty-Two
Rebecca

"Could you be any ruder?" I blurted as soon as Dale left. "What part of being nice to him did you not understand?" I took a seat at the kitchen island, refilling our champagne glasses.

Karina's jaw dropped, then snapped closed. "Do you think a leopard can change his spots? What makes you think he's going to be there for you this time?"

She walked over and laid a hand on my shoulder. "I just don't want him to hurt you again. You are the sister I never had. If they hurt you, they hurt me. Plus, who's going to keep an eye out for you. Look what happened when I didn't... you ended up with Phillip."

My eyebrow arched higher than usual. "Are you serious? That's your excuse for being mean? Give me a break. Please tell me you were not rude to him because of my ex, I shook my head slowly, "Don't you think I knew Phillip was wrong for me. That's why we went our separate ways. The fact he thought my life should revolve around his was a major reason we would never work out."

Karina lifted the champagne flute to her lips, but not before raising it in the air in a toast, a half-smile on her face. "You're catching on. Self-realization is important and recognizing how you are worth the effort. Any man who wants to be with you has to earn it."

I touched my glass to hers. "Okay, I promise I'll be on the alert for men who want to trifle with my heart."

A knot of emotions burned in my center at her words. Karina's concern for me was genuine. We practically grew up together then left for New York to study later on. She trusted no one. She joked it was the nature of the beast. As a very successful spin-doctor out of Manhattan, her job required cleaning up her clients' messes. Of course, her instinct was to help me clean up mine. Especially the one named Dale.

As a kid, she practically lived at my home. Her absentee parents spent their time traveling around the world, leaving her as an afterthought with her grandmother and a revolving door of nannies. We'd been in each other's lives from grade school through college, but all she knew of Dale was how he'd dumped me after a summer fling and broken my heart. I'd never shared with her the truth of what had happened that summer. I'd been so humiliated.

I turned to my best friend and said, "Please, give me the benefit of the doubt. I know what I'm doing this time. If I can put this behind me, I'm asking you to do the same." I lifted my flute toward hers. "Now stop being such a party pooper. You need this outing as much as I do."

She sighed. "You're right. Fun's been out of my vocab for far too long. All I do is work, cleaning up other people's scandals. Tonight, we're going to party." She raised her eyebrows once, twice. "Plus, I didn't tell you why I flew into Miami."

"You're right, we got so caught up with calling Ken and everyone, I forgot to ask."

"As of tomorrow, I will be a homeowner in the state of Florida? I bought a pied-à-terre in South Beach."

My jaw dropped in pleasant surprise. "I'm so excited. I've missed our brunches and hanging with you."

She placed an arm over my shoulder and knocked her hip against mine. "It will be like old times before you left the city to pursue your career as a producer."

Life was coming full circle, I was returning to the scene of where everything started our friendship, love, and even heartbreak. A ball of emotion clogged my throat, this time I prayed we had a different ending.

* * *

Our party of twelve arrived at Fran's by eight p.m., and once again, it amazed me how this dive bar in the middle of nowhere, was standing room only. Townies mixed with the city crowd. The loud music drowned out the noise from the pool table area and the bar lining the wall. They had dimmed the lighting to center the crowd on the stage and bar area. As soon as we entered, Levi, who'd been standing close to the entrance, made a beeline to greet us. I would bet next season's ratings it was to play interference, to run off any guy who tried to hit on his girl.

Who would have believed Levi would have fallen as hard as he did when he first met Marisa? Or that Marisa who had seen working with Levi as giving into the patriarchy would be head over heels in love?

To convince him to work with her had been like pulling teeth at the start of our venture together.

A hand trailed down my naked back and a rush of pleasure jolted me when I turned to face Dale. "When I saw you enter, all I wanted was to carry you over my shoulders caveman style and be alone with you."

My skin grew hot and excitement fluttered deep in the pit of my stomach. Sentiments like that and I would totally let him have his way with me. I'd worn a backless halter top and silk dress shorts in black, wanting exactly this reaction from Dale. Our morning lovemaking was still fresh in my mind as I chose what to wear this evening. Although we'd only seen each other four hours ago, I had been looking forward to being with him in a fresh setting, not work-related. His burnt copper hair combed and gelled, his five o'clock shadow gone, and wearing an ironed chambray blue shirt, a surge of electricity ran through my veins.

I turned to smile up at him, "Then I accomplished what I set out to do."

"Oh... what was that?"

"Make you notice me in a room filled with people."

He gave me a crooked smile. "My brother's not the only one who's going to need to fend off the savages tonight." His lips dipped to my collarbone, inhaling me before placing a light kiss behind my ear. Warmth spread through me, and I seriously wished we were alone.

I arched into him in the bar's darkness. I was counting on our movements being unseen. But who was I kidding with this crowd? They most probably had their cell phones out taping us.

"I'll always notice you, regardless of how you dress.

From the first time I met you. You were always the axis I wanted to circle." His expression faded from playful to serious, and my heart swelled with a feeling I had thought long since dead.

Our group had moved farther into the bar, but we stayed back, surrounded by the other customers of the bar. I wanted this momentary privacy to clear up some issues we had. His arms went to my hips to pull me in closer as he moved us toward a wall lined with old license plates from top to bottom. His head moved from left to right, scouting the area before he leaned in and kissed my forehead.

"Becca, I need to kiss you. Levi thought I was just hanging out with him to chew the fat while he waited for Marisa. He didn't know how badly I wanted to be with you tonight. You take my breath away every time I'm in a room with you." His eyes were reverent as his lips lowered to mine just a peck, once, twice, and three times, causing a tingling deep in my stomach.

"You were hard to ignore that day in the library, too. I guess something fated us to meet. I originally planned to go to England with Karina that summer but changed my plans last minute and met my family in Miami. Hey, speaking of friends, I wanted to apologize for Karina's behavior at the house, she promised me she wouldn't repeat...." My breath came in tiny pants as he cupped my face, and placed more light kisses on my brows, followed by my nose, cheeks then a soft peck on the lips. I clung to his broad shoulders. The entire room seemed to spin as I felt the most incredible pleasure ever.

"I'm going to kiss you now." His larger body hiding mine from onlookers had me hypersensitive to every brush against my breasts, hips, and thighs. I was about to combust in a dive bar on the outskirts of Miami.

When his tongue dipped between the seam of my lips, I brought him in closer, opening myself to him, our tongues tangling, the taste of beer on his lips. His sandalwood cologne comforted me when surrounded by the aroma of beer and greasy food. The house lights started flickering on and off to announce a new set of musicians starting their set, and I jumped out of his arms. We were too old to be caught necking in public by our friends.

We made our way to the tables that the brothers had reserved ahead of time. Marcos and Jeremy were already chatting up Sarah. Karina gravitated to catching up with Ken and his husband. Corrine kept a vigilant eye over Sophia as she spoke with Carlos and Noah. No way was there going to be a repeat of the incident that had them in a hospital the last time they'd come here. Noah had pledged to be Sophia's watchdog when he wasn't on stage. He was so blind to the way she looked at him when she thought he wasn't watching. Major crush going on there. I hoped it didn't end in heartache.

Dale pulled me toward empty seats at the table, pails filled with water and beer chilled in ice buckets on the table. "Beer or water?" He must have seen my frown. "If you want something else, we'll need to order it at the bar or flag a server."

"Water for now, please. I need to hydrate. I forgot how much Marisa loves tequila."

"You don't drink tequila?" He seemed almost disappointed.

"Please. We started doing shots on the bus on the way over as we sang. But I'll fully admit I'm a lightweight."

He opened the bottle before passing it to me, taking my hand in his and placing it on his thigh hidden from prying eyes.

Marisa and Levi sauntered over to sit in front of us, I removed my hand from his body. I wasn't in the mood for twenty questions from Marisa or anyone. What we had was still too new. Levi and Dale started talking about my parent's library when Marisa sidled her chair closer to me. The men had stood up from their chairs, signaling that they would bring us drinks from the bar.

I turned in my chair toward Marisa with a shit-eating grin on her face, and I couldn't help but ask, "What? Why are you looking at me that way?"

Her face turned innocent. "Nothing, this is my normal minding my business face." The gorgeous Latina signaled with a circle to her beautifully made-up face. "It's just great to see you both being civil to each other. It was mighty uncomfortable watching the whole I'm ignoring the elephant in the room. I guess my all-knowing Nana was right once again."

She leaned closer to me. "She told me Dale was transparent and wore his heart on his sleeve, and he loved you. She insisted still rivers run deep, and he was hiding his pain behind that devil-may-care attitude of his."

I moved closer to her so as not to be overheard. "We're feeling it out. I'm doing my best to be openhearted now. But to be honest, with so much going on, I just want to live in the moment. I'm not sure if you're aware of this, but we dated years back and then went our separate ways."

I felt comfortable sharing this with her. Maybe not too comfortable, but finally comfortable enough. We'd bonded through so much in the last month. If there was anyone who would understand heartache, it was the woman in front of me, having witnessed the death of her parents.

Her hand reached for mine and squeezed before letting go. "Yeah, Dale might have told me a bit about you guys."

My eyes widened at her words. "He spoke about us?"

"Well, to be honest, I enticed him with Nana's cooking. Then I confronted him to explain why you both were acting so funny. I thought he was hitting on you, and you were too polite to tell him to go fly a duck." She laughed as she said this.

I sighed, then let out a deep breath, "No, we'd been so in love that summer eight years ago, ready to tie our lives to each other." I let out a deep sigh. "We were too serious for being so young. I don't have to tell you. It didn't end well. He broke my heart, and that was that."

Marisa wrang her fingers. Her eyes troubled as she bit her lip, then just blurted it out. "Fuck it. He didn't tell you all that happened. I love him and you too much to let you think he's an insensitive asshole. There's more to the story of why he didn't show up. Ask him. He didn't make me promise not to tell you. I know firsthand how dangerous keeping secrets can be."

* * *

Noah and his group brought the house down, they were popular and regulars at the bar. The music played in the background, and my friends had left the table to be closer to the stage. Marisa and Levi had long gone to play pool against The K's, as I call Ken and Karina.

Dale must have figured something was off. His warm palm went to the small of my back as he leaned in to ask, "Are you okay?"

"Fine," I said.

An empty answer he didn't buy for a second. "Do you want to go somewhere else?"

I nodded, afraid I'd contracted Marisa's diarrhea of the mouth and would blurt out without thinking through what it was I wanted to say, and I didn't want to compete with the loud music. He reached out and clutched my hand, pulling me along beside his hard length as we walked toward the red exit sign in the back. We walked in silence, hand in hand, toward the parking lot.

His white truck was far enough removed from everyone that we had some privacy. I had deliberated whether to say anything, but Marisa's words replayed on a loop in my brain. All I focused on was that Marisa knew something I didn't. I hadn't wanted to throw Marisa under the bus, but I needed to figure out how to get the information he wasn't telling me. Maybe my timing was off, but I found there was no better time than the present. If I couldn't handle the answer, I would survive. I'd done it before. I could do it again.

He took the key fob to the enormous truck and pressed it open, placing his hands at my waist and lifting me as if I were as light as a feather to sit on the car seat facing him. With the car door open and as far as we were from the entrance, this was as private as it was going to get. He planted himself in front of me, arms crossed, his eyes searched my face, reaching into my thoughts.

"Okay, now speak," he said. "Something happened between my going to look for drinks with Levi and my return."

I shrugged and swallowed. This was hard, but I was going to tell him. "You're right. It was repeated to me, and I have been trying to figure out how to broach the subject without getting the messenger in trouble." My stomach dropped at the thought of what we had to say to each other. Both of us had been keeping secrets all this time.

His brows slanted in a frown as he took a step, moving closer, his upper thighs grazing my knees, taking my hands in his. With a sigh, he let out, "What did Marisa say to you? She's the only person who spoke with you after you arrived in a great mood."

I held on to his hand like a lifeline. The chill that crawled up my spine had nothing to do with the balmy temperature outside. "What haven't you told me about the night we were planning to elope? "

For a moment, he froze with shock. Whatever he'd expected me to ask, it hadn't been that.

Then his eyes grew liquid and soft, not focused on me but some internal thought, his voice solemn. "Do you remember the day before we were to elope? We met in the pool house to make our final plans."

I nodded, but I didn't say a word. I didn't want to interrupt the flow of his thoughts and narrative. We were both so fragile now, and any wrong word could ruin whatever progress toward truth we might make.

"Well...we were not the only ones in the pool house that day. We just didn't realize that we were not alone." My eyes widened at his words. I tried to remember what we had said and did. "When you sneaked back to the main house, your brother had been in another room and confronted me about our plans. I was honest with him. It wasn't like I could deny it. He'd heard our conversation." His shoulders lifted to his ears then dropped.

Dread filled the pit of my stomach because I could imagine how that conversation went. Charles would have been twenty-five and an extremely overprotective older brother. I could just imagine all the shit he must have said to Dale, but Dale wasn't a weakling or a coward. Something didn't add up.

"What did he say to you that made you change your mind about our plans?" I shivered, an uneasiness in my chest at what I might hear.

His mouth formed a grim line. "He asked that I listen to him before I got defensive and flew off the handle. That I should consider both our futures and what getting married so young could do to it. You having to give up on your dream school and losing your trust fund, you not finishing college was too much to ask of you. I didn't want to shoulder the burden of making you choose between me and your opportunities, especially when I couldn't offer anything in return. Plus, hiding our feelings for each other from everyone and going behind our parents' backs was starting a relationship on the wrong foot." His shoulders slumped at the end of his heartrending words.

I bent my knees against my chest and buried my head between them, hugging myself with my arms. My voice came out muffled as I buried the hurt once again, seeing how everyone else had decided what they felt was the best for me. No one trusted that I could make my own decisions, determine what was best for me. An empty sensation filled me to the marrow. "Wow, all that. My brother interfered in our lives, decided for us, and you agreed without consulting me or even giving me a heads up."

His voice was low and broken as he raked his fingers through my hair and smoothed his hand down my back, causing goose bumps on my sensitive skin. "Becca, I'm sorry. I didn't have the strength to walk away from you. I wanted you too much. If I'd told you everything, you would have said screw everything just to spite your brother. And the last thing I wanted to do was throw Charles under the bus, my brothers are so important to me the last thing I wanted was to alienate the only one you have."

I couldn't even look at him. "So, what if I did? It was my decision."

That got him quiet.

I lifted my head from my knees. The only illumination around us came from the neon lights above the dive bar rooftop, but I could see the regret in his eyes reflected at what I'd said to him. There was a lump in my throat as I braced myself for his reaction. "If we're going to be truthful with each other, you might as well know something I withheld from you. You weren't the only one that had a secret that day. I was pregnant. I didn't know how to break it to you, it wasn't like we planned it." A weight had lifted from my shoulders, and I felt lighter than I had in years. Confession was proving good for my soul.

Dale's voice cracked, his fingers pinched his eyes, then he released them and asked, "What happened?"

"I left and returned to campus. You never answered my calls, so I figured I was doing this on my own. I don't know if it was the depression or my lack of eating and sleeping, but I lost the baby in my second month. My friends all thought it was an acute case of heartache. At eighteen, we can be drama queens. I couldn't get over the guilt for a long time." I swallowed hard and bit back tears.

Large hands cupped my face as he brought his lips to my forehead and muttered against my skin, "I never stopped loving you. My heart's breaking for what I put you through, baby. Forgive me for letting you down."

"We let each other down." I suppressed the tears swelling in my throat. This was too much. The pain. The regret. The shame. The desire. The man in front of me.

But as though sensing I needed help carrying that weight, he wrapped his arms around me, folding me into his body. He whispered over and over into my ear, "I've got you, baby. I've got you."

Chapter Twenty-Three
Dale

I was numb with what Rebecca had shared with me. No wonder she'd hated me all these years. I would have resented the fuck out of me as well. With her trembling body in my arms, all I wanted to do was hold on to her, feed her the strength I had failed to give her years ago.

Covered in darkness, the twenty-foot sign above the dive bar, the only illumination around us spelled out Fran's with a giant red arrow pointing towards the locale. We held each other, consoling ourselves as my mind replayed the woulda, coulda, shoulda. My heart was beating so hard it pounded its way out of my chest.

She sat in my lap, one arm molding her to my body and the other threading through her hair, and all I wanted was to comfort her with my touch.

I pulled back when her breathing returned to normal. I caught hold of her shoulders and held her back, so I could see for myself her beautiful face. "Babe, do you want to go back in, or do you want to go home? We'll do whatever you want. You call the shots."

She pushed herself off my lap, but not before placing a gentle peck on my lips as she stroked my face and traced her fingers over my features. "Let's go back in. I brought my friends and the *Renovated* crew with me. My leaving would bring up too many questions from everyone. Believe me. If I don't show up, I'll have Karina and Ken in my face tonight. I don't want the third degree."

Still shaken by her words, I stood up from where we were sitting. The only woman I had ever promised to love in this world, and I'd let her down. What did that say about me as a man? Was I capable of standing by her and making her proud? Was I even worthy of being her man when I'd failed to be there when she needed me most?

As we walked back to the bar, neon lights the only illumination, Rebecca pivoted to search my face, and something gave her pause. Because she stopped mid-stride and swiveled around toward me, "Dale, you hear me now." Closing the distance between us till we were inches apart, pointing her index finger into my chest, "I don't need to be a mind reader to figure out all the misguided guilt you have ruminating in that brain of yours. I need you to snap out of this funk. You and I were teenagers, we loved and lost, but we've matured and know what we want now as adults,"– she took a deep breath in and let it out,– "the one thing I've realized is I can't fight my feelings for you anymore. What we had and what we can be is still worth fighting for."

When we returned to the bar, Rebecca insisted on a bathroom pit stop, so she could fix her face as she told me. Noah and his group had already finished their set, and the dance floor was empty but for a few stragglers. The sound system above us played whatever Spotify mix the bartender had chosen for the night. Tonight, they were playing old rock songs. My arm hugged her waist, with her body tucked into mine.

Once we got closer to our table, I didn't miss that there were more than a few eyes on us. A mix of curiosity or maybe some disapproval reflected back at us. Rebecca must have felt those same judgmental eyes on her because her hand tightened on my waist. But before we took our seats, she turned in my arms, grabbed my shirt to bring me closer, and kissed me worthy of a *Nicholas Sparks* movie, except for the tears. My heart hammered in my ears, whistles and catcalls brought me back to the here and now. When she pulled away, heat spread through her cheeks, and she murmured, "I think we've made it obvious now that we're together. I own this. How about you?" then she smiled as she turned to sit next to Karina.

Karina grinned at Rebecca. "We all got the message, and it was crystal clear."

The table returned to whatever conversations were going on before our arrival, as if what we did a minute ago hadn't disrupted the space-time continuum of our group.

Once I settled in the chair next to Rebecca, I grabbed an ice-cold beer from one of the buckets sitting in the middle of the table. My brothers Levi and Jeremy watched me as I took off the bottle cap. "Is there a problem?"

The worry on Levi's face turned up a notch. "I hope you know what you're doing. You can't screw around with this one. There are repercussions to this if it doesn't work out."

That's Levi, always fixated on the business side of things, not that I can blame him. He'd never known me in love. I hadn't bothered with anyone seriously after Rebecca. And to

Levi, anything that disturbed the bottom line of the family business was not to be tolerated.

Jeremy's eyes were shrewd as he gave me the once over, and in his typical get to the point style, turned to Levi and said, "Don't be an ass. She's no-hit it and quit it. He's loved her since he met her." *There, I guess my brother knows me better than I thought.*

I took a sip of beer and said, "Rebecca has always been the one. I will not fuck it up this time. Plus, is it too much to ask that you have my back as I had yours when you went after Marisa?"

My brother had the decency to look ashamed at his words and hit my bottle with his. "Sorry, you're right. I'm an asshole for even doubting that your feelings for Rebecca aren't legit."

Jeremy, who was sitting to my right, just slapped me on the back, "About time." I grinned at his words, "Yeah, it was time we cleared things up between us."

I turned toward Rebecca, who was chatting away with her best friends from college.

Sarah, who had been in an animated discussion with Marisa, turned to Rebecca and announced, "Did you tell them yet of your brilliant idea to showcase *Renovated* with the charity auction?"

Other than the background noise, you could have heard a pin drop at the table. Everyone shut up to listen to what Rebecca had to say. I could tell this wasn't the moment or place she wanted to bring this up. I almost felt sorry for Sarah, who realized she'd messed up too late.

Rebecca stopped mid-sentence whatever she was about to say to Ken forgotten as she turned towards Sarah, her eyes widening, shaking her head. "I hadn't yet presented it to them. I had planned to speak with them once I could iron out the details and logistics, plus I'm not sure if the network will back me."

Sarah's cheeks turned bright pink, "Oh my, I'm so ... so sorry. I let the cat out of the bag. Or as my mother would say, put the cart before the horse."

Jeremy moved closer to Sarah, leaning forward to buffer her from her boss and everyone else, if need be, which surprised the hell out of me. Jeremy wasn't anybody's knight in shining armor.

Levi and Marisa were now paying attention to whatever was going on because now no one was talking, just listening to the conversation taking place in front of them.

"It's okay. I guess now is as good a time to bring it up as any," Rebecca turned her attention to Levi and Marisa, "I hadn't wanted to mention this until I knew if it was plausible, but I don't see why I can't tell you what I have planned. Nothing's written in stone, but I'm proposing to the network that we auction both Renovated hosts services to the gala in Nashville. It's all for a good cause. Various charities benefit from what they collect from that night, and we can get a great promo for our show. We can tape the bidder's renovation, and Home Network will foot the bill. It's a win-win all around. They'll make money off the sponsors and TV time, while the money from the auction will go straight to the charity."

Levi's eyebrow lifted in question while Rebecca opened a bottle of water in front of her and took a sip. The wheels were turning in her brain, but she remained silent as Levi asked her. "What does that have to do with us?"

"Well, I suggested we offer the services of *Renovated's* newest hosts," she answered.

Levi lifted his hand for her to stop in mid-conversation. "What? Do you want us to renovate in Nashville? Rebecca, I'm not sure why anyone would be interested in us, especially giving us money for a charity, when they can hire a local and not have to pay through the nose for it. What about the logistics? We're starting the two homes back-to-back for the show. We might spread ourselves too thin. Plus, Chance Brothers have other clients we've postponed because of taping the show." His face was grim.

She didn't sell my brother on the idea. Not at all. And if he didn't agree, none of my other brothers would either.

She placed her elbows on the table, the palms of her hands in front of her, "Listen to me before you decide. Look at this as an opportunity to bring a lot of money to a charity that needs your help and creates goodwill and exposure to our audience. Also, just like we do here, you will work with a Tennessee crew that is licensed, of course."

Marisa cut into the conversation at this point. It surprised me she'd waited this long to make her opinion known. "Levi, she's right. Other hosts have done the same thing. It gives brand awareness to the show. It elevates the show by placing us in a different category, were giving something back to the community."

"I'm not convinced that this is a good idea. Who cares about us in Nashville that they would bid on our design services?" He shrugged matter-of-factly. Rebecca's mouth opened in surprise, then snapped shut before saying, "Are you kidding me? You guys are celebrities. Of the reality TV type, you're now a famous dating couple. Newsfeeds eat that stuff up. There will always be someone that will pay to have the bragging rights of saying Levi Chance and Marisa Sanchez, the design duo of *Renovated,* did this job."

Karina lifted her drink and yelled, "Very true, and I would know. Everyone, please raise your glass to Renovated."

Rebecca lifted her hand for a high five, and they smacked their hands and laughed. "Damn right. To Renovated! Tequila shots for everyone. We need to celebrate. She waved the server over and placed an order for the whole table.

Some gaffers, cameramen, and video tech guys from the crew of Home Network lifted their glasses and yelled, "Church!"

Levi looked at me with a questioning look on his face, and I mouthed to him, "Slang for agreement."

Levi then turned to Marisa, "Fuck, I'm going to need to walk with an urban dictionary at this pace to keep up with the new terminology."

She pressed her face to his for a selfie, "Don't worry, Grandpa, I'll be your interpreter and keep you relevant."

When the server arrived with shots and everyone had one in front of them, Rebecca lifted hers in the air. "To *Renovated,* to this first season, excellent ratings, advertising sponsors, and our hosts, who make it look easy. "

To this, the table all yelled, "Church!"

This time, it was my turn to stand by the woman I loved. I brought her closer to me and kissed her shoulder, whispering into her ear. "You did well out there, defending your point. Levi is stubborn if you can get Marisa on board. He'll follow."

She grinned and leaned in closer and whispered in my ear, "It's the power of the pussy." Then she winked at me. "It moves mountains and men to Nashville."

Chapter Twenty-Four
Dale

Rebecca had departed last night with her friends and the Renovated crew on the party bus at midnight. She had an early staff meeting tomorrow morning, and they were going to film the new client's episode promo and still shots. It seemed she wanted to have this done before some presentation she needed to give to the bean counters and bigwigs at the network.

God only knew in what condition everyone was going to be tomorrow when taping. A few of those guys were so drunk they could hardly stand. She'd had the bus driver supply everyone with bottles of water for the return trip back to Miami.

Last night, our heart-to-heart made me realize how many loose ends needed tying up if I wanted to be with Rebecca. One of the biggest was lying in a hospital. I woke up this morning to find Carlos sitting at the kitchen table, his computer open and some medical reference books strewn on the table. At five-thirty a.m., it was still pitch dark outside of our Mom's Victorian house, but the oinking sounds of the pig frogs and the bellows of the alligators had a symphony going on that could wake the dead.

I walked over to the coffee maker and inserted a pod to brew myself a cup. "Damn, I hate the mating season. Those grunts sound like they're outside the door."

Carlos looked up from the computer he had been typing at. "Yeah, it's white noise to me now. I'm so used to it. Hey, what are you doing up so early? You're not working today?"

Marcos was eight, I was seven, and Carlos, being the youngest, was four when we came to live with Jack and Kate Chance. We all arrived at the same boys' home in the same week. It was a temp area till they found us a foster family. We'd bonded to each other instantly, being the youngest and newest residents. We clung to each other for comfort and out of fear. When our Mom came into the home, she refused to separate us, and Dad went along since he lived to make her happy. Mom had been a product of the foster system, and even with three kids of her own, she took us home.

Just going to see my birth father in prison would force me to face the darkness that might be inside me. The fundamental flaw that proved that the woman I loved had been better off without me then. I also had to tell my brothers, who on a whole would tell me to hell with him. They would feel no remorse letting him rot after what he had done to me as a kid.

"I need to face some personal demons." I scratched the two-day growth of hair on my face. It wasn't like I wanted to impress the man.

His eyebrows lifted, his eyes focusing on me for real now. "What the hell does that mean?"

I had the visitation application approval letter burning a

hole in my pocket. I had said nothing to my brothers because I wasn't sure if I'd go through with it till last night. But my conversation with Rebecca only reinforced that I needed to put to rest parts of my past.

"I received a letter from my birth father a month ago. It sat unopened in my night table drawer for a few weeks before I decided to read it. He's in a prison in Okeechobee, and he's been diagnosed with terminal cancer. When I called to get permission to visit him, I was told they had moved him to a hospital facility close to here."

Carlos closed the computer top, a pensive look on his face. "He what?"

"He sent me a letter."

"And you..."

"Just got approved to visit him in the hospital."

He shook his head. "Not cool, bro, keeping those types of secrets. You should have at least mentioned something. We're always here for you."

"I know you are, but some things have come up with Rebecca that made me realize I needed to deal with this part of my past."

His eyebrows furrowed as he gave me a clinical diagnosis and he wasn't even a doctor yet, "Man we've all got shit to deal with from our past, but I'm not sure if this is the health- iest way to deal with it. We're your brothers, you shouldn't keep stuff like that from us, it's pretty obvious that this has been on your mind for some time."

"He wants to meet me after all these years and he's asking for forgiveness." I took another sip of the coffee and helped myself to a donut from a box left on the table. Once I bit into the glazed chocolate treat, a churning in my stomach made me put it back down.

I looked down at the old, scratched farm table where we had sat as a family and would have discussed our problems, guilt-filled me as I spoke. "Don't think I don't know that. I hadn't planned on visiting him. My attitude when I received it was to let sleeping dogs lie and all. Now I want closure on that part of my life. It never played out, but it's haunted me for a long time. And not just me. Everyone who gets close to me."

Or tries to.

Carlos raked his hand across his scalp. "I'm sure the blast from the past was the last thing you expected."

"Are you saying you would have expected it?"

He shrugged. "I don't make as many enemies as you."

The guy had a point. My dad wasn't my enemy, but he was the tree, and I was the apple. Visiting him might be the only way to see how close I'd fallen from him.

Carlos must have seen the concern in my expression. "Do you want company? I can go with you. Be your support system –in case it gets intense."

Carlos, as my wingman, probably would make me feel more confident, but that was why I couldn't bring him. If I couldn't face my biological dad without him, I sure as hell wouldn't be able to face Rebecca.

"I'll call you after," I said.

"You sure?"

"Of course I am."

Even I could hear that I was anything but.

* * *

I drove two hours to get to the county hospital and the hollow feeling in the pit of my stomach made its home there once I parked my truck and followed the instructions to the wing in the hospital that was set up to care for inmates. Once I checked in and passed through security, the guard asked me to wait in a holding area. The white walls contained various signs showing standard protocols for this institution and the expected behavior. The astringent smell of cleaning products surrounded me. Others were waiting in this room, and no one made eye contact. A buzzer sounded, and another guard came through a mechanized opening that separated the patients from the rest of us.

Pointing to me, he asked, "Are you Dale Chance?"

I nodded as I approached him. "Yes."

He waved the paperwork in his hand at me and signaled for me to follow him. "This way, please."

Our footsteps echoed in the empty hallway as I walked beside him in silence. I followed him down a hallway that took us out of the main building to an annex with a sign above the doorway that spelled Infirmary in block letters. The guard inside took my papers and unlocked the next wave of security doors.

I'd known this was an infirmary, but it was still a prison infirmary. And yet instead of a glimpse of prison cells, or bars, or anything I'd expected, the guard took me down a hallway that made the place look more like a hospital than a prison.

Terminal cancer, I reminded myself. He wasn't here to serve out his sentence. He was here to take his last breath.

When we arrived at a sizable glass-encased room that contained patient beds and a nurses' station, he turned toward me. "Wait here. The nurse will take you over to visit your father."

Thank God I had a second before the nurse did, because when I glanced over, there he was. A twenty-five-year older version of me. My father.

* * *

Even from here, I could see his emaciated state. Cancer had consumed his body. He lay sleeping, some machine measuring his vitals. His skin was yellowed and paper-thin. I looked up from the man in the bed to the nurse.

"How long?"

Shrugging he said, "We do not know. He's sometimes lucid. Good days and bad ones, you know how it is with these types of illnesses. We have him feeding by vein." He stops and stares at me. "You're his son, aren't you? You're a carbon copy of him."

"Yeah, I am."

The man spoke in low tones, not wanting to disturb the other patients. "He's in the last stages. The doctors don't expect him to last too long, not much more they could do for him."

"Is he in pain?"

The nurse shook his head before answering, "He's on morphine. It was the best they could offer him. I can give you some time with him. I'll be at my desk." As he returned to walk back to the nursing station, I sat down in the plastic chair by the bed.

I looked at this stranger who'd given me life and waited for any type of emotion to fill me, but I had nothing. His chest rose in shallow breaths, frail and rail thin. Pulling my chair closer to his bedside, a loud scrape from the legs brought the nurse's head up from whatever he was doing.

I lifted my palms as I faced him. "Sorry."

The nurse lowered his head back to his paperwork and I returned my attention to the man in the bed. Eight years ago, I let fear keep me quiet. I wouldn't do that again today.

I said what I needed to say in a low voice. I said what I think my father wanted to hear. I said what I hoped he could take with him.

"Abbot, if you're in there somewhere, it's me, Dale. You asked me to come to offer you forgiveness. Well, I'm here now. You can leave this world in peace knowing that, at least for me, I did alright. I was one of the lucky ones. The family who adopted me gave me a home, an education and taught me what it was to be loved. I guess there's not much more I can say, but to tell you, I have a life I'm proud of, a family who loves me, and there's a woman I love."

A tear leaked from my birth father's closed eyes and his fingers lifted slightly in response to my words, I gave us both the closure we needed to get on with our respective paths.

I walked to the attendant to let him know I was ready to be escorted out.

* * *

When the guard returned my property to me, my brothers had left no less than ten messages. But there was only one person I wanted to talk to, and she hadn't messaged me.

Her phone rang twice before she picked up "Hi."

"Hi. Where are you?"

"Wrapping up the footage of the new promo shots, the new home we're renovating."

I could hear people talking in the background. "Who else is there?"

"Your brother and Marisa are here with the camera crew."

So no one she couldn't get away from.

But only if she wants to.

"Can I meet you? I'm not close. It'll be about two hours."

There was concern in her voice as she answered. "Two hours away?"

"I know. Heck of a drive." The words wanted to come out now, but the phone wasn't the right way. "I'll tell you about it when I get back."

"You sound off. Are you okay?"

I let out a deep breath. It felt like I'd been drowning for the last two hours, and I'd finally come up for air. "Meet me in two hours. I'll tell you everything."

Chapter Twenty-Five
Rebecca

We had wrapped up the client's interview and promo pictures with Marisa and Levi at the new client location. They presented the prepared before and after pictures to the new clients for the show. They were newlyweds and had bought the house the wife had grown up in.

The biggest attraction—or opportunity—was that the place hadn't been renovated since the seventies. It still had avocado-green appliances and pink and blue tile in the bathrooms. Getting it into this decade would be a major overhaul and, with just a little luck, a ratings giant. Fortunately, my TV hosts were up for the challenge.

I said goodbye to the crew as they packed up the video equipment into the van when Levi and Marisa walked over to say goodbye.

"Hey, you guys, I need to sit with you both. I promise it will be fast. We need to discuss what I mentioned last night about the special project I had in mind for you. I saw a coffee shop by the strip mall close to here. Can we meet there in five minutes?"

Levi looked down at his phone before looking up at me, "Sure, I'm supposed to meet with some clients that want a quote, but not till later on."

Marisa rolled her eyes at me and nodded as she said, "I'll follow you in my car. I didn't come in from your direction, so I don't know which place you're talking about."

All three of us entered the quaint coffee shop called the Last Bean. The vibe was reminiscent of a New York Deli. Pastries, cakes, and cookies were behind glass cases for the clients to choose from, reminding me I had nothing in my stomach since last night. Once seated in a booth, our server took our order for three cups of coffee, and I insisted on slices of blueberry, peach, and strawberry pie. I needed all I could to sweeten the deal as I presented my plan for the auction.

"I wanted to apologize to both of you. Last night in a bar under the influence of lots of tequila was not how I planned to put forward my idea for both of you to take part in the charity."

Marisa was the first to reply. "I know I can only answer for myself, but I think the optics alone will be great for the show. Our name as a design team will have more recognition, and not just because of my past."

Marisa's response hadn't surprised me. Her career catapulted when, as a YouTube vlogger, she caught the interest of the network. She had grown a fan base by teaching the weekend warrior how to take care of their homes themselves. She was more in tune with how the algorithms worked in branding *Renovated* as the show to DVR.

Now Levi was a different matter, and I knew this would

be a harder sell since his interests lay in growing his family construction business, and he'd never set out to be a TV personality.

"Rebecca, my biggest concern is the licenses and working with a crew that's not my own. Plus, our hands are pretty full as is. I don't care to spread myself too thin. You do that, and things fall through the cracks."

Marisa, who was sitting on his side of the booth, swiveled in her seat to face him. "Levi, look at the big picture before you shut the idea down."

I interjected, "She's right, Levi. The exposure would be fabulous for the ratings."

Levi's eyes widened. "I'll do a lot of things, but for free?"

"It's a charity."

"And?"

Marisa rolled her eyes. "Charity means free."

He shrugged. "I'm not a charity."

"Your time would be free," I said. "But Home Design Network will pick up all the expenses for the construction."

Marisa turned to me. "Count me in. When I needed your help, you were there for me. This is the least I can do for you."

Levi gave her an annoyed look. "Not leaving me much option to say no."

"You can say no. I told you I was all for it this morning. I'd love to give you some more time, but she needs a decision from us."

It was nice to know that Marisa had my back, regardless of her boyfriend not being on board. She could make her own decisions and would stick to her guns. I guess that came from running her own construction outfit that she'd inherited from her grandfather.

As we finished the pie between the three of us, I again said to Levi, "Think about it, but remember other hosts on TV do shows that benefit charities. In your case, someone is bidding on your time and design for their home. Could be good publicity." I looked up, as though a headline were written in the air. "Levi the hero, champion of charity causes."

"Champion of free shit, more like it." He shook his head, but the corners of his mouth were turning into a smile. "Let me talk to my brothers. Maybe we can work something out."

* * *

I opened the front door entrance for Dale just as he parked his truck in the driveway. When he walked up to the entrance, I stepped aside to let him enter. His smile didn't reach his eyes.

There was tension in his stance as he asked, "Hi, you alone here?"

"Yes, Yolanda left to pick up her husband from dialysis. I told her to take the rest of the day off. Which was perfect timing because I gathered you wanted to be alone."

He followed me into the entertainment room, which had a very well-stocked bar. I was walking straight toward the wooden marble-topped bar when I asked him, "Can I get you a drink? You look like you could use one. My father keeps a well-stocked bar."

His voice, husky with emotion, stopped me in my tracks. "Becca, what I need isn't at the bottom of a bottle."

I took a deep breath. We'd been through a lot together, but most of it had been painful, and almost none of it had been as good as this last little while. What could have hurt this chiseled rock so badly that he let himself express a simple need?

"Just tell me what you need," I whispered, and my heart sent a jolt of electricity through me.

"You," he said. "Just you."

Unable to stop myself, I took one step toward him, and he closed the distance between us, engulfing me in his warmth, surrounding me with his scent of clean male and fresh-cut wood that sent me straight to my knees.

He came to the floor with me, and we leaned into each other in silence.

This wasn't like him. Not at all. Something big must have happened.

Something big could still happen, I reminded myself.

"Are you okay? Do you want to talk? I'm here for you."

He brushed his knuckles down the side of my face, then just picked me up as if I weighed nothing.

"What are you..."

He lifted me off my feet to place me on the bar's marble top a few feet behind me. Now we were eye to eye, the loose orange maxi dress I had changed into when I got home bunched around me as he stood between my open thighs. His hands at my hips, as mine traveled from around his neck to cup his cheeks, his body pressed closer to mine, and my sex pulsed at the apex of my thighs.

Maddening and distracting as his touch, I forced myself to speak. "What's wrong? This isn't like you."

His fingers trailed from my ankles to my knees, spreading

233

them farther apart as he moved in closer. The feel of him brushing my legs caused the muscles low in my stomach to clench. He lowered his face to my neck and whispered in my ear, his hot breath against my skin. "Hon, I promise to answer all your questions, but please, for now, let me forget for a little while."

It was almost a whisper, but I was so attuned to him, my head fell back as heat spread through every inch of me. My insides were melting as his fingers trailed lightly around my thighs, reaching my apex.

Then his desire-filled eyes lifted in surprise and my breath caught in my throat with a touch of embarrassment. I'd had no idea what he was going to talk about, so I'd come prepared for, shall we say, more than one intense outcome.

"No underwear," he said, and thank God for the smile he couldn't resist. "Was that for me?"

"Who else would it be for?" I said, but then we were both laughing.

When we were quiet again, he said, "Could this moment be more perfect?"

I bit my lip hard around the smile that tugged at my mouth. "I wanted to have the least amount of clothes to take off tonight."

The dimple on his cheek appeared as his eyes locked with mine.

He lowered his head to place kisses on my lips, cheeks, and jaw. One big firm hand bracketed my thigh, then roamed my upper thigh as the other stroked me. I shivered from the delicious sensations running through me as his fingers circled my nub and then pressed inside me. He repeated the movement till a cry escaped my lips when a hot, searing bolt of pleasure struck me.

"Oh... dear God," I barely got the words out before he lowered his head to consume my lips, groaning into my mouth.

His mouth was leaving mine to trail down my jaw, neck and latch on to my nipple, sucking hard on one then moving to the other, each pull of his mouth reaching my core. He gave me a gentle bite that had me struggling for my breath.

"Don't stop. I'm close."

"Again?"

The pride in his voice nearly sent me over the edge.

"Again," I said.

His thumb continued encircling my clit as his finger rubbed inside my upper wall, ravishing me and building the tension in me till my hips were lifting, reaching for the orgasm just within reach. I continued stroking his cock, my thumb circling his head till he pulled his hips away and, with a raspy voice, asked me, "Becca, I need to be inside you."

My eyes opened wide, and I couldn't help the words that slipped out of my mouth. "I'll be your home this time," I said. "Come inside."

My eyes strayed to his as I lowered the zipper of his jeans. The desire and intensity hypnotized me as he watched me cup him with one hand as I stroked his silken length with the other from hilt to tip.

"I can't wait any longer," he said.

I nodded and took him in my hand and guided him inside me. He arched his back, driving forward, both of us groaning at the same time.

"You're so hot, soft, and mine," he growled into my ear.

I'd been so close to the edge that his voice and his body and his will pushed me over, and then I was lost to the sensation. He was in me, I was around him, and for at least this moment, that was all we needed.

Mine, he'd said. The word I'd wanted him to say eight years ago. The word I'd secretly dreamed he'd say ever since.

What else had he come here to say?

* * *

My fingers raked through the waves in his hair as his head lay on my breast. Our breath and heartbeats coming down from the orgasm, our bodies satiated, but my mind wandered back to the elephant in the room.

I tapped the hand that lay on my breast. "Dale, are you ready to talk?"

He lifted his head enough to meet my eyes, and once again, the haunted look that he'd arrived with was back, but he nodded and lifted himself off me, rolling me on top of him as if reluctant to sever the connection.

He pulled me closer, his arms around my waist before he began, "I went to visit my birth father at the hospital where the prison sent him."

My hands lay on his chest, just above his heart. "Why? After all these years, why did you feel the need to visit him now?"

"He has pancreatic cancer and wrote to me, looking to make peace. I didn't owe him anything, but after all we said to each other last night. I'd failed you when you most needed me to be there for you. I didn't want this hanging over me."

My heart broke for the man in front of me and for the

child he was when all this happened to him. Instinctively my body arched into his seeking to offer comfort. "Were you able to talk to him?"

"I was too late. He's all but gone. Hooked up to a bunch of machines, more dead than alive. But I told him I held no ill will toward him." He let out a breath that I'm sure he didn't realize he was holding. My arms tightened at his side hoping to transfer strength and support, not with words but with my actions.

He gathered me into his arms and held me snugly, peace surrounded us as a large weight lifted from what was between us. I placed a kiss above his heart, lifting my face to watch the emotions flit across his face. His eyes were closed, but he wasn't done talking. There was a reason I didn't know about Dale's birth father. A reason he wasn't still in Dale's life. A reason I suspected Dale was about to tell me.

I kissed his chin and his mouth swooped down to capture mine, his lips were warm and sweet as his mouth descended on mine. He lifted his lips from mine and whispered, "Becca, don't feel sorry for me. I never wanted you to know the ugly side of my past. But I needed to come clean with you, because how can we have a future if we can't confront our past.

His words caused a strange sensation to tighten in my throat. "You sharing this means so much to me, and I can't say my heart doesn't hurt at you having to experience what you have. But I understand you wanting to confront the bogeyman."

After a bit of time, Dale opened his eyes, a certainty in them. "Him abandoning me in that motel room was the best thing that ever happened to me. I got placed with the Chance family, and it turned out alright."

His arms wrapped around me as mine went around his neck and he tucked my head under his chin. I wasn't sure who was consoling who, but we stayed that way till we fell asleep, as desperate for our dreams to hold us as to prepare us for what we'd face tomorrow.

Chapter Twenty-Six
Rebecca

I woke up at five-thirty a.m. with a sleeping Dale by my side. I observed the rise and fall of his chest, the stubble on his jaw, and the ridges and valleys of his body. My heart rate quickened as I replayed last night in my mind. After bingeing on Chinese takeout, we headed upstairs to shower. I insisted he stay, and he decided not to go. The intimacy of bathing became more than washing the day off for us both, another opportunity to relearn again each other's bodies, what turned us on, what worked — what didn't. Warmth spread through me as I watched his eyes flutter open, and his eyes found mine in the bedroom's darkness.

He turned on his side, so he faced me. "What are you doing up so early?" His early morning voice gruff as he broke the silence.

"My flight out of Miami is at eight this morning. With all that's been happening, I forgot to mention it to you last night. There's a presentation I need make to a bunch of pencil pushers at headquarters tomorrow. Plus, Sarah made appointments with some donors for the gala." Pushing myself up to sit up from where I lay, the linen sheet fell to my lap. His eyes moved to my naked breasts, then up again to my face.

"How long?" His eyes never leaving mine.

"Not sure, exactly. My mother has also scheduled meetings with the charity committee, after which I'm back to Miami."

His eyes widened as he sat up as well. "That long? What about Renovated? Don't they need you around?"

I smiled and answered. "There's a two-week window before I'm needed. If I can get everything done, I'll be back sooner than later."

"Who's in charge, if you're gone?"

"The videographers are under orders to tape when Levi and Marisa start the demo with the clients. We usually cut a few takes for the audience, something funny or insightful for the viewers. I should be back long before you miss me."

"I'll miss you."

Moving closer to his warmth, "I'm going to miss you, too. But now that Sarah's here, I can let go of some responsibilities."

His hand slid from my shoulder to my wrist, and an electrifying shudder reverberated through me when he said, "Well then, let's not waste any time."

* * *

My mouth had fallen open at my brother's curt response to my petition. I needed to remind myself to close it before imaginary flies entered it.

"What do you mean, no? Aren't you going to give me

any type of explanation? You're just dismissing my idea without listening to my argument?" My voice rose in frustration at the man in front of me with every sentence I bit out.

The conference room of Home Design Network headquarters was state-of-the-art. Scented grapefruit and orange blossoms perfumed the air. Custom office chairs surrounded the long oval table. But now I missed the salt air, the tropical breeze, and the view of the ocean. I scheduled this meeting over a week ago with my brother, and he'd agreed to meet me this morning. I had arrived earlier than planned because this confrontation was a long time in the making. He needed to stop meddling in my life.

The sleeves of his Oxford shirt rolled up, he sat amid a pile of spreadsheets and folders. I guess it's true what they say *heavy is the head that wears the crown*. I came with coffee for both of us and homemade banana walnut muffins that Mother brought home from the Blue's Bakery.

His hand went to his forehead, his eyes sharp and assessing. I placed the coffee and muffin before him and sat down. "Thanks', those from Blues?"

I grinned as I lifted my coffee to my lips to take a sip, "Yup, consider it a bribe."

He lifted the muffin took a bite, I waited as he chewed and swallowed. Then his attention was back on me.

"Look," he said, his tone all but dismissive. "I'm meeting with the board tomorrow. Do you think this is the time to discuss your promo project?" He picked up the muffin and took a bite out of it, as though we hadn't agreed to meet.

Wait. Was it possible he didn't even remember?

"Did you forget you agreed to meet this morning?"

His sudden intake of breath said it all. Not that he would admit it. "Don't see it on my calendar."

"I can send you the text as evidence."

Now he was looking at his phone. "I'll just delete it."

I leaned forward and looked up at him. "I'm not leaving."

He looked at me with a new expression. Maybe it was my tone, maybe it was the fact that so much else had already changed, but he straightened his shoulders. He could see I meant it.

Which didn't mean he saw me as a worthy adversary. But it did mean I could prove to him whether I was one.

"Impress me then," he said. "I'll listen. Explain how Home Design will benefit from a charity event. What's your plan?"

I let out a breath I hadn't realized I was holding, my heart beating so fast I thought it would pop out of my chest. I was being asked to perform for my dinner, "Our newest Home Design team will get exposure outside of our network and bring more brand awareness to *Renovated*, which will increase our market share and our sponsors will pay more for advertising time. Other hosts lend their names to charity. We've even made competitions where the winner gets the money applied to their charity of choice. Marisa and Levi are a winning team. The audience loves them, and you've even signed them on for an extended contract. What's better, we'll establish a minimum bid. I'll get Marisa and Levi to donate their time. It would promote the show, our network and, better yet, get me to my numbers. Sorry, had to add that in, since the organizing board placed a monetary goal to be reached, and I'm as competitive as the next girl."

He shook his head. "It would take us six months just to figure out the logistics."

"Logistics? The breakdown I sent you already has them done for you. Line by line. Did you even bother to read it?"

He shrugged. He wasn't flustered. He wasn't bothered. And whether he was taking me more seriously now, he hadn't been when I sent him the breakdown.

I stood and loomed over his chair as much as I could without actually being a towering person. But my personality was as high as Everest, and I knew the key to persuading the man in front of me. He was a self-centered person, and self-centered people just needed to be reminded of what was in it for them.

"Are you kidding me? You don't imagine there would be interest in this. Well, let me inform you that home renovation is a four-hundred-sixty-five-billion-dollar industry and emerging competitors are erecting their networks as we speak. Even *Netflix* is on the bandwagon."

He looked up and rolled his head left and right, tossing the idea around in his head. "I do like *Netflix*."

I had him with the money. Now to close him with his heart. "I'm sure this might sound self-serving, but the cause is important, and more than that, this means a lot to Mother. So back me on this."

He assessed me again. He wasn't intimidated, but I didn't need him to be. I just needed his help.

"I don't know," he said. "It's a big ask."

"Bigger than you asking Dale to break up with me eight years ago?"

Charles practically sucked all the air out of the room with his sudden intake of breath. He rose from his chair and walked toward the window. Did I say he wasn't intimidated? Well, that question had floored him.

Now he knew, didn't he? I'd come prepared.

His hand raked through his hair. "Can you blame me for trying to protect my baby sister? How old were you, eighteen? He was your first everything, love, lover. And you were ready to tie your wagon to him for the rest of your life. I'm sorry if watching out for you has you mad at me. You would have lost everything, your trust, finishing at Columbia, to do what? Be a construction assistant's wife?"

I practically guffawed. If this conversation wasn't so important, I'd have walked out. "What if I had?"

"Come on," he said. "You know I'd love you if you chose to live in a sandbox with a hot dog vendor. That's not what this was about."

I crossed my arms, unconvinced. "Then what did you say? Be specific."

He hesitated. "I only asked him to give you more time to figure out what you wanted in life. Grow into the woman you would become."

That wasn't as bad as what I'd thought, but it was still bad. No person had the right to make my decisions for me. Not the decisions themselves. Certainly not when I would make them.

"Charles, you should have said something to me. I stayed away for eight years, wasted so much time to end up in the same place. What are you going to do to push him away from me now? You're always deciding about what's best for me, regardless of what I want. You, Dale, Dad's illness, when do you let me decide for myself?" I spoke with as reasonable a voice as I could muster.

"You're right. Why do you think the library needed a new design? It wasn't Mother that had the architectural firm design the new layout. It was me. They were under contract to say it was her."

My palm went up and stopped him mid-sentence. "Wait, you manipulated the library redo. Why bother? Wait —does Mother know?"

"Just enough." He nodded as he raked his hand through his blond hair. "I've felt guilty about what I did, more times than you can imagine. Dale was afraid that he wouldn't be strong enough to tell you it was off, and I agreed. I'm aware of how persuasive you can be. All you would have to do is give him a reason, and he would have run off to marry you. But all he had to do was look around at the luxury that surrounded him, and he could never take you away from that."

"Charles, there was a perfect reason. I was pregnant, he didn't know it, and when he rejected me by never showing up or answering my calls, I said nothing." A pained expression filled his face, "I miscarried a month later." My voice was little more than a whisper.

His face fell, and he pulled me into his arms and hugged me. "Oh, Rebecca. I'm so sorry. I wanted to make amends for my actions by placing you and Dale together and seeing where it led."

Moving out of his arms and sitting down again, "I thought you didn't want me in Miami. You fought me on starting production there."

"Because my hardheaded sister was only going to fight harder to make her dream a reality. You weren't happy in New York. You were just biding your time with that pretentious lawyer."

"That's assuming a lot."

He shook his head, I guess in a futile attempt to shake off his guilt. "But look at you now. The whole world in front of you. And I mean it, you've impressed me." His broad smile reached his eyes, spreading small lines outward.

My voice broke and cleared it before saying, "Well, I guess things played out the way you wanted them to because we've started seeing each other again. We're giving it another go. This time, you need to stay out of my relationship. But, enough about me and my personal life. Are you going to back Renovated for the Black and White Gala?"

He sighed. "Let me sleep on it. What are your plans today?"

I looked down at my watch. My first appointment was at nine thirty. "I have meetings with donors all day, today and tomorrow. The least I can do if I'm going to ask people to donate their money or time."

"But I'm having dinner at home tonight with our parents. If you come over, I'll see you then. You'll give everyone the good news in person."

* * *

My phone rang as I walked into my parents' home from the garage to the main house. Dale's name flashed on the screen, bringing a smile to my lips. His voice would be a balm after going from one donor meeting to another all day. Giddy as a schoolgirl getting her first call from the boy she liked I answered the call, "Hello...you have perfect timing. I just walked in."

"How did it go? Did you get what you needed?" there

was concern in his voice, this wasn't a condescending interest in the little woman's hobby. He genuinely was worried about how it went.

My tone was grim as I explained, "Not all I set out to do. The gala is coming up. I have a week to get this done, and my brother's got other stuff on his mind. I presented the idea the pros, and the cons, and he said he still needed to think about it."

"Well, maybe stuff like that takes time to decide."

"It might take time, but we don't have the luxury of it. He's got to make an executive decision and trust that what I'm recommending we do will work out to the benefit of the network."

"Then I hope he listens and backs you."

"We also had a moment, and we cleared the air. He promised to not meddle in my life. Now all I need is for him to okay my plan."

Dale paused. "Listen, I spoke with Levi, he really didn't sound very enthusiastic."

My stomach plummeted to the floor, even if the network agreed I needed my hosts on board. "Oh...that doesn't sound good, is there a problem I don't know about?" I sat down at the kitchen island.

He cleared his throat. "My brother had a family business meeting, and there might be a problem with timing and projects that are in the pipeline. I just wanted to give you the heads up, so you should consider other options."

"I'm out of ideas here, Dale. This was the best I could come up with."

"Becca, what happens if by chance the network says no?" There was concern in his voice.

"Dale, not you as well. I need you to have faith in me. Stand with me. I can't be doubting you're in my corner. I'm always swimming upstream here."

"Whoa, Becca, you're jumping the gun. I am and will always be on your side. I'm aware that I let you down once, but you can't always be throwing the past in my face, or there never will be a future." The truth of his words stung.

"I never mentioned the past. But you're right. I can't resent you for what you did, or we will never heal. I can't keep coming back to my old resentments. Either my brother backs me, or he doesn't, but he'll have to take me seriously. If not, other networks will back me."

There was silence for a moment before he asked, "Is this about those job offers you received? What about us?"

My stomach dropped and a sinking feeling enveloped me because, what about them? In all this, I hadn't considered that I would fall in love again with Dale. Saltview was where he lived and where his family's business was. He would never leave it. Maybe now was not the time to decide between them or my future with Home Design. Was this my fear becoming a reality? Our getting attached to each other again was complicating what I had set out to do.

"Look, I'm going to be pretty busy for the next week, and I can accomplish everything that needs to be done for the show here at headquarters. Sarah will be busy anyway, setting up the office with Jeremy's help."

I could almost imagine Dale on the other side of the phone, his fingers raking through his short copper burnished hair, walking from side to side with nervous energy, as he did. "You're shutting me out. Aren't you? Is this payback for what I did?"

"No, but I need to focus on what's happening here."

"Translation, you are avoiding me. Even if this isn't payback," he said without emotion and continued. "Look, it's been a long day," he said. "Probably for both of us. Maybe we should just get some rest. You've got a big night ahead of you, right?"

He had a point. He had a lot to focus on, and so did I.

Earlier, I'd faced Charles and done okay. But this time, he would have my father with him.

* * *

Dinner was an informal affair when it was just the three of us. The chef my mother contracted to prepare her, and Father's meals had left everything set up in the fridge. My parents were on a health kick, it seemed, because the meal was halibut and three sides of vegetables.

Father was already sitting down, placing broccoli on his plate. I lowered myself on the chair next to him where the housekeeper had set a place before leaving for the day. I kissed him hello, placing the linen napkin on my lap. I picked up the plate with caprese salad and served myself the tomato and mozzarella drizzled with olive oil.

Unwilling to wait for someone else to break the ice, I smiled at my father. "How are you feeling?"

Handsome in a well-groomed sort of way, anyone else that wasn't me would call my father a silver fox, "Honey, I'm fine. I'm taking medication, the procedure went well."

"I'm sure it did," I said, trying my best not to be frustrated by his constant focus on image. But we were family. I just wanted him to be honest about his health. "But you can tell me. I can take it."

He studied me for a moment. "I know that this might upset you, but I need you to maintain appearances. You've grown up in a family that balks at convention. We're Walton's."

I nodded. We'd grown up listening to my father make these generalized and entitled comments all our lives. And Mother? She was standing in the doorway, listening to us but as oblivious to how Dad's comments affected me as ever.

"Yes, we are Walton's, but this Walton in particular has felt excluded from the family dynamic. You both hurt my feelings by not telling me what was happening to you. I can keep a secret if this was about a power play to move Charles into position without opposition. I wouldn't have blabbed it to the press."

"Of course, we trust you. I just didn't want to speak of this at all. I was assured by my urologist that the treatment would take care of the prognosis. All your mother and I want to focus on is enjoying what's left of our lives together. I was ready to pass the baton, and Charles was in a position to run with it. Now, are we good? I've read the statistical sampling done on *Renovated*, and you have a winner there, you've made your family proud."

"Then why are you pushing for me to come back and run the foundations? Don't you get it, I'm happy in production. I want to create content for the network, I want to contribute in that manner. And if this is because you're worried I don't have a man by my side, you don't have to be. I can fend for myself. I don't lack for company."

He served himself fish before passing me the platter, making a grimace as he turned to my mother who had been uncharacteristically silent as we spoke. "Honey, somehow I didn't need to know that, did I?"

Mother gave me a sly look. "As long as no one is getting hurt, our daughter is a grown woman who can do as she pleases. But if Dale hurts her, I'll kill him."

Chapter Twenty-Seven
Dale

All I needed was one word from Rebecca. A single text. A two-second voice mail. But we'd been in radio silence since our last talk. And I know the gurus say to lean into the mystery, but I couldn't help but fear the space between us signaled how far we were about to fall.

At my workshop, I smoothed my hand over a varnished tabletop. The clear epoxy resin had hardened the wood's natural grain. The table I had just finished was going into my new home. It was a fine piece of art, one that I would receive a nice sum for. But this one was special because I had created it with Rebecca in mind. She'd been my inspiration throughout the whole design and creation. The crunch of gravel outside my workshop announced cars and the slamming of doors with the unmistakable voices of the cavalry coming to see what had happened to me.

A truck door slammed close to me. "Dale, you in there?" Jeremy called out.

"Duh, of course. Where else does he go when he's upset?" Marcos answered.

Jeremy yelled out again in case I needed a hearing aid, "Well, if you would answer our texts, we wouldn't have to storm over here. We brought pizza, so we're all coming in."

I made my way toward the exit of my workshop and called out so they would hear me. "Wait, I'll be out. I varnished a piece in here, and the fumes are strong."

I walked out to the gravel parking lot and outside stood all my brothers. This was an intervention.

"Why are you all here?" I looked from Levi to Carlos, who'd arrived in another truck.

"Because we love your dumb ass, and we're going to kick some sense into you," Noah said.

"Something's wrong. You've been avoiding us the last few days, and we're here to share the burden. Invite us in. We have pizza and beer." Levi said as he brought out the pizza from Jimmy's, the only pizzeria in town, while Carlos and Marcos held the beer and soda in their hands.

I knew they weren't going anywhere. I might as well invite them in. "Follow me but take the boots off before you enter the house. I had the floors sanded and stained this week."

As we sat at the counter, everyone with slices of pepperoni in their hand, Jeremy broke the ice. "We know something happened between you and Rebecca. You've been moping around. Don't think we haven't noticed."

"How did you find out?" I couldn't hide the glumness from my voice. I hadn't told anyone anything, as usual. But I wasn't good at hiding much of anything. Certainly not the truth.

"Sarah," Jeremy said. "She commented that Rebecca wasn't her usual self over the phone. She didn't give me any details, but somehow, it's related to you. We want to know what you did this time."

"Same as always. I didn't have her back when it mattered, so she's got good reason to think it'll happen again. I've fucked up and let her down. The show, the charity, and our past has created a perfect storm." I took a sip of the beer in front of me. "I might have wiped away any chance I ever had of getting back with her. My wanting to get her back collided with the purpose of why she came back to Florida in the first place."

"Have you called her?" Noah asked.

"No. I've tried closing that gulf. I think I'd just hurt her again, maybe she can't forgive me for having let her down." An eruption of soda came out over the top as my hand clenched the can. "Shit–Shit–Shit." As I grabbed the roll of paper towels on the counter and started mopping up the liquid.

"Hold on, *Hulk*, no damaging the canned goods," Jeremy said as he lifted the pizza box to keep it from getting soda on it.

Levi swiveled to face me again. "Well, I came over because the *Renovated* charity event is a go. Our fearless leader went into the eye of the storm and had the network backing a fifty-thousand-remodel, with a bunch of advertisers coming on board. But instead of some rich donor bidding on us to do the construction, *Renovated* is going straight to the charity itself. Which also makes Marisa over-the-top happy because she was on board from the beginning."

Carlos gave a knowing look to Noah, "Levi's thrilled because if Marisa's happy, then she'll make Levi happy."

Levi gave them a dirty look, "Get your heads out of the gutter."

Noah pointed to Carlos as he said, "Don't look at me. That was all him."

My heart did a flip-flop, and it exhilarated me that Rebecca would achieve what she wanted, but I wasn't there to stand by her side. "I'm glad she got what she set out to do."

I mopped up the liquid with a paper towel about as sad as a person could mop. Slowly, languidly, like the liquid was my pain and it was all I had left.

Marcos slapped me on the back of the head. "Do we have to do everything for you?"

I swatted away his hand. "Hey!"

"If you love her, go to her," he said.

"Just like that?"

"It took you eight years to get this far. Don't stop now when she's standing right there waiting for you."

Chapter Twenty-Eight
Rebecca

Marisa and Levi were being prepped for the promo pictures at the foundation today. They had flown in yesterday evening so they could be here bright and early for the taping. Wardrobe and makeup had arrived early at their hotel to make sure the brand was spot on. That meant jeans and a soft blue chambray shirt rolled at the sleeves for Levi and a layered V-neck T-shirt that flattered her bust so she wouldn't look boxy for Marisa. Marisa had proven that women were more than capable of tackling home renovation and charming a TV audience.

My *Renovated* hosts met me at the foundation, where we did an initial walk-through with the director and some staff, getting an overview and discussing the primary concerns. The center had seen better days, interiors were drab, furniture was worn, and they did not divide the space for better utilization. Once, this was a house of worship, but now the facility's purpose was to allow social interaction and job integration skills. The students worked in a buddy system outside of the center at shelters and different local businesses that helped with the cause.

Some improvements had to be made to the facilities to make them more practical, user-friendly, and meet the end users needs. We walked through a set of rooms dedicated to meditation, sensory, computer, art spaces, and then, the kitchen. Creating a priority list of what they needed most was today's priority. Based on their observations, Levi and Marisa would then give them options to choose from. The official taping would start when choices were made. Renovated would recreate the walkthrough with the director and present the ultimate design for the audience to celebrate.

I took a step away from everyone to check my phone. Still no messages. A dark, sickening grief filled my heart. I'd been texting and calling Dale for the last two days, but no response. Did I screw this up? In all our conversations, he was the one opening up, saying he loved me, asking for another chance. Now, dread rolled through the pit of my stomach had he stopped caring. Did he give up on me?

My mind kept replaying my last conversation with Marisa as we went over the details of the expectations and budgets that Home Design was approving. The group from the foundation had walked off to follow Levi while he'd asked for details on a room that the kids used to decompress in when they felt sensory overload. I took advantage of the privacy to ask Marisa how everyone was. She'd read right through my question to the answer I was looking for.

"He's in a funk and has kept to himself. We've tried to have him over for dinner, but he just works at your parents' house and goes home." Marisa's shoulders lifted in a shrug.

Guilt weighed on my conscience. "I tried calling him, but

he's not answering. I'm concerned." Had I finally pushed away him away? After all, my brother was just as involved in keeping secrets from me, and I was still talking to him. Dale had suffered just as much as me, each of us in our own way, but I coped by turning my feelings into indifference.

Marisa rested a hand on my arm, "Rebecca, I love you like the sister I never had. Without you, I wouldn't be here right now." She paused, as though hefting the significance of what she was going to say. "I'm going to tell you something that may be hard for you to hear, but you don't deserve to have things kept from you."

I steeled myself for what she was going to say. It never ended well when someone prepped you to receive news.

Marisa looked left and right before turning back to me. "What were you thinking? This man adores you. You're both crazy about each other." Placing her hand on mine, before continuing, "You get your shit together as a couple, decide to make a go of it, and then you pushed him away."

My shoulders tightened. I hadn't expected to feel this attack, nor feel this emptiness. "We have a history that you're not aware of," I added.

Levi was making his way back toward us with the camera crew and the director of the foundation. She turned towards me, so her back was to them, and nodded. "You're right. I'm not aware of the details about what went down between you both. You figure that out for yourself if what you had was worth fighting for. We both know nothing of value comes easy in life."

Then she turned towards where the crew was standing to join Levi for some last photo ops. I looked down at my phone once again. Nope, no calls received in the previous half hour.

Restored

* * *

My mother's text as to my estimated time of arrival had popped up on my phone for the fifth time just as I walked through the door. Her own personal hairdresser and makeup artist were waiting at the house to prep us for tonight's event.

Forty-five minutes. That's all I had once I arrived home to shower and be ready to leave for the gala event. I had promised Angie, the coordinator, that I would arrive early to double-check the silent auction donations had the correct place cards and descriptions in front of them. I hadn't counted on the delays on my way back home. The first had been a contract crisis between the landlords of the Miami building and a matter of me wanting a full private bathroom at the satellite location. The second was an existential crisis of my own, as I ate a late lunch with Levi and Marisa. We discussed the next phase of our growth as a show and how we would implement the time constraints that having a project out of state was going to have on our schedule. I couldn't help but notice how much in love they both were with each other. Only further reminding me that neither had told me what was happening with Dale.

* * *

I arrived at a quarter to seven at the hotel. I dressed in a simple white one-shouldered evening gown that skimmed my body and trailed to the floor in honor of the event's namesake. Once there, I searched for Angie, the activity coordinator and point person at the hotel.

She stood in the middle of the melee dressed in her usual

armor of an elegant silk black suit, small heels, pearl earrings, and her silver hair in a sleek bob. She commanded the room as a general to her troops, directing the florists and event planners to their specific locations. Over fifty hotel employees were busy fixing arrangements and placing cards at tables. We were working on getting to the finish line. Musicians were fine-tuning their instruments and practicing before the event, and the hotel staff had installed an enormous dance floor in the front of where the musicians would be playing. Angie had overseen this activity since I could remember.

Look at her. She'd started as my mother's assistant and now ran the show.

She greeted me with a hug when I walked into the ball-room, "Rebecca, so good to see you again. It's been so long. "

"It has."

An employee with a box of candles asked a question, she answered him then returned to me, "When was the last time you attended one of these?"

"Over seven years ago. I was living out of state, plus you know that this has always been more of my mother's gig than mine." I added with a smile.

"That's true, but it's never too late to come over to the dark side." her mouth quirked with humor.

I knew where this not-so-subtle hint was coming from and let it pass without comment. "Angie, when I was told that it was you in charge of organizing the event, I knew the benefit was in expert hands. And I don't want to take away from your time. But I arrived early to check on the donated items. I don't want to upset anyone if they don't have the right names on the place cards."

She nodded in complete understanding, "No problem at

all, we have two security guards watching over all the items that were donated for tonight's event." giving me a knowing look, "You can never be too careful, and the last thing we need is a missing item via sticky fingers."

I agreed as I followed her out of the grand salon toward an adjacent room right off it. We passed two grave men dressed in suits. They had security written all over them. Angie waved to them as we passed the entrance. The men, all business, nodded in greeting. The set-up of the room had tables covered in fine white tablecloths that pooled on the floor. Angie had placed sheets of paper taped to the front of each item up for auction, pens set by their side for people to write in their bid.

"Rebecca, do you have the names of the different donors so that we can cross-check them?" Angie said as she looked through a thick folder in her arms to retrieve her list.

I opened the folder that I had brought with me with a breakdown by name, description, and value of the donated item. I looked around the room to start my foray into the more than a hundred items placed when my eye gravitated toward a table sitting to the far right of the room.

Without a word, I made a beeline in the direction of the beautiful sixty-inch round table to ensure my eyes were not deceiving me.

The reclaimed pinewood with hand-finished work was the same one I'd seen in Dale's work shed. My hand traveled over the variations in the wood. The salvaged wood planks were uneven, some bowed and cracked. Each imperfection, nick, or nail mark revealed a part of history and provenance. Something like our relationship, it started new and innocent but was now reclaimed and renewed, the scarring and aging had created growth and beauty.

Somehow, this table, with its intentional flaws, was a simile to my relationship with Dale. I lifted my eyes to Angie's questioning look.

Bewildered, I asked, "How did this table get here? Who brought it?"

Picking up the folder she'd laid down on the table next to her, she retrieved the list. "It says it was an anonymous donation. They didn't want to be named. We inquired as to provenance, but Levi Chance requested we accept it. And honestly, how could we not? The artistry is stunning. We should get a substantial amount for this table?"

Baffled, I nodded in agreement, though there was an ache that blossomed in my chest, "You're right, it is stunning, and should bring in a nice sum to help the foundation. Did you see who brought it in?" My sense of loss brought me close to tears at the auction of this table.

Angie pursed her lips and closed her eyes as if recalling the memory. "Hmm, I believe it was Mr. Chance and someone whom he introduced as his brother."

We finished up with my list as fast as I could. I had a few calls to make. My only problem was getting a certain someone to answer them.

* * *

I walked from the ballroom to the lobby of the hotel and made a call. It rang once, twice, and by the third ring, someone picked up.

"Hello," Marisa answered.

"Hi, it's Rebecca. Where is he? I just saw the table he made at the silent auction. I know he's here."

There was silence on the other side of the line before she responded. "The gig is up. But, I knew nothing about this till we returned from lunch with you, and Levi went down to help him bring in the table."

"Okay, I believe you. Where can I find him?" I could hear the desperation in my voice. My heart hammered in my ears.

She spoke low, so I could barely hear her over the noise in the busy hotel lobby, "He's in Room 401. And Becca?"

I'd been about to blast away faster than the Road Runner. "Yeah?"

"Good luck."

* * *

Once in front of Dale's hotel room, a knot of emotion burned in my center. I took a deep, cleansing breath as I hit the door-bell button on the side of the door.

I heard a shuffling sound and a response that I couldn't quite make out. My stomach did flip-flops.

What if he already gave up?

A bare-chested Dale answered the door with a towel wrapped around his waist and another towel hanging off his neck as he dried himself off. The sight of his bare body had me speechless. My sex pulsed, standing so close to him, and I was at a loss for words.

"Rebecca?" goose bumps rose at the sound of his voice.

I opened my mouth to speak, but words failed me at first. Tears threatened to spill from my eyes. "You're here. Why haven't you answered any of my texts or calls?"

263

I might have sounded prickly, but I felt justified.

"You asked for space. I understand if this isn't what you wanted, but I don't know what else to do."

"So...you iced me out?"

He closed his eyes and rubbed them. "Let's not do this in a hallway."

I walked in as if I hadn't noticed the muscles of his shoulders and chest, the marked abs, and the fine *V* of hair that traveled to beneath where the towel knotted at his waist. Once I was in and standing in the middle of the hotel room, he asked, "How did you find me? I'd wanted to surprise you."

"How surprised did you think I would be when I saw the table that only you could have made?" My voice broke, but I continued. "That was for your first home, and you brought it here. Why did you do that?"

Dale stood up now from the seat he had taken on the bed, capturing my hand in his and pulling me toward him. He pulled me onto his lap. My body melted into his heat, my softness against all his hardness. A delicious shudder went through me as he spoke. "Hon, there's no home for me if you're not in it. Plus, if this was important to you, then it is to me." His hand went to lift my chin so that our eyes met. "Becca, I will always be here for you. This time when you run, I'll run with you."

I sucked in a harsh breath and trembled with the desire that surged within me. Fire streaked between my thighs. "I'm so sorry, so wrong for the taking out my frustrations with my family out on you. I thought I lost you again."

He ran his finger down my bare arm. "Becca, you never lost me. I was always yours. We just lost our way for a while, but we made it back to each other."

She whispered, her voice husky with emotion, "I love you. And this time I'm not letting you go."

"And I'm not letting you go," he said, his sadness melting into warmer feelings. His mouth lit up with a seductive smile. "Becca, you look fantastic."

"Oh, I know."

"It'd be a shame if someone messed up your hair and makeup."

My hand reached for the knot that held his towel and twisted it off him. "Very shameful."

A growl escaped his lips when I took him in my hand and stroked him from root to tip. Once, twice, three times. His deep, shuddering breath let me know how turned on I was making him.

"Babe, I've missed you. I need to be inside you." He expelled his breath in a steady, slow hiss.

Nuzzling him on the edge of the bed, I lowered the side zipper of my dress, letting the one-shouldered number pool at my feet, standing there in a thong and nothing else. "Becca, I'm head over heels over you. Come here. You are so sexy, you've always been my wet dream. You know I love you, don't you? You never have to doubt that." His voice was guttural as he watched me, stroking himself with his right hand as he extended the other to bring me closer. I was mush in this man's hands. As I got closer, he skimmed his finger over my lower lips. His finger found me wet and ready for him. He circled my nub rubbing featherlight circles there. "Do you want me here, now?"

"Yes, I've missed you so much." I could barely get the words out and winked as I admitted. "Some parts more than others."

"Then come sit here, because he's missed you a lot too."

He caressed my hips, bringing me in closer and lifting me, so I was straddling his thighs. His muscular hair-roughened thighs against my smooth skin, making them jelly as my wet heat moved over his straining shaft. Sliding over him, teasing him, he thrust his hips, impaling me on his length, letting me set the pace.

I moved my hips at first, accommodating his size, then faster. With fevered kisses, he took my mouth with unrelenting passion. His muscular hands clasped me as he pumped inside me, shifting his angle to graze my pleasure spot. His mouth latched on to my nipples, teasing them with his teeth, then blowing on them till I cried out.

"You're beautiful, and you're mine. Tell me you're mine." His minty breath fanned my skin.

My hands went from his shoulders to his cheeks. I blinked back tears as I looked straight into his eyes. A flush prickled over my skin. "I'm all yours, Dale." My teeth nipped his shoulder, and then my legs clasped him harder.

"Becca, are you close? Because I don't know how much longer I can hold on before I come inside you," he said with gritted teeth.

Was I close? I was all but there.

I ground my core into his, and my body exploded as his hands pressed me into him to receive his release.

* * *

We arrived an hour and a half later at the Black and White Gala, just in time for the presentation by my brother of the project that Renovated was going to do on behalf of the

Home Network. He called Levi and Marisa, to the stage and in the background on gigantic screens, the footage taken as they did the promo shots was playing. We could tell crowd loved the idea just from the clapping that drowned out the last of what my brother was saying on the podium.

Dale's arm was at my waist as he pulled me in closer and whispered in my ear as he placed a tender kiss at my neck, "Congratulations, you make me so proud to call you mine. You have nothing left to prove."

I lifted my face to give him a peck on the lips. "You're right, I don't and having you by my side only makes things better. Have I told you you're totally rocking that tux? You look so hot right now."

His lip lifted in a slight smile. "I was just glad you knew how to do the bow tie, but I'm actually looking forward to taking it off for you later on."

My mother stood with my father, presiding over the event like the queen bee she was, surrounded by her worker bees. She waved me over as soon as she saw us, I swirled to face my beautiful man, my brows lifting in question, "You ready to meet the parents as my boyfriend?"

He took my hand in his. "Becca, I've been waiting for that invitation for the last eight years."

Epilogue
Dale

Four months later

"Babe, the camera crew is ready to roll. Are you ready?" Rebecca yelled from the door of my workshop.

Today, the show would be partially taped in my woodshed. They'd already taped me over the week as I created a table for a client from start to finish. When they televised it, what took me a week to create would replay back to the Renovated audience in fast-forward within five minutes.

Usually, I'm the behind-the-scenes type of guy, but this happens when your wife's the show's producer. I looked down at the plain gold band on my left hand that had the words '*better late than never*' engraved on it. After waiting so long to call her mine, I still couldn't believe how lucky I was to wake up next to this woman every day.

We'd flown to Vegas last month for some Television

Exchange Convention, which she needed to attend. I wasn't letting her get away again, and when we passed the chapel of love, I got down on one knee and, going with gut instinct, proposed. And when she didn't hesitate to say yes, we walked in and eloped as we'd planned eight years ago.

When we returned as Mr. and Mrs. Chance, the in-laws were not at all happy that they had not thrown their only daughter a wedding celebration. Thinking of them as my in-laws had been challenging at first, but Susan and Louis Walton turned out to be very supportive of the entire relationship. They insisted on celebrating an official wedding on the Walton Compound in Nashville for friends and family, and we'd agreed as long as it was kept it too just that.

I completed the Walton library, and with my design changes, it appeared in some well-known home design magazine. Bringing more requests for custom work than I could handle, so much so that I was training others to help me with the work. The custom table that I had donated to be auctioned off for the gala event had shown up a month later as the centerpiece of the library.

But better than all of that? When Rebecca walked into the finished library and saw my table front and center, the waterworks didn't stop till she was hiccupping in my arms. Susan later explained that when she knew that I'd made it and had placed it for auction, she'd outbid everyone for the right to take it home. She told me later that she wanted to own an original piece by her son-in-law, with a knowing look on her face.

My beautiful wife walked into my workshop, boss face on, all business. "Dale, they're going to be recording soon. Remember that the key to this is not to focus on the camera, just act like it's not there. You're having a conversation with the hosts of the show. When Marisa and Levi come in, he's going to introduce you as his brother. Levi's also going to be explaining why they are here today. Marisa will ask you the details of what she needs for the clients, and you'll fill her in on the process. You give your input if they ask it of you. In the end, Marisa and Levi are the hosts, and the show rotates around them."

"I won't flub my lines," I said, drawing her into my arms and placing a light kiss on her forehead.

Her eyebrows lifted, and she nodded. Who was she kidding? We both knew she thought I was going to freeze on camera. We had been practicing for close to a week. It seems my mouth shuts down when the camera crew's around, and I must remind my brain that I have to speak.

"I know you won't. I just want this to go well for you. Who knows, you might become a regular on the show whenever they need to create a custom piece for a client," she said as she pecked me on the lips with her mouth.

A car door slammed, and we could hear a discussion going on outside the workshop doors and the voices were only getting louder. It was Jeremy and Becca's assistant Sarah, having another disagreement.

"Jeremy, I told you the guy was just being helpful. He said he would drop off my purchases, on his way home from the store.

"You can't be that naive. The guy only wants to get in your pants."

"Are you frigging kidding me. Jeremy Chance, you take that back. The guy could be my father."

"Honey, have you seen yourself, no one is confusing you

with their daughter." Jeremy's voice got gruffer.

I turned to the woman in my arms, "Hon, let's go outside. The air in here is...toxic, with all these chemicals. Plus, I think we need to diffuse whatever is going on outside, they should just get a room."

She placed her hand over her still flat belly. The gold band on her finger glinted in the sunlight. "Right, let's walk outside. This is still so new to me."

Pregnancy hadn't done anything to shrink her feelings for me. The way her body felt about me. Or the way all of me felt about her.

"Well then, let's not take chances." I kissed the top of her head, my hand around her waist as we walked outside to meet the crew.

* * *

Thank you so much for reading Restored I hope you loved reading about Dale and Rebecca. Find out what happens next in a bonus epilogue when you click on my newsletter. SIGN UP FOR NIKKI KILEY'S NEWSLETTER AND RECEIVE A BONUS EPILOGUE OF RESTORED.

https://dl.bookfunnel.com/fv3vjwio83

* * *

If you loved Restored and want to read about how Levi and Marisa's fell in love, please read Renovated the book that started the series.

https://geni.us/AvAVQS

THANK YOU!

Acknowledgments

Writing a book can be a very daunting and solo endeavor, but having the support of friends and family makes the journey easier. To my first fans, Nikki Lopez, Rica Alos, Michelle Villamil, Stacey McCloskey, Lui M. Concepcion and Patricia Kiley all of your eagle eyes make for a richer more evolved story. I thank you all for your feedback and input. Kira you were my silent companion and will miss you always, I know there is a dog heaven for you.

Thank you to my amazing editors who helped this become a reality Jessica Snyder Edits(Developmental), Stephenie Edits(Line), My Brother's Editor(Proofread), and a very special thank you to Sarah at Okay Creations, for creating the book cover that I envisioned.

To my family, you are my all. Thank you for your love and support and especially your belief in me. I love you!

About the Author

Nikki Kiley is an author of Contemporary Romance who lives in a tropical paradise. A voracious reader, who felt transported and transformed by the stories she read, since she was a young girl she dreamt of writing stories that would entertain and move her readers, like she was and still is, by talented authors.

Finding herself working from home during lockdown, she could not resist the opportunity to make those lifelong dreams a reality. An accountant by profession, when not working the day job of running a medical office, she spends hours crafting and writing stories about characters – everyday heroes and heroines - earning their chance at love.

She makes her home in Puerto Rico with her very handsome husband, and her two young adult children.